What people are saying about

The Traitor's Child

Exhilarating and provocative, this is one hell of a religious thriller.
Peter James, bestselling author of over 30 novels

The Traitor's Child is a haunting and heart-breaking novel of betrayal and conspiracy, in which the roots of one family's sordid secret burrow so deep beneath the pillars of the Church, they threaten to bring it crashing down. Gripping and thought-provoking to the end.
Karen Maitland, bestselling author of *Company of Liars*

Fantastic, exciting and a real page turner. Unputdownable!
Barbara Erskine, bestselling author of *The Ghost Tree*

The Traitor's Child

Will one family's guilty secret lay bare
history's biggest lie?

The Traitor's Child

Will one family's guilty secret lay bare
history's biggest lie?

Mark Townsend

ROUNDFIRE
BOOKS

Winchester, UK
Washington, USA

First published by Roundfire Books, 2020
Roundfire Books is an imprint of John Hunt Publishing Ltd., No. 3 East St., Alresford,
Hampshire SO24 9EE, UK
office@jhpbooks.com
www.johnhuntpublishing.com
www.roundfire-books.com

For distributor details and how to order please visit the 'Ordering' section on our website.

ISBN: 978 1 78904 375 4
978 1 78904 376 1 (ebook)
Library of Congress Control Number: 2019941540

A CIP catalogue record for this book is available from the British Library.

All characters - apart from the obvious historical ones - in this publication are fictitious and any
resemblance to real persons, living or dead is purely coincidental.

Design: Stuart Davies

UK: Printed and bound by CPI Group (UK) Ltd, Croydon, CR0 4YY

We operate a distinctive and ethical publishing philosophy in
all areas of our business, from our global network of authors to
production and worldwide distribution.

My wife came up with the original title, The Girl Behind The Glass.

Amazingly, since then over 70 more books with 'the Girl' in the title have been published, so I needed to change it.

My wife gave me the original inspiration for this story and has been a wonderful support during its gradual 'coming to life'.

I dedicate it, therefore, to Sally, my beautiful wife, soul mate and best friend. Xxx

Also by this author

Gospel of Falling Down, 2007 - 978-1-84694-009-5

The Wizard's Gift, 2008 - 978-1-84694-039-2

The Path of the Blue Raven, 2009 - 978-1-84694-238-9

Jesus Outside the Box, 2010 - 978-1-84694-326-3

Jesus Through Pagan Eyes, 2012 - 9780738721910

Diary of a Heretic, 2013 - 978-1-78279-271-0

Acknowledgements

So many people have influenced the writing and 'polishing' of this book. I am utterly indebted to them all, and will be forever grateful to them for helping make my debut novel a reality. I do hope I have not missed anyone out in the following words.

Writers who have been a huge inspiration to me and who graciously offered their expertise and advice during the writing of this book: Nimue Brown, Barbara Erskine, Jane Fallon, Essie Fox, Cara Hunter, Peter James, Karen Maitland and Phil Rickman.

Editors and experts from the literary world who offered invaluable advice throughout the process: The Cornerstones Literary Consultancy, Ed Handyside, Dave Gaylor and Kimberley Young.

Friends and family who kindly read the manuscript and offered their thoughts and advice: Lauryn Boston, Philip Carr-Gomm, Adrian Gibb, Chloe Gray, Catherine Gurney, David Harris, Steve Harvey, Paul Kerr, Marlene MacPhall, Pennie Lodge, Aisha Mann, Sam Mann, Dianne Pallett, Erinn Painter, Joanne Shield, Deborah Townsend, Jamie Townsend, Sally Townsend and Kim Trombly.

My Publisher: Huge thanks to the team at O-Books and Roundfire Books for taking my words seriously and seeing enough potential to invest in them.

Cover artist: An enormous thank you to my daughter Aisha Mann for her exquisite art work. I'm so proud of you.

Prologue

A gust of wind blows an olive leaf across the sand and a lime-green lizard emerges from under the rocks. It lies motionless, as if in deep contemplation. The occasional flick of the creature's pink tongue is the only movement as it licks the hot air. Another gust shifts the leaf a little further and the lizard disappears back into hiding.

The man doesn't notice. Beads of sweat drip from his turbaned head, stinging his bloodshot eyes. A blink relieves them, bringing back his sight. He opens his hands. Red skin and weeping blisters betray many hours of pulling back heavy oars. He leans against the tree, moving his head out of the sunlight and giving his aching back some support. The date palm is his only shelter.

It's just a matter of time before they reach him. His task is complete, save for one last trial. What he's written is safe but they won't stop until they've found him *and* his words – and destroyed them both. His sole comfort is the certainty that his account is secure. It's already on its way into hiding and is, by now, far across the sea. He's left no clues and will not buckle when the torture comes. He knows what awaits him will be close to unbearable, but bear it he must – he has to. There will be no escape.

The lizard re-emerges and this time the fugitive sees it. The tiny flicking fork evokes images of the serpent himself.

A movement from behind, and a shadow. The lime-green portent is gone. His accusers have arrived.

Part One

Dam
Origin and Etymology: Middle English *dam, dame* lady, dam
First Known Use: Thirteenth century
Also Ma-dam – A procurer,
colloquially called a pimp
(if male) or a madam (if female),
is an agent for prostitutes who collects part of their earnings.

Chapter One

Amsterdam, 1981

The red velour curtains swished back into place, re-trapping the damp heat and, along with it, the heavy, lingering scent of cheap perfume and sweat. Dressed in black lace bra and pants, Maggie watched the fat man remove his dark hat and sunglasses. She'd been through this ritual a thousand times but there was something different about him. His bulk accentuated the narrowness of the bed that stood there like a low-level massage couch, and the room itself seemed to cave in around them, its red neon-lit walls giving the impression of a hotel room in hell.

He said nothing as his puffy hands reached up to undo the buttons of his overcoat and remove his black scarf. He could have been a private detective with his homburg and shades, or even a mobster. But what Maggie didn't expect to see was that familiar slice of priestly white linen wrapped around his neck.

Oh my God!

After three long years in this hell hole, she'd become accustomed to the weirdest eccentricities of her clients and their tastes but she'd never, as far as she knew, been bought by a man of his profession before, and it revived the darkest memories: the stark, echoing clang of the bell that summoned them to chapel; the tip-tapping of children's shoes on polished tiles; dark corridors followed by unintelligible Latin; clang...another bell – this one for breakfast; eating warm slop in silence; humiliation; fear; tears. And – *oh Christ...*

Pushing the thoughts away Maggie flicked the hair out of her eyes and took a deep breath. 'So, what would you like?'

Moments later the priest was sitting on the bed in his underpants. A small basin stood by and above it a mirror. A tissue dispenser was taped crudely to the wall and to the side

4

stood a chair, over which the man's dark jacket and trousers were draped. Underneath lay his polished shoes and, sprawled across them, his black clerical shirt. His scarf, hat and overcoat were hanging on a peg behind the door, the dark glasses jutting out from the pocket.

Relieved that his request was for standard sex, she moved over and sat next to him. He smelled of stale cigarettes and incense.

Incense. Those haunted thoughts: humiliation; fear; tears. And – *oh Christ…Blood – so much blood.*

* * *

Lying on her back, Maggie faced the ceiling mirror and numbly registered his grey-haired back glistening with perspiration as his buttocks rose and fell in a laborious steady rhythm. No words – just the occasional grunt. Then she noticed her own face, her silent grimaces beating in time to his heavy thrusts. Her young vacant eyes were like those of a hope-dashed prisoner gazing aimlessly through the bars of a cell.

Another jolt to the past: the rage; the fist; the face; the swish of the girl's arm.

Blood – so much blood.

His bulk pressed down on her. His panting quicker. His putrid breath hot against her neck.

Apart from the flashbacks the only other sensations were the vibrations coming through the wall in the form of a muffled melody. Her neighbour, Chrissy, always insisted on her radio being tuned in to Hilversum three during working hours. Maggie could just about make out the words of a new song, *Scary Monsters,* from the country of her childhood. She'd known more than a few of them in her short life.

Again, the memories seeped in: *What in Christ's name's going on here?*

5

Oh Jesus. Oh God. The pale, lifeless body, stretched out on the hard, wooden floor and punctured like Saint Sebastian.

Blood – so much blood.

Ten minutes later and the priest was gone.

Normally she'd be straight back behind her window, beckoning more potential punters as they shuffled past, but she needed a few moments. The girl lifted a quivering hand to the tip of the unlit cigarette in her mouth and found herself having to steady the lighter with her other hand. As she drew in the soothing smoke so she began taking in who had just fucked her for money, and the terrifying place to which his presence had just sent her.

How long had it been now, since the murder?

Chapter Two

Amsterdam, 1981

'Get out the way you crazy bastard!'

The sudden sound caught his attention and, momentarily distracted, Eric looked up to see a group of brightly coloured bikes passing by, one of them almost colliding with a smiling Japanese tourist who was standing in the road.

The guy jumped out of the cyclist's path just in time, before hopping back to take a polaroid of his friends outside a shop. This was a city where visitors photographed everything. Not just the usual targets of historical architecture and prominent landmarks, but dope dispensing coffee shops that oozed noxious smoke, bikes stacked up and chained to bridges, shop windows filled with pornographic postcards low enough for children to gawk at, and other tell-tale sights of this *city of tolerance*. Occasionally a tourist would risk a quick snap of a red-light worker behind her glass window, but whenever a camera was unveiled in those streets her friendly tapping for attention would turn to angry banging. *Do not take photographs of the sex workers* was a warning drummed into the head of every visitor to Amsterdam's Red-Light District.

Eric was sitting outside *Café het Paleis*. The canal was busy with boat trips and the streets were alive with shoppers, tourists and bicycles. The city was busier than he remembered, especially considering the time of year. Back when he was resident, Amsterdam was much quieter in late spring, but he hadn't seen these streets for two decades. He looked at the book again and his stomach churned as he turned to the next page.

Eric's mother had died young, leaving him at the mercy of his unaffectionate father – a business tycoon and hotel chain owner – and older brother. She was twenty-five years younger and, though constantly intimidated by him, she'd always been able to protect her youngest against the other two males of the household. But after her death it was constant bullying. His father had never ceased to heap praise on his eldest son, Peter, while simultaneously scorning Eric as a wimpish mummy's boy and an embarrassment to the Van Kroot name. It was obvious why he favoured Peter, being such a chip off the old block, but Eric never did understand why his father had taken such a profound dislike to his youngest. Even on his death bed, with both sons present, the old man looked only at Peter. Hence it came as no surprise when Eric learned to whom the family estate had been left.

With loud cheers and oriental grins, the crowd outside the shop congratulated the photographer on his photograph, which had clearly just appeared before their eyes instantly.

Eric ran a hand through his hair. His eyes may have been on the Japanese tourists but his mind was elsewhere. Half-dreaming, he reached for his jacket. He'd had the same tweed for years and, along with home-made elbow patches, it had become something of an abiding comfort to him, a symbol of stability in his unstable world. Together with his faded brown cords and liver-red ankle boots he could have been mistaken for a trendy high school teacher. Handsome for a forty-five-year-old man, Eric still caused the occasional head to turn. He was of medium height and had not yet gained the signs of slower metabolism. He was frequently informed that his penetrating blue eyes smiled permanently, due to the attractive lines that framed them.

His cigarette had burned to the end without him taking more than a couple of puffs. It lay in the ashtray like a cremated corpse. The revelation had almost been too much for him. He carefully put away the book, gulped down his cold coffee and left.

Eric hadn't seen his older brother for over twenty years. Peter's image still haunted him, as did the sound of his rage.

Peter Van Kroot, standing with his fists clenched, snorting like a bull. *She doesn't want you! She hates you. So get the fuck out of our lives you cheat. And if you ever try to see her again, I swear I'll kill you.*

He'd never forgotten those words, nor the tone with which they were delivered. He still loved his brother and he still loved Ella. What would it be like to see them again? He couldn't imagine. He didn't even know if it were possible. Would Peter still hate him? Would he still see him as a traitor?

Chapter Three

South Wales, 1970

The Black Crow, they called her, and when she flapped and squawked and spat she could make a girl piss herself in terror. Pissing yourself, the worst offence. Do it and you end up wearing your wet knickers on your head. Hannah had never got used to Sister Dominic.

Her earliest memories were of the convent. She'd lived there since the age of two, after being brought across the Channel by foreign nuns. She couldn't remember them but often wondered whether they were as cruel as Sister Dominic. Not all nuns were such bitches, though. Sister Simon was quite the reverse and, for someone so young, was never afraid to stand up to her elders if she thought they were in the wrong, but where was she now?

Hannah could feel the eyes glaring down at her.

'You're a worm,' she said, as she sniffed away something moist. 'Your parents didn't want you, but we took you in. And how do you thank us?' Some white froth flew out and landed on the girl's bare foot. 'How do you thank me?'

Hannah didn't answer. What was the point? She just watched the frothy blob ooze down between her toes. The dormitory's wooden floorboards were cold and hard. They creaked as Hannah tried to wipe the spit off with her other foot.

Feeling as frail as a china doll, she searched the room for support but there was none; the other girls knew better than to challenge Sister Dominic's authority by offering sympathy to her prey.

Hannah was eleven years old and slighter than most of the girls. She wore a coarse fabric nightgown like the others, though Hannah's had been pulled up to reveal her stick-like legs – whacking targets for the nun. Her eyes were heavy and she could feel her nose running onto her top lip.

Shivering, she raised her head.

'Don't you dare!' The nun struck the girl across her cheek and more phlegm splattered out.

Hannah knew very well not to look directly into Sister Dominic's eyes when she was in one of her rages, but she was confused. She'd been smacked many times and usually for nothing. But this was for something – something that had displeased the Sister more than what seemed reasonable. Even in her fear and pain, Hannah wanted an answer. What was it she'd said? What had so got under The Black Crow's robes that she'd swooped into the dormitory and dragged Hannah out of bed by the hair?

Most of the orphans had lived at Crucis Home For Girls for as long as they could remember, though a handful had known life outside, and sometimes Hannah thought it must be even harder for them. To help her get through the tasks and chores she often allowed herself to dream of a life beyond the high walls.

She imagined waking up in the warmest, cosiest bed, with fluffy pillows and the softest eiderdown – and no clanging bells or screeching voices. She dreamed of delicious breakfasts, hot baths and gentle soap. Remembering things she'd heard from the other girls, Hannah often pictured a mum and dad reading her bedtime stories, trips to the park, protective big brothers and a little sister who she could dress up and put ribbons in her hair. She would gladly make a bargain, a deal. Anything to get away from this place. But who could grant her such a wish? Not God, that was for sure. He was not one to make bargains with. Every girl knew that. To Him, as to Sister Dominic, orphans were nothing.

Hannah's face burned. She would not look up again and she would not hope for any answers tonight. Sister Dominic was too cross. For now, she'd have to stand there and take whatever the nun had in store.

11

* * *

Though life was hard at Crucis, Hannah had always been a content little girl. Her earliest memories were mainly happy, especially from the time Sister Simon arrived. Sister Simon was Hannah's best friend, though she'd been told never to call her that when anyone else was around.

Sister Simon was different. She stood out from the others, not just because she was kinder, but she also wore different clothes. It was the first thing Hannah had noticed about her. Up until then nuns looked like huge black birds, with their long dark gowns. The only part left visible was the tiny slice of face surrounded by a tightly fitting white wimple. But Sister Simon wore a shorter white veil and no wimple. She didn't wear the long black robes either; just a skirt and jumper. Hannah had never seen a nun's hair until she met Sister Simon, and hers was long, glossy and the colour of sunshine. And instead of moth balls and damp she smelled of freshly cut flowers. With her clear blue eyes and wrinkle free skin she didn't look much older than the oldest of the orphans.

Not long after the new Sister had arrived, Hannah, who was then just six years of age, asked her why she wore such different clothes.

'I'm what's known as a postulant, Angel,' she said.

'A poss-too-lunt angel?' Hannah beamed. 'You're an angel? I knew it, I knew it.'

The Sister chuckled and hugged Hannah. 'Oh you funny thing. I was calling you Angel. No, I'm a postulant, which means I am trying to discover whether I should be a nun.'

'Oh.' The moment of joy left Hannah as quickly as it had come, her shoulders now drooping like a wilting flower.

'Now then,' said the Sister. 'Why the sad face?'

Hannah looked at the floor. 'So you might not become a nun? And if you don't you'll have to leave us.'

Sister Simon knelt down and gently squeezed Hannah's arms. 'Don't worry. Being a nun is all I've ever wanted.' She smiled. 'I don't intend to leave.' She brushed Hannah's nose gently. 'Anyway, I'll be made a novice for a few years before I take my final vows, and I'll still wear a white veil while I'm a novice.' She stood up again.

'And will you still wear these clothes Sister?'

'Why, do you like them?'

'Oh yes Sister.' Hannah nodded. 'I can see your face.'

Sister Simon smiled, and Hannah thought she could easily have been an angel.

The postulant nun leaned forward and, cradling the little girl's cheeks, kissed the top of her head.

'Go now, Angel, and join your friends. I'll see you later.'

Whenever Hannah was sad, she would fill her mind with happy thoughts of her favourite Sister. One in particular stood out. She was only eight at the time and, as she awoke to the angry clanging of the morning bell, felt a sensation that every girl feared. At first she prayed it was something else – dampness caused by the heat perhaps, or maybe another girl had spilled something on her during the night? But then the familiar smell hit her. Oh No!

Terrified she crept out of bed hoping she could reach the washrooms without attracting too much attention, but the dark stains on her nightgown were too visible.

One of the girls noticed and started a chant that soon spread around the dormitory. 'Hannah, Hannah, ginger head. Hannah, Hannah's pissed the bed.'

Within minutes, the dormitory door flew open and Sister Dominic's piercing shriek silenced the noise. 'What's the meaning of this?'

After she'd forced one of the girls to explain she turned slowly towards Hannah, nose curled up. 'Right, you little skunk. There's only one way to cure this.'

13

Hannah was left on her own, crying and standing in the corner with her wet sheets piled up in a smelly heap on top of her head. The girls had gone to morning mass. There she stood, eight years of age, shivering and sobbing and wishing to God she'd not been so disobedient as to wet the bed.

Suddenly there were footsteps coming from outside, moving quickly, getting louder, coming closer, until…

'Hannah!' Sister Simon's shocked face peered across the room. She rushed over, threw off the wet sheets and pulled the little girl into her arms, rocking her and whispering, 'Shhhhh, it's okay now.' Tears of sadness and relief fell from Hannah's eyes as she sobbed.

Sister Simon then took her to the nuns' own bathroom and washed her with her own sweetly scented soap, and Hannah could smell those familiar freshly cut flowers on herself. She had always remembered her favourite Sister's kindness and her comforting words. *It was just an accident. It's nothing to be ashamed of.* But she also remembered Sister Dominic glaring at Sister Simon in chapel the next morning, and afterwards the young sister following her superior like an obedient puppy.

It was around that time that Hannah had started asking why? Not out of any mischief – just a growing interest in why things are, or are not, the way they are. And it wasn't long before it started getting her into trouble. On one occasion she asked podgy Sister Matthew why the food the girls had to eat didn't smell as nice as the Sisters' meals.

'Insolent little brat,' shouted the nun, as she put both hands on the table and pushed herself up. 'How dare you judge what we eat?'

'But…but,' said Hannah, shaking her head and backing away from the fast approaching mass of black fabric and wobbling fat. 'I wasn't. Honest. Sister, I wasn't.'

It was too late. Hannah had to spend the next day's meal times in the chapel praying for forgiveness and nursing a freshly boxed ear. But it didn't stop Hannah's questions. Some of the nuns gave up discussing things with her because they knew the conversations would never end. There would always be another *why*? Even some of the girls were tired of her. A few of them teased her, and said she needed to ask so many questions because she was dumb.

As Hannah reached nine Sister Dominic began to find her inquisitiveness quite impossible, often resorting to smacking her but, as the nun said, she just couldn't seem to drive the questioning devil out of the little worm.

Chapter Four

De Stooterplas Island, 1981

It was Eric's first sight of this stretch of road for over two decades, and he remembered it as if his last visit had been yesterday. As a protected 'area of outstanding beauty' it was largely unchanged, apart from a few new restaurants along the main road to the island.

The Van Kroot residence was situated on the outskirts, just north of Amsterdam, close to a green park known as *Het Twiske*. It was a fenced off estate, the grounds of which took in most of what was essentially a small island jutting out into *De Stooterplas Lake*.

The taxi dropped him at the gates and the driver agreed to return in two hours.

'Thanks,' said Eric. 'If I'm done before that I'll wait here for you.'

As the taxi drove away, Eric turned to face the mansion at the end of the long drive. His stomach churned. He then strolled over to the left side of the gates where the intercom system was fixed to a chest-high metal post. He leaned over and pressed the button. High above him a pair of seagulls squawked.

'Van Kroot residence, how can I help?' said the voice over the intercom.

'Er,' said Eric, suddenly aware of how real it was, 'I have a meeting with Mr Peter Van Kroot for 10.30am.'

'Mr Van Kroot usually sees people at his office in the city.'

'He agreed to see me here. It's not a business meeting.'

'Very well,' said the voice. 'Your name please?'

'Um...Wim Gossel. I have a message for him from his brother.'

As Eric waited at the intercom he took out his cigarettes, lit one up and inhaled deeply. He closed his eyes to release the calming smoke. Was this a crazy idea or what? How was Peter going to react? An image of him came into Eric's mind, as he was the day he last saw him. Like a bull, snorting and spitting rage.

The voice caused him to jump. 'Mr Van Kroot will see you now Mr Gossel.' Then the gates clicked, jerked slightly and began opening.

Eric paced up the long drive and, as he gradually approached his brother's huge home, his mind wandered back to another time, when their father was still alive. It was a bright spring day and the young Van Kroot boys were playing hide and seek in the vast island garden. Eric was out of sight behind the shed that housed the swimming pool heating system, but chubby Peter was coming closer. Eric crouched low and tried to make himself as invisible as possible, pulling a sack of freshly mown grass over himself.

Peter shouted, 'Come on weasel, where are you?'

Eric was determined not to be found, remaining silent and completely hidden. After a while Peter started showing signs of impatience. 'Okay, I give up, where are you?'

A victorious Eric, winner of the game, stood up waving his arms. 'Over here.' Peter stormed over. Big brother Peter. Bullying brother Peter. Older brother Peter now calling Eric *cheat* for hiding where he had.

Eric's memory played back the finale of that game as he remembered himself limping back to the house in tears, blood trickling from his nose where his brother had punched him.

He blinked, shook his head and looked up. He'd reached the front door and, seconds later, it opened. A tall blond man, who Eric supposed was his brother's personal assistant, stood in the doorway. His expression was icy and he had the remains of a black bruise under his left eye.

'Follow me,' he said, and Eric stepped into the house in which he'd grown up.

They crossed a familiar hall to a closed door on the other side and Eric noticed that the same family oil portraits still hung at equal intervals along the wall. The personal assistant knocked once and entered, closing the door behind him. After a few moments he re-opened the door and beckoned Eric in. The large room was just as he remembered – polished oak floor, mauve velvet curtains, bay window and, in front of it, a huge oak desk, behind which sat Peter Van Kroot.

Chapter Five

South Wales,1970

'All stand.' The voice was frail, breathless and belonged to a man. Apart from the occasional delivery boy who might be spotted loitering near the gates, or the rare visits of a father dropping off a new orphan, Father Francis was the only male they ever saw. And those two English words always marked the beginning of mass. The rest was in Latin.

Hannah liked the chapel. It didn't have the stale damp smell of the dormitory, or the dustiness of the study-rooms. The chapel's scent was always sweet. Even though Father Francis only swung his smoky censer on Sundays, it lingered there throughout the week.

And it was crammed full of interesting things to look at. Unlike the drab walls of the corridors and classrooms, the chapel was lit up by brightly coloured glass, telling stories from the Bible and history. Behind the altar stood six huge brass candlesticks, all polished and shining, and behind them was a painting that always captured Hannah's imagination. It was in three parts, the central section depicting the crucified Christ, blood gushing from the wounds on his head, hands and feet. But it was the side panels that intrigued her the most. The one to the left showed the disciples with Jesus at a table, one of them – a red-haired man – dipping something into a bowl, and the one to the right depicted the same man swinging from the branch of a tree by his neck, a pile of coins scattered on the ground beneath him. Whenever she asked about it, she was told not to think about him but *focus, rather, on Our Lord who bled and died for us all.*

Mass itself was a nonsense to Hannah, who had approached the moment of her first communion with growing dread. A nun's shrill voice still rang in her head. *It's a miracle. The bread turns into the very flesh of Christ himself. But you'd better be careful my dears. Sinful girls fall to the floor, dead.*

Yet there were no deaths on that day, nor any visible miracles. Even after the magic words had been spoken by the priest, it was still nothing more than a tasteless wafer.

But at least the daily mass was an escape from the nuns and their chores. It was also the time of day when her questions bombarded her the most. Why did Father Francis talk in that strange language? Why did the girls have to tell him private things through a little window? Why was the friendly Jesus that he talked about so different to the strict Jesus of the nuns?

She could remember all the stories the priest told. Her very favourite was the one about the boy who ran away from home and spent all his father's money on himself and his new friends. And who, when he'd run out of it and lost all his friends, went home to face his father. Hannah's favourite part of the story was when the father threw his arms around his son to welcome him home. Why weren't the nuns like that? Would Sister Simon become like the rest of them?

Sometimes her imagination took her even further. One day she would find her mother and father, and they would welcome her home like the little boy in Jesus's story. Of that she was certain.

Hannah knew nothing of her parents. She didn't know her family name. She'd arrived at the orphanage without even a first name. It was the nuns who'd decided on Hannah, but some of them referred to her simply as Number Fourteen. And there was the other name, the one that Sister Dominic sometimes used for her, Maggie, but she never understood why. The nun had used that name as Hannah was dragged out of her bed a few evenings before, and she still had no idea what she'd done wrong. All she knew was that she'd offended the Sister so much that neither of them had had any sleep that night. *I'll teach you, Maggie.* Hannah's daydreaming never stopped. Her mind fluttered constantly from one scene to another. The nun's voice was etched into her head. *Think you know better than me do you? Think you're clever? How dare you mention* his *name in my lessons. How dare you?*

Hannah tried desperately to recall the incident. Why was it so bad? She remembered Sister Dominic droning on and on about the all-embracing mercy and forgiveness of God, which had triggered a series of questions.

'So Sister, is there anything that God cannot forgive?'

'Impertinent child. Are you trying to trick me?' The nun's eyes flared as she folded her black-sleeved arms.

'No,' said Hannah. 'I just want to know how wide God's arms are.'

'Foolish girl. God doesn't have arms.'

'But, please Sister, don't Catholics believe Jesus is God? Because he has arms.'

Sniggers rippled around the classroom.

'Don't play games with me girl!' The nun unleashed her hands and clapped them together as if swatting an imaginary fly.

'I'm not Sister.' Hannah felt on the verge of tears. 'I promise. I'm just trying to understand. I want to learn. Please.'

Sister Dominic sat down. 'Very well. Let me try to answer.' She looked up at the crucifix on the wall, gazing at it briefly before focusing on Hannah again. 'Yes child. Catholics do indeed see Jesus as the Second Person of the Blessed Trinity and therefore as God in human form.'

Hannah looked at the crucifix. 'And is it right that Jesus forgave the thief who was next to him on the cross?'

'Yes child. The thief asked Jesus to remember him, and he told him he'd be with him in paradise.'

'And the tax collector?'

'Yes child.'

'And the woman who'd been caught sinning?'

'Yes.'

'And even those who ordered his death, saying "*they know not what they do?"'*

'Yes, Jesus forgave them all.'

Finally, Hannah had asked whether Jesus forgives the poor imperfect souls in purgatory who are prayed for at every mass, and again the nun's reply had been *yes*.

For some reason Hannah's memories faded at that point. She couldn't seem to remember what had happened after that.

Mass concluded and the girls were marched out of the chapel in single file. At the head of the procession was Sister Matthew, whose huge black habit flapped like a pair of gigantic wings. The corridor's floor echoed as the children's shoes tapped out a clip-clopping beat.

A tall, boyish girl called Rose turned around and smirked at Hannah who was directly behind her. She turned back before the nuns saw anything.

Rose waited a few seconds, then turned her head slightly and whispered through the side of her mouth, 'Oi, watch this.'

Chapter Six

De Stooterplas Island, 1981

'Hello brother,' said Eric.

His huge body jolted. 'But, my assistant said – '

'I wasn't even sure you'd agree to see a friend of mine. I made the name up.'

Instinctively the older brother crossed himself and Eric noticed how his fat arm struggled to reach. He'd always been big, but there must have been eighteen stone of him behind that desk. His thinning hair was still worn slicked back like a Wall Street stock broker, and yet it was an even deeper black now. *My God he must dye it.* His face was damp and there were small veiny blotches on either side of his nose. Eric could hear a faint whistle as he breathed.

The look of shock drained from Peter's face. His eyes narrowed and his nostrils flared. Putting both hands on the desk in front of him he pushed himself up slowly.

'What the fuck do you want?' he growled.

'I don't want anything. I have something for you.' Eric smiled.

'Huh? What could I possibly want from you?'

'I assure you, you'll want this.' Eric patted his jacket pocket.

Peter glared across the desk at Eric, studying him and allowing the intimidating silence to build.

'You'd better sit down then.' He let himself collapse back into his own seat.

Eric crossed to the chair at which his brother had nodded. Peter leaned back in his own, an enormous leather armchair, and then reached forward again for the packet of cigarettes on the table. He didn't offer Eric one.

'Well?'

'Wait. Before I give you what I've brought,' said Eric, still standing, 'let me first ask of Ella. How is she?'

Peter flinched, as if he'd just been given a doctor's jab. Then his head sank as he leaned forward and faced the desk. 'She's dead.' A tear fell onto the newspaper in front of him. He raised his head, eyes now filled. 'But I warn you…don't ask about her.' His top lip curled up and revealed a set of tar stained teeth. 'Don't mention her. Don't even think about her while you're here.'

Eric felt his knees start to give way. Two decades had passed since he'd last seen her, but he'd never stopped thinking about her. He held the chair to steady himself and eased himself down. His mind was swimming but, reluctantly, he dropped his questions about Ella. The news of her death had stunned him, but he was there for an even more important reason than the welfare of his ex-lover.

'Okay, I'll explain.' Eric took a deep breath. Any mourning for Ella would have to wait. 'After I left all those years ago, I needed to get as far away as possible.'

Peter grunted, lit his cigarette and inhaled.

'So I decided to find work on a cruise.'

'You said you had something for me.' Peter blew the smoke across the table.

'I'll come to it. First I need to explain how it came to me.'

Peter took another big puff.

'I found work with a company that specialised in Caribbean fly-cruise breaks for rich Americans. It introduced me to a land I felt the strangest connection to. We visited many islands and parts of Central and South America, but it was Mexico that really hooked me. I'm not sure what it was about it. But, after one of the dockings, when customers and staff were able to explore for a few days, I found myself wanting to stay. Of course I had to go back and work out my agreed terms but, once I had done so, I took the first opportunity to return. And that's where I've been for close on twenty years.'

'What's this got to do with me?' Peter's voice was hard as granite.

'I found something.'

'Found what?' Peter shifted in his chair.

Eric raised one finger. 'I'll get to it in a minute. Just listen.'

Peter slumped back and let out a wheezy sigh.

'I took to the Mexican culture like a duck to water. I learned Spanish quickly. I even learned a little of the old language – Yucatec Maya. I made a living by working in bars and spent my free time exploring the cultures. I say *cultures* because there are many in Mexico. I visited *Chichén Itzá* and other ancient sites and grew fascinated by the way our own Catholic faith is able to incorporate the older pagan ways.'

Peter sniffed.

'But then I came across another community. One with whom I felt an even deeper connection. On the surface they were Catholics like most Mexicans, and yet they were different. Something about them really intrigued me.'

Peter glanced at his watch.

'I also kept noticing a strange little symbol around their premises.'

'What symbol?' said Peter. 'A religious symbol?'

'No, not really religious. More totem-like. Something that I'd seen before but couldn't remember where.'

The desk intercom buzzed. Peter pressed the button. 'What is it?'

'Mr Van Kroot, there's a telephone call for you from your office. Would you like me to transfer it to you?'

'No Vince. Take a message. I'll call back later.'

'Very good, sir.'

'When I returned to my lodging, I asked one of my friends about the community I'd come across. She was an English research student called Penelope. I explained where the community was located and this was the first time I heard the term *Maranos*. She didn't know much about them, but said they were often shunned by other Mexicans. She'd once overheard them described as *filthy Maranos.*'

Peter looked at his brother through the smoke. 'What's that mean?'

Eric felt his heartbeat speed up, his words coming faster. 'This is where it gets exciting. Have you ever wondered about your own ancestors? Our grandfather built his hotel empire from scratch. We've always known he came from very little. It was his strong Catholic faith and work ethic that gave him the will to achieve, but have you ever wondered who we were before all that? Centuries before?'

'What are you trying to suggest?' said Peter, glaring. 'That we're South A-fucking-merican?'

'No, let me continue. Please. I want to tell you what I learned from this community before I give you what I've brought.'

Peter leaned back and stretched out his arm to glimpse his watch. 'You have half an hour. Then you can get out.'

Eric closed his eyes to picture the scene. After a moment he opened them. 'I was determined to get to know this community, so I got myself a job in a local food store – one that I'd seen members of the community use. Gradually a few faces became familiar and, over the course of time, they warmed to me. I knew better than to pry, so I just made sure to look after them well and be as helpful as possible. One man in particular stood out. He didn't come to the store as often as the others but, whenever he did, he'd always have a few words to say. After a while we had exchanged names. His was Señor Mendez. Abrim Mendez.'

Peter coughed, and looked at his watch again.

'I waited many months for an opportunity to present itself, and then one finally came. It was Christmastime and Señor Mendez had called by to order a package of special produce. He accepted my offer to deliver the package personally when it was ready. At last I was able to visit the community, or at least drive my van into their courtyard. When I arrived, Señor Mendez greeted me and was thrilled when I offered to repeat the favour whenever he required anything else. I told him he could simply call by with a list of produce and I'd deliver it. Payment on delivery.'

'Look, is this going anywhere?'

'Yes. Please let me continue. I promise, you'll be amazed.'

Peter sighed, reached for another cigarette and signalled with his hand for Eric to continue.

'After many more months of delivering various items to Señor Mendez, who by then had insisted I call him Abrim, I finally felt able to ask him the question that had burned within me since I'd first asked my friend Penelope about this community. I was unloading the last box of vegetables when Abrim offered me a drink. Moments later we were sat at a table in the sunshine with a cold lemonade.'

'And?'

'After a few minutes of small talk I decided to take a chance. "Abrim. Please forgive my ignorance if this is in any way impertinent, but does the term Maranos mean anything to you?"'

Peter blew a thin trail of smoke across the desk. 'Well, did it?'

'Yes, he flinched. I closed my eyes, shook my head and was ready to apologise, when he stood up and said, "Eric, over the last year you've become a friend to this community and I have come to trust you. So I will tell you our story, and I believe it will not only answer your question but set you on a new path of your own."'

'Odd thing to say.'

'Very. But it turned out he was some kind of mystic. You know...like a seer.'

Peter shook his head. 'Oh for Christ's sake.'

'He *knew* though. For some reason he knew that I was *meant* to ask him that question. Señor Mendez looked into my eyes and said, "Eric, the word Maranos was once a term of abuse. Our community have suffered greatly because of that word and what it means. Eric we are Jews."'

Peter's eyes widened and he took another long draw on the cigarette as Eric's memories continued to unfold.

'He described how his ancestors were Jews who'd been expelled from their homeland back in late fifteenth-century Spain. He told me how they were dispersed throughout the Mediterranean, ending up in Italy, North Africa, the Netherlands and beyond.'

Peter's left eye twitched.

'The Netherlands!' Eric's heart was beating faster.

Peter's eyes narrowed. 'I don't like the sound of this.'

'I've done it,' said Eric. 'I've traced our family. I know where we came from. Like those Mexicans, we too came from fifteenth-century Spain. We, too, brother – are Jews.'

Peter jumped up from his chair, banged his huge fist on the desk and roared. 'How dare you?'

'Peter, I – '

'Get out now before I take a fucking club to your head!' He reached to open a draw in his desk.

'But I have something for you. I need to leave it with you. It will explain everything; even about the little symbol I mentioned.' Eric reached inside his jacket pocket and pulled out a package.

'I don't want anything from you. You come here, lying about who you are, waltz into my private room twenty years after I swore I'd kill you for fucking my wife!' Peter pulled the club out from his drawer. 'You have one minute to get out of here.'

'Please, Peter. Please at least take this.'

'Fifty seconds.'

'Brother.'

'Stop calling me brother. No brother does what you did. You're not my brother. You're not even human. You're a traitor. And now you want to add to my pain – my misery – by claiming I'm a fucking Jew?'

'It's true. *This* will prove it.' Eric held out the package.

'Twenty seconds.' Peter held his watch up to his little brother. 'You killed me when you betrayed me. And you killed Ella when you got her pregnant.'

Eric's hand dropped. He felt like his brother's club had been thrust deep into his stomach. 'Pregnant? Ella...Ella was pregnant?'

'Yes, you sad fool. You not only lost your whore, you lost your whore's brat, too. That creature was given up for adoption as soon as she was born. Now fuck off.'

Eric sank into the chair. 'I had a child? I *have* a child? *I have a daughter?*'

'Yes.' Peter calmed slightly. 'Ella died giving birth. I decided to entrust the child to a Belgian Order of Sisters. They took her into care and told me she'd be taken to a Catholic children's home in Britain when she was ready.'

'I have to find her.'

'You won't. She left without a name and there are no records. That was my condition. I paid good money. And I wanted that to be the end of it. I've not thought of her until...' Peter glanced at Eric and their gazes met. The older brother almost looked guilty, '...until – um – until you showed up today.'

Eric rose from his chair, looked at the package in his hand, and went to put it back in his pocket.

'Is that what you wanted to give me?' asked Peter.

'Uh...yes.' Eric was too shocked to think straight.

'Leave it on the desk. I'll take a look later. Now get out.'

Chapter Seven

South Wales, 1970

'Which one of you brats was it?'

Sister Dominic stomped back and forth in front of the blackboard. The gloomy classroom had been the girls' base for the last two hours. In one hand the nun held her favourite cane, a beating stick so precious that she'd named it.

'You'd better speak up soon, or we'll start…' She raised the cane for effect '…at the front. And *Agatha* won't stop until we've found the culprit.'

In the other hand she clutched something else, something very small but significant.

Hannah was standing next to Rose. She reached up on tiptoes, raised her lips to the taller girl's ear and whispered, 'Rose, you have to own up, or we'll all get it.'

Rose turned and smirked.

'I'm going to count to five!' yelled the nun.

Grudgingly the tallest girl in the room slunk forward. 'It wer me Sister, I dun it.'

The previous day, while the girls were out in the yard, Rose found something on the ground. She wasn't sure where it had come from or what it was for, but she guessed it had fallen from something, perhaps when the delivery boy had been. Whatever it was she knew she could have some fun with it.

Rose was one of the girls who'd been sent to Crucis from the outside. Her talk was as dirty as the outside toilet block, which never seemed to get cleaned. She never talked much about her life before, but Hannah guessed it had not been as nice as the others who'd come from out there. Once, during bath time, Hannah had noticed the scars on Rose's back and often wondered why her nose bent to one side.

Rose was older than all the girls in Hannah's dormitory, but for some reason the nuns had placed her there. Perhaps it was because she couldn't learn as quickly as the others. Whatever the reason Hannah liked her being around. She made her laugh.

But this was serious.

The nun held a tiny object at her fingertips. 'Come here girl!'

Rose stepped forward.

'Wipe that grin off your face,' said Sister Dominic. 'Raise your skirt and tell me what possessed you?'

'Dunno.' The girl shrugged.

Crack. Agatha swished down and struck the back of Rose's bare legs, before recoiling like a snake.

Hannah flinched, imagining the shock of pain. Rose's hands became fists and her whole body went rigid. She was clearly trying to overpower her instinct to scream. This girl had already learned not to let the tormentors get their way. The crow wanted nothing more than to have Rose collapse into a pleading heap on the floor, but she was tougher than that. Hannah willed her not to give in and wondered when *Agatha* would take a second bite.

'Poor Sister Matthew is in the infirmary because of you!' Sister Dominic's face was red like a beetroot. 'You're a guttersnipe and a toad!' She half closed her eyes, lifted her face and looked down her nose at Rose. 'You'll be a nothing forever.'

Two hours earlier, the girls had been marching back to their dormitory after mass when something terrible happened. Sister Matthew turned the corner of the corridor when she lost her balance and fell wobbling backwards, landing on the stone floor like a huge pudding. The scream, followed by a heavy thump, had echoed down the passageway as the two nuns at the rear hoisted up their habits and ran to the front. They had arrived to find poor Sister Matthew lying unconscious, a gradually widening puddle of yellow liquid surrounding her lower half.

Rose had nudged Hannah. 'She's pissed 'erself. The fat cow's pissed 'erself.'

Moments later, more Sisters had appeared, some of them resorting to panic, flapping around like headless chickens. Then Sister Dominic arrived.

'Quiet! Stop this at once.' She looked down at Sister Matthew and, grimacing at the sight and smell, ordered two of the nuns to take the girls back to their dormitory.

The girls had been back at their beds for no more than a few minutes when they were summoned and promptly escorted to the classroom, to wait. It was now 8.30am. They'd already been deprived of breakfast, but only two of them knew what it was about.

Sister Dominic held up the little steel ball so all the girls could see it. 'I don't know where you found this,' she said, 'but you're going to wish you never had.' She grabbed Rose by the scruff of the neck, dragging her from the room and slamming the door as they left.

The remainder of the lesson was taken by Sister Kevin, an older nun who had to sit down to teach. She never shouted or smacked like Sister Dominic, but there was something else about her that frightened the girls. Sister Kevin had ill-fitting false teeth that, every so often, dislodged and popped out the front of her mouth. Whenever it happened at least one of the girls would scream and get into trouble.

Helping Sister Kevin was Sister Simon, now a novice. To Hannah she was the same sweet Sister Simon.

Sister Kevin's voice was tinny and strained. 'Girls, I hope you've all taken note that we will not tolerate any misbehaviour here?'

'Yes Sister,' they said together.

There was a knock at the door and another nun entered. She walked over to Sister Kevin, whispered something in her ear, and left.

Sister Kevin coughed. 'Alright, I need to leave.' She used her stick to push herself up onto her feet. 'Sister Simon will be in charge. You will all be obedient won't you?'

'Yes Sister.'

'Sister Simon will remain here until you've all finished your reading, after which she will bring you through to the yard for your hair inspection.'

'Yes Sister.'

The girls dreaded hair inspection. The big nurse who stood at the end of the queue enjoyed nothing more than grabbing handfuls of hair to search for the tiny imposters. She didn't care how much she pulled and scratched and tore at the little heads in front of her. But the girls dreaded something more than just pain. Each time this happened at least half a dozen poor unfortunates, whose hair had proven infested, were frogmarched to the room adjacent to the infirmary and sheared like sheep.

So far Hannah had managed to escape the shears herself.

Sister Simon walked to the centre of the room and looked around the class. 'Okay girls, finish your reading and put up a hand if you struggle with any words.'

Part of each morning was spent reading a chapter of a Gospel in quietness. Hannah had been told it was to complement the reading out loud, and help them to develop a discipline of daily Bible reading.

'Yes Hannah,' said the Sister. 'What word are you finding difficult?' She walked over to Hannah's desk and looked down at her open Bible.

Hannah peered up at her friend, feeling the tears flood her eyes.

'What is it Hannah?'

'I'm worried Sister.'

'Worried? About what Hannah?' The Sister put her hand lightly on her shoulder.

'You're going to be made into a proper nun soon aren't you?' She gazed into the angelic face.

'Well, yes, probably Hannah. But we shouldn't be talking

about that during lessons should we?'

'No Sister. Sorry Sister, but I'm scared.'

'Scared? What of Hannah?'

'That you're going to change. Turn into...'

A girl towards the back of the classroom sniggered, and Sister Simon spun around and shook her head. She turned back to Hannah.

'Girls, I'm hopefully going to be taking my full vows in the next few months, but I'll still be the same old Sister Simon.' She smiled, stroked Hannah's hair and whispered, 'I promise.'

Chapter Eight

The Testimony of Ezra Van Kroot, Amsterdam, 1535

It is, as they say here, the year of Our Lord fifteen hundred and thirty-five and I know not where to begin, but start I must, for I do not have long.

Yet, as I lean into this writing desk, my heart thumps so heavily that I can barely hold my quill without shuddering. Outside, the town awakens gradually out of its slumber. I hear the faint yelp of a dog barking in the distance, followed by another and then another, each slightly louder than the last. They mark their territory as the night watchman stalks, damping out the street lamps on his way. I grimace at the heavy clanging of piss pots being carried to the edge of the canal, splashing out their stinking contents.

I have checked the oil and wick and am satisfied the lamp will last. Though morning breaks, these shutters will remain closed until my task is complete, for a different form of darkness has engulfed me and thus I feel burdened to write, lest we do not survive this time. Who will tell our story if not I? And who will pass on the secret?

Our city, our once great New Zion, is falling. Only yesterday I beheld the savagery of their acts. What is it within men that renders them capable of such bedevilment? Never have I witnessed such a repugnant sight in peaceful Amsterdam. I retched so violently that the bile burned my throat. Forty unclothed men and women they were, naked as the day they were born. Anabaptists, and foolish enough to offend the Catholic authorities. Nudity and naivety were their only crimes. They bled. Their freshly cut out hearts hung like hideous decorations in Dam Square, a statement that said *do not cross the Church*. But I am running ahead of myself. To speak of the present I must first visit the past.

I was born on an eventful day, not that anyone in our locality would have known. It was the first of November 1478 and we lived in relative peace *for Jews*.

Our home was the little town of Muxacra situated on the eastern corner of the Kingdom of Granada. I confess, it is agony to think of her as I write these words. Oh Muxacra, sweet Muxacra, how I miss you. How I dream of your captivating views of blue ocean waters. How I long to, once again, walk your narrow streets and greet my old friends in the market square.

Our rulers were Moors and, according to their calculations, the year was 882. We Jews had the oldest dating system. For us it was 5238 but, I ask you, does God keep count? Has He the slightest interest in our mathematics? Nevertheless, because I now live as a loyal citizen of a Dutch Catholic city, I shall continue to use the Christian calendar here.

The latter period of Moorish rule has since become known as *La Conviviencia*, the getting along together, when our three communities lived in reasonable harmony. It was not that our town had been free from all unrest, but trauma seldom arose from within our own walls. Rather it came from the outside, for it was a frontier town. And, though we made up three distinct religious families, we always managed to tolerate one another. We were, after all, the three faiths of Abraham and thus cousins.

We Jews had lived on the Iberian Peninsula for centuries, well over a Millennium in fact. We had lived under the Romans, the Visigoths and the Moors who, through various Caliphates and Emirates, had ruled for the last eight centuries. They knew the land as *Al-Andalus.*

La Conviviencia was not perfect. We did not have equal rights with the Moors, but we did have opportunities for scholarship, medicine and trade, and enjoyed the freedom to worship as our traditions commanded us.

However, Moorish power had weakened, and we could see

the borders of Christian Castile creeping ever closer. There were frequent skirmishes as Castilian forces chipped away incessantly at Granada's boundaries.

Though context is crucial, the Jewish history of Iberia is not my primary purpose for this testimony. I write these words to safeguard a far greater story. My family carry a great and grave responsibility. We are custodians of a secret, a secret so devastating that only the first-born sons are ever entrusted to it. And even then, if the next in line is not deemed worthy or strong enough to bare it, it must skip a generation.

I myself, as first-born son, was handed the privilege when I was just ten years of age and far younger than would have seemed wise, but the circumstances were exceptional. The fact that I feel it necessary to write these words now proves how important this secret is, but I cannot pass it onto my own son. I dare not, after what I've suffered. God forbid the same unspeakable fate befall him. So, if this document has found itself in the hands of a descendant, I only hope you know what you must do.

Chapter Nine

De Stooterplas Island, 1981

Peter Van Kroot watched his brother cross the room and leave, closing the door behind him.

Then his eyes fell to the far side of the desk and to the package Eric had left. Using the club, he pulled it towards him. Sat behind his desk he opened the wrapper and took out a little leather book. The cover was worn and the title barely legible. All he could be certain of was the date, which had been stamped boldly into the leather: 1535. He shivered as a cold sensation ran down his spine, from the nape of his neck to his coccyx.

He then opened his drawer once more and, replacing the club, retrieved a little case out of which he took his spectacles. Placing them on his nose he held up the book and opened the cover to the first page. Though it looked like a professionally produced book, it had no identifying marks of either publisher or printer. On the inside cover it said simply *The Testimony of Ezra Van Kroot. Amsterdam, 1535.*

Chapter Ten

The Testimony of Ezra Van Kroot, Amsterdam, 1535

I was bequeathed the secret at the age of ten. How vividly I remember it. My father and I were in our boat. A Castilian fishing village was situated just north of Muxacra and we had to be ever diligent not to cross into its waters.

We had anchored and were untangling the nets, preparing to make our first cast of the day. A slight breeze blew across the waters cooling our bodies and silver shoals darted in and out from under the boat. Looking towards the shoreline I could see the white buildings on the hilltop that was my home, and who could have wished for a more perfect home?

Yet my father did not seem himself that day. He was quiet and his eyes were glazed, as if he were under some kind of enchantment.

'Father,' I said, but he did not respond. He simply continued to work on the nets and gaze into nothing. 'Father.'

At last he stopped, his face now turned to mine. He smiled. 'Ezra, you are a good son.' He bit his lip and breathed deeply. 'There is something I must ask of you.'

His words and manner unnerved me. I felt myself tremble.

'I should have waited until you were of riper age but...'

'But what Father?'

'But there are reasons why I must do this now.' Truly I had never beheld him this way before. 'Ezra, a storm is brewing. It was set in motion the very day of your birth, when they unleashed the dreadful human beast they call the...'

It was then that my father introduced me to a word I would never forget. A word that has since brought terror whenever I hear it. A word that burst into my mind when I saw those poor

Anabaptists writhing in agony as their beating hearts were cut out.

My father looked deep into my eyes and swallowed. 'Inquisition.'

Chapter Eleven

South Wales, 1970

Her pale grey face was lined deeply and powder dry, like a baker's work surface, but Hannah had always found her gentler than the younger Sisters. Occasionally she heard the old nun talking to a girl in the kindest way, even using terms like *my child* and *little lamb*. Yet she was still capable of instilling fear. When Mother Angelica spoke, everyone listened, the other nuns included.

Rarely did she visit the girls' dormitory. Only the most important matters would bring her there, one of which was a death – either a nun's or an orphan's – but this was uncommon. Another matter that brought the old nun was more like a birth, and that was why she'd appeared this morning.

'Girls, I want you to welcome a newcomer to our family. This is Lucy.' A tiny little girl with light blond hair stepped out nervously from behind the old nun's habit. She had big sky-blue eyes and the smallest mouth. Her dainty nose was turned up slightly. She was carrying a neat little bundle of clothes.

'Go on then my dear.' Mother Angelica pointed at an empty bed. Lucy hesitated at first, but then inched her way across the room as all the girls watched. Her bed was next to Hannah's.

'Girl Fourteen.' Mother Angelica's voice sounded as old as she looked. 'Remind me of your name.'

'Hannah, Mother.'

'Ah yes. Hannah. I'd like you to look after Lucy until she finds her way.'

'Yes Mother.'

'And see that she gets everywhere she needs to on time!'

'Yes Mother.'

Hannah waited for the Reverend Mother to leave and turned

to the new girl whose bottom lip trembled like a leaf and whose eyes were filled with tears. 'It's okay,' she said. 'You'll get used to it.'

Lucy stood by the side of her new bed and put the little bundle of clothes on the mattress. Then she turned to Hannah.

Hannah smiled. 'You'll need to change into those before we go to breakfast, Lucy.' Immediately Lucy started to undo the buttons on her blouse.

'No, not like that. Let me show you.' Hannah unfolded the bundle and laid the clothes out on the bed for Lucy to see. She then picked up a garment. 'This is your nightgown Lucy. Whenever you change, you need to put this on before removing your other clothes. Here we get changed under our nightgowns. It's a sin to show your body, you know.'

One of the girls let out a sarcastic laugh.

Hannah watched as Lucy put the big gown on. 'Now, you need to remove the clothes you're wearing and put them neatly in the little cupboard by the wall.' Hannah pointed to a wooden bedside table. 'The other clothes are for wearing now. These are what we all wear here.'

Lucy stared at the colourless dress and apron that lay on her bed.

'I know they're not pretty,' said Hannah, 'but we have to wear them here. It's the rule.'

Lucy had arrived just before breakfast, which was her first taste of life at Crucis. The girls filed into the refectory and stood silently behind the chairs. Then an elderly voice bellowed across the tables in words that no girl understood, but all knew by heart. *Benedic, Domine, nos et dona tua, quae de largitate tua sumus sumpturi, et concede, ut illis salubriter nutriti tibi debitum obsequium praestare valeamus, per Christum Dominum nostrum.* Mother Angelica always said the benediction before meals, but the girls never saw her because the Sisters sat at the far end behind a screen. The delicious smells that drifted out from behind that screen made eating the slop they were fed even more difficult. Watery porridge was all the girls had to look forward to in the mornings.

After the benediction they were allowed to sit. Hannah turned to Lucy, putting a finger to her mouth. No talking was permitted in the refectory.

Just as Lucy began to spoon the first mouthful in, another voice started up. This morning it was Theresa's turn to read from the book of Holy Scripture. Hannah remembered the first time she asked why the Bible was read at meals. *We feed our souls as we feed our bodies, child.*

Lucy stayed close to Hannah throughout the rest of the day but there were no opportunities to talk. Mornings were always spent in the classroom, whereas afternoons were set apart for the various forms of manual work the children had to perform, and all of this was supposed to be done in silence. They could have talked at break time but Lucy had been called for by one of the Sisters. It wasn't until after vespers, and they were back in their dormitory, that the girls were granted permission to talk for half an hour before lights out.

'So Lucy,' said Hannah, as she sat on her bed next to the new girl, 'where are you from?'

Lucy looked on the verge of tears. She didn't even seem to notice Hannah's question.

Her voice was like a tiny bird's. 'Mummy will come for me. She promised.'

'When did you last see her?' asked Hannah.

The little girl turned to face her new friend and a large tear ran down her pale cheek. 'Yesterday.' She wiped her face with her hand. 'Daddy left us and mummy said she couldn't look after me or my sisters until things change.'

'Change?' asked Hannah.

'Mummy has no money. She needs to be able to work which means us being sent away.' Her bottom lip quivered, her eyes closed and she sobbed into her hands.

'Oh Lucy.' Hannah hopped off her bed, reached out her arms and the two little girls hugged each other.

Chapter Twelve

De Stooterplas Island, 1981

'How could it be? How could it fucking be?'

Eric sat on the side of the road not far from the intercom system he'd used no more than an hour before, and there he waited for the cab. His head was down and his face was cradled in both hands. With eyes closed he felt like he was recovering from ten rounds with Rocky Balboa. Nothing could have prepared him for what his brother had told him.

Eventually the cab arrived and a friendly toot brought Eric out of his trance, and though the driver attempted it a handful of times, there was no conversation on the ride back to the hotel.

* * *

The next morning, Eric only had one thing on his mind.

Chapter Thirteen

South Wales, 1970

The classroom's grey walls were bare, save for a wooden crucifix that hung like a terrifying warning against misbehaviour. The high ceiling was filled with floating dust particles that sparkled as they drifted in front of the sun's rays shooting through the metal-framed windows. Cobwebs hung high up in the corners, each one home to a spider who clearly hoped not to be noticed.

As Sister Dominic entered, the girls rose to their feet, all eyes focussed on the blackboard as they were commanded. Eventually they were given permission to sit back down at their desks.

It was then that Hannah noticed the girl standing next to the nun. Her head hung like a sack of washing, her shoulders were slouched and a thick black mop of hair covered most of her face. It was definitely her, but she never normally stood like that.

'Find your chair, toad,' breathed the nun. 'And remember what I told you.'

It had been a month since Rose was dragged from the dormitory.

'Yes Sister.' With her head still facing the floor, the big girl found her desk, pulled out the chair and sat down.

Sister Dominic turned to face the blackboard, grabbed a piece of chalk from the well at the bottom and scratched out some numbers. Still facing away, she said, 'Take out your Holy Bibles and turn to the Gospel of Saint Luke, Chapter Eight.' She tapped the blackboard with the chalk. 'And for those fool enough to have forgotten how to find it, it's on this page.'

After the rustling of pages had stopped, the nun looked directly at Hannah. 'Maggie, it's your turn to read today.'

Hannah looked up and the nun added, 'You will like this passage my dear.' The faintest smirk flashed across the nun's face as Hannah picked up the book and stood to read.

Clearing her throat, she began. *And it came to pass afterward, that Jesus went throughout every city and village, preaching and sharing the glad tidings of the kingdom of God: and the twelve were with him, and certain women, which had been healed of evil spirits and infirmities, Mary called Magdalene, out of whom went seven devils, and Joanna the wife of Chuza Herod's steward, and Susanna, and many others, which ministered unto him of their substance. And when much people were gathered together, and were come to him out of every city, he spake by a parable: A sower went out to sow his seed: and as he sowed, some fell by the wayside; and it was trodden down, and the fowls of the air devoured it…*

Hannah was used to the daily reciting of a chapter from the Gospels. They'd been through each of them more times than she could number. But why did Sister Dominic say she would like this passage?

Vespers finished, and the girls were marched back to their dormitory. Hannah knew she could now talk to Rose but wasn't sure whether to leave it for a while. As well as the one on the side of her face, bruises were visible on Rose's arms too. She sat on her bed hugging her legs, rocking slightly – eyes fixed on nothing in particular, but staring intently.

Hannah thought back to her own last incident with a nun, and still had no idea why she'd been dragged from the bed by Sister Dominic. The only clue was The Black Crow's words, *how dare you bring his name up!* But she couldn't remember bringing anyone's name up, and she knew it would not be wise to ask what this meant.

She then remembered the morning's scripture reading. Why did that bitch say things and not explain?

She felt a little tug on her nightgown and, turning around, saw Lucy. Even though Hannah was slight, Lucy was tiny in comparison. Her huge eyes seemed out of proportion as they glanced in Rose's direction.

Lucy whispered, 'Who is that?'

'Oh of course, you don't know Rose do you?'

The little girl shook her head.

'She's my friend, but...'

Lucy's eyes widened even more.

Hannah lowered her voice as much as she could, '...but I think it's best to leave her be for a while.'

Lucy gulped.

'Oh don't worry. I don't mean that.' Hannah smiled. 'She's just tired, that's all. She's been in an accident and has had a few weeks in the infirmary. Do you know what an infirmary is?'

The little girl shook her head.

'It's where poorly people go to get better.' She smiled again and reached out her hand touching Lucy's.

Suddenly there was a huge bang and the heavy dormitory door swung open hitting the wall. A black figure stood in the opening, filling it completely. Her flabby mouth was turned down and her eyes were like thunder as she hobbled over to Rose with the aid of a walking stick. It was always hard to judge the age of the nuns, because so much of them was covered up, but by the lack of lines on her face, Sister Matthew must have been one of the younger ones. She was much fatter though, like a pig, and that might have made her face seem smoother.

Then another nun came in.

'Right girls.' It was Sister Dominic. 'Lights out and into bed. I take it you've all said your prayers?'

'Yes Sister,' they said in unison.

'Have *you* said your prayers?' Sister Matthew stood over Rose with her arms folded.

Rose simply nodded, her eyes still staring into nothing. As she pulled back her blanket and got into the bed, the hovering figure inched a little closer to the bed and whispered something, before moving away.

Sister Dominic was still by the main entrance. 'Sister Matthew,

I need to see Mother Angelica about something. I'll leave you to do the final check before switching the lights off.'

'Yes Sister Dominic.'

As Sister Matthew turned away from Rose's bed she limped up to the far end of the dormitory and, moving slowly down the central aisle, made her way towards the entrance, glancing back and forth at each girl. Hannah felt her coming closer, and then she stopped – right next to Lucy.

Peering down at the new girl, she said, 'What's this then? A dormouse?'

'Her name's Lucy, Sister.' Hannah sat up to address the nun. 'She's only been with us a while.'

'I'm sure she can speak for herself,' wheezed the nun.

But Lucy didn't say anything. She lay there with eyes as wide as saucers, sheets pulled up over her nose.

Hannah watched as Sister Matthew stepped closer, uncurled an arm and reached a podgy white hand across to the little girl's head, her fingers stroking her hair. Then, in a sickly-sweet voice, she said, 'There there, shy little Lucy. Sleep now. Plenty of time to talk later.'

Hannah, still upright in her bed, noticed that across the dormitory someone else was sitting up and peering at the nun.

As if she could sense it the nun swung around to face Rose. 'Go to sleep creature,' she said as she swished away from Lucy's bed, completing her inspections quickly and flicking off the light switch as she left.

* * *

Hannah didn't get much sleep due to Lucy's sobbing. But as the morning bell shocked her awake, she became aware of another sensation. She turned her head and realised she wasn't imagining it or dreaming. Lucy was in the bed with her. Terror! The crows would go mad if they saw. Too late.

'What's this?' The shriek was deafening. 'Devils!' cried the nun as she flew up the aisle towards the girls. 'Evil little devils!'

Sister Benedict only rarely visited the girls' dormitory. Usually it was Sister Dominic or Sister Matthew's role. Sister Benedict was older than both and, though not as cruel, she was feared in a way the others weren't. It was her appearance that made her so terrifying. She was extremely tall, thin and stooped, with a narrow face whiter than chalk. And, the most unsettling part, a blind eye that had the appearance of the underside of a slug.

She could see perfectly well through the other one, though. Her hand was dragging Lucy from Hannah's bed.

Hannah protested, 'Please Sister. She's new and is missing her mother so much. Her nights have been filled with horrible dreams. I let her lie beside me because she was so upset last night. Please believe me.'

'Perverts! I've never seen anything so disgusting!'

Lucy's sobs were inconsolable. Hannah pleaded.

'Oi, leave em alone!' Rose was standing by her bed and, as Sister Benedict turned to see which imbecile had dared to challenge her, she added, 'please Sister.'

'Don't you *Oi* me, you little slut,' said the nun. 'You probably encouraged this. This…degenerate behaviour.'

'Yeah, yeah you're right Sister. It wer me. Don't blame em. I erd the new girl cryin and saw Hannah tryin to comfort er. I told er she should let er lay beside er for a while. You know, to comfort er. It wer my idea.'

Hannah couldn't believe that Rose was standing up for them.

'Very well. But don't think I won't have my eye on you three.' With a skeletal finger the nun touched her good eye. 'I can spot depravity a mile away…even with just one.'

And she was gone.

Lucy was still sniffling and wiping away tears, Rose was back in her bed and Hannah was deep in thought. What had happened to Rose? She'd never have done that before. *Stupid girls deserved a right beatin for doing that,* is what she'd have said.

Hannah then noticed Lucy padding across to Rose's side of the dormitory. And, as the little girl drew closer, Rose broke out in a big smile. Hannah had to blink. She was not used to seeing Rose like this.

Chapter Fourteen

Amsterdam, 1981

'Let me see him. I demand it.'

'Impossible,' said the voice. 'Mr Van Kroot has given me strict instructions not to let you in. Please don't call again.'

'At least pass on my contact details and a short message,' said Eric.

'Very well.'

After he'd given the name and address of the hotel, Eric said, 'My message is this. Brother you have every reason to hate me, but please just give me a clue as to how I might find her. Do this and I will never bother you again.'

'Good day sir.' The other end of the line clicked.

Eric replaced the handset and walked to the window. Down below, the morning streets of Amsterdam were already busy. A small group of young men staggered past. Eric watched as one of them stopped to piss against the wall. A youth on a bike who was about to ride past him, crossed the street and hurried by on the other side. A young woman walking in the other direction did her best to ignore the urinating youth and scurried on. She looked about half Eric's age and, as she walked, the sound of her heels beat out a steady rhythm of high-pitched clip clops until they faded into the distance. He wondered how old his own daughter would be.

The kettle reached boiling point and Eric poured some water onto the brown contents of two little sachets he'd just dumped into a small cup. It tasted foul but he needed the caffeine. He glanced at the empty glass and half empty bottle of Jack Daniels on the bedside table.

As he sat on the bed and allowed the hot remedy to do its work, he tried to recall the conversation. What had Peter said about the nuns? What were they called? *Shit, shit, shit.*

The only thing he could remember was that Belgian nuns had taken her and handed her over to a British order. Who could help him? Who could he ask?

Then it came to him.

* * *

As Eric made his way towards the huge city library his mind drifted back to his last visit to a library in Amsterdam, a city that boasted over twenty-five of them.

He recalled the excited telephone conversation with the archivist at the *Biblioteca Ets Haim.* She'd found something. He'd rushed there that morning, and waited nervously in the reception area of the oldest Jewish library in the world. What could it be?

Eventually the archivist brought him an old leather covered box with a strange stick man figure branded onto the lid.

Mr Van Kroot, I believe this item was hidden back in the early forties, together with a lot of other material. This was the period when Nazi personnel or sympathisers would have destroyed anything like it. I'm not sure where it came from prior to that, or how it ended up being preserved and protected here. It may have simply been gathered into a general store of Jewish artefacts that found their way here over the last few decades, but I can tell you that, not only is it marked with the symbol you have enquired about, it also bears your family name.

* * *

Eric snapped out of his daydream and made his way up the main steps of a very different public library.

The *Centrale Bibliotheek* was an impressive building situated on the *Prinsengracht.* Eric thanked the assistant who led him to the area on Roman Catholicism and pointed out the small collection of books on religious orders. He took them to an empty reading table and sat down, notebook and pen ready for any details that might help him.

After an hour of looking up every index reference to Belgian and British Roman Catholic convents and searching for possible connections and clues, Eric started to doubt whether he was going to find anything.

'Shit,' he muttered, 'what the fuck am I going to do?'

The cough jolted him. It came from behind and he turned around instinctively.

'I couldn't help noticing what you were reading.' The old man was dressed in the dark suit and a shirt to match, causing Eric to freeze.

'Can I help?' asked the priest. A kindly smile broke out across his lined face. 'You seem to be – forgive me – a little upset.'

Chapter Fifteen

South Wales, 1970

'Sister, can I ask you something?'

'Of course you can Angel.'

It was the afternoon break and Hannah had taken advantage of Sister Simon being on duty. They were standing together near the outer boundary. Just then a dove flew down from a tree and landed on the top of the wall. Hannah looked up and smiled as he sat there watching them silently, then she turned back to Sister Simon.

'When did you first want to be a nun?'

Sister Simon laughed. 'Well that's a big question, Hannah dear, and I don't think break time is long enough for me to answer it, but you've given me an idea. Perhaps I should ask the Reverend Mother's permission to talk to you all about it in class sometime?'

'Oh yes Sister.' Hannah couldn't stop herself from bouncing up and down. 'I'd love that.'

'Do you think the other girls would be interested?'

'Yes, yes, I know they would.'

'Alright,' said the Sister, 'I'll talk to her soon.'

The dove stretched out his wings and flew away. Hannah watched him. Then she looked across the yard and saw Rose with Lucy. Over the previous few weeks Lucy's night time episodes had lessened and Hannah noticed she was spending more break times with Rose. Since the morning Lucy had been caught in Hannah's bed, Rose had noticeably softened. She'd returned to the dormitory quite different after her month in the infirmary. She was like a new person. Hannah had never seen her smile, except for when the grin betrayed malice rather than happiness. Now Rose smiled at Lucy whenever she passed her.

Maybe she just needed a little sister?

* * *

It was a particularly hot summer morning. The night had been sweltering and many girls had found it hard to sleep.

Mass had finished and the girls processed through the corridors. Hannah walked next to Lucy. Rose was three girls ahead. Suddenly, and without any warning, the larger girl collapsed. She just dropped, hitting the hard floor with a crash. The girl next to her screamed and Hannah noticed a trickle of blood flowing from Rose's nose. Then Rose started trembling and her body shook wildly for a few seconds. And once again she was still.

Sister Dominic spun around at the front of the procession. 'What's all that noise?' She darted towards the commotion.

Lucy moved closer to where Rose was lying.

The little girl knelt down, sobbing and held her friend's hand. 'Rose, Rose, wake up. What's wrong? Please. Rose.'

'Get up, and get away from her.' The crow towered over Lucy, face contorted like a hideous gargoyle.

Lucy didn't move quickly enough. 'I said move!' A hand shot out from a black sleeve, like a viper's tongue, grabbing the little girl and pulling her off the floor. She pushed Lucy backwards to the circle of girls that had formed around Rose.

One of Rose's eyes opened briefly, and then closed. Hannah held onto Lucy's hand in case she tried to reach her friend again.

'Alright girls,' Sister Dominic said, 'You are all to go back to your dormitory calmly. Sister Matthew and I will take Rose to the infirmary. Don't worry. She's just fainted. It must have been the heat.'

Back at the dormitory Hannah tried to comfort Lucy. 'She'll be okay. Like Sister Dominic said, she just fainted because of the heat.' But was that really true? Hannah wasn't at all certain.

'Yesterday she told me she had a headache,' said Lucy.

'Really?'

'Yes,' said Lucy. 'And Rose said something about a doctor who'd seen her while she was in the infirmary.'

'What did the doctor say?'

'He said she might have had a fit or something.'

'When Lucy? She's never fainted like that before?'

'She told me that she'd felt very strange after the nuns had hit her. And she also said that she'd been told to tell the doctor she'd fallen over and knocked her head.'

'I did wonder about the bruises. So how did she get them?'

'Sister Dominic whacked her across the side of her head with a shoe, Hannah. With Rose's own shoe.'

'Oh no. They've done this to her, haven't they? They've given her fits.'

* * *

Rose returned to the dormitory just before bedtime prayers. She was brought back by Sister Dominic. After the nun had left, Hannah very carefully crept out of her bed and crossed the room to where Rose was lying.

'Rose, Rose, are you okay?'

'Shhhhhh. Yeah I'm okay, go back to bed.'

Hannah did as she was told and, as she lay there looking up at the ceiling, her mind began to fill with images of the last few weeks. She thought of Rose rolling the metal ball up the corridor, sending Sister Matthew crashing to the floor in a heap. She could even smell the putrid aroma as she imagined the huge nun lying there in a puddle of piss. She remembered Rose being dragged off. Then she thought of Lucy's first appearance at Crucis where, at the end of that day, the two of them ended up hugging and crying together.

She daydreamed of Rose's return from the infirmary and the

bruises on the side of her face and neck, of Lucy and Rose sitting together in the refectory, of Rose rocking back and forth in some kind of dream and of her collapsing this morning. The blood from her nose. What was going on with her?

Her eyes grew heavy as she drifted into sleep…

Within moments she was dreaming of being back in the classroom with Sister Dominic. She looked at the crucifix and asked, '*And is it right that Jesus forgave the thief who was next to him on the cross?*'

'*Yes child. The thief asked Jesus to remember him, and he told him he'd be with him in paradise.*'

'*And the tax collector?*'

'*Yes child. His forgiveness is ever-flowing.*'

'*And the woman who'd been caught sinning?*'

'*Yes child.*'

'*And even those who ordered his death, saying "they know not what they do"?*'

'*Yes, Jesus forgave them all.*'

'*And he forgives the poor imperfect souls in purgatory who we pray for at mass?*'

'*Yes.*'

'*I think he even forgives poor Judas.*'

Silence. And a scream. And pure rage. And a hard knock to Hannah's head. And more silence.

The morning bell clanged and Hannah woke up. So that was what it was. That was the name. Judas. But why did he upset the nun so much?

Chapter Sixteen

The Testimony of Ezra Van Kroot, Amsterdam, 1535

I listened as my father explained. 'Ezra, have I not told you that the time is coming when our town might be overthrown. We have talked about it have we not?'

'Yes, Father. But you said the people who live over there...' I looked towards the northern part of the coast, 'are angrier with the Moors than they are with us. And that they would probably allow us to remain here.'

'That is true, my son. But there is something else. Something that will mean far graver changes for our family than merely a new set of governors.'

He stood and, holding the edge of the boat to steady himself, reached down with his other hand and took one end of the net. Instinctively I got up and took the other end.

As we cast out, my father said, 'I have to keep our family safe. I need to make sure that no nets are set to trap you, your mother or brothers. I must protect you all from those who would harm you.'

I studied his face. He suddenly looked so old. His once sparkling eyes now looked lifeless. He was not an old man by any measure, but long days of fishing in the hot sun had aged his features and bleached his hair. Salty hot wind had transformed his face into an old dry drinking skin. The bags under his eyes twitched as he struggled to tell me what he had prepared.

He sat down. 'My son, our people have never been far from trouble and any peace we have known has not lasted. For some unknown reason we have always been unwelcome, wherever we have chosen to make our home.'

'But Father,' I said, 'we have been welcome here have we not?

Who has ever wished us harm in *Muxacra*?'

'Yes, Ezra.' He smiled. 'Our family have lived here for many summers, and we have been fortunate. No one cares much how we pray here, but the same is not true across the border. Indeed, it is not a border any more, but a barrier. And if that barrier comes down...' He turned away and looked out to sea, '...we will be forced to hide our identity and become Christians.'

Chapter Seventeen

South Wales, 1970

Hannah had her hand up.

'What is it, child?'

It was breakfast and Sister Dominic was on duty. Hannah didn't know how to begin. She knew what she had to ask, but she was also aware that it might trigger another beating. She'd felt sorry for Judas ever since she asked about the red-haired man in the chapel painting. Sister Simon had told her the story of how he betrayed Jesus and felt so sad about it that he hung himself. Hannah wondered whether Jesus actually needed Judas to do what he did, or the story wouldn't have worked. But she kept those thoughts to herself.

'I'm sorry Sister, but I want to ask you something…in private,' said Hannah.

'What? You don't get to speak to me in private. How dare you! If you wish to ask me something, ask me now. Come on girl, what is it?'

Hannah gulped. 'Alright. Sister.' She glanced around at all the young faces looking at her. 'Why was it so wrong to mention Judas the other week?'

The nun narrowed her eyes and leaned forward. 'It wasn't so much you mentioning him, it was your blasphemous presumption to pardon him.'

'But Sister, all I said was that I thought Jesus would have forgiven him.'

'*All you said!* That would have been enough to have had you burned a few hundred years ago.' Her eyes were now wide open and bulging.

Hannah shuddered. 'But that's what's so confusing, Sister. Why all this talk of doing such beastly things to people in the name of God? Burning people. Surely Jesus would never have wanted to burn people? And surely he would have loved Judas, even if he was also angry with him?'

The crow starting twitching and her face deepened in colour. 'But that's not true. You wicked girl. How could you think that? He was a devil – an imposter. He was a dirty Jewish monster who sold Our Lord to his death.'

'But Jesus even forgave those who crucified him, Sister.'

'You're a true child of evil aren't you?'

Hannah found herself energised. Stronger. Braver. 'You've always hated me. Why? What have I done?'

'I'll tell you what you've done girl.' The nun's eyes and face were red like a demon's. 'I'll tell you what you've done!'

The other girls were silent. They dared not interrupt Sister Dominic, and now they watched and waited – waited to hear what it was that she hated so much about Hannah. But she said nothing. The nun just stood there peering at Hannah, as if suddenly dumb.

About five minutes went by with not a word from anyone.

'Alright,' said Sister Dominic, 'girls on the front table, you can lead today.'

And breakfast was over.

All the way back to the dormitory, Hannah wondered why Sister Dominic didn't tell her. And then she knew. It was because the nun didn't even know why she hated her. That was it.

Chapter Eighteen

Amsterdam, 1981

They pushed themselves through a crowd queueing up outside the Verneer Café and finally reached the enormous neo-Gothic building. Father Ambroos unlocked the door and turned to Eric, his smile fading. 'We used to keep it open day and night.' A sadness moved slowly across his face like the shadow of a cloud.

'Those were the days,' said Eric, as they entered the Church of St Nicholas.

The streets had been busier than normal for an Amsterdam mid-morning. The streams of bicycles had been hard to fight through, like an army of worker ants on their way to and from their nest. The familiar sounds of bike bells ding-a-linging, excited tourists in what seemed like a thousand different languages and gongs and chimes from the many town clocks and towers added to the feel of a thriving cosmopolitan city. And then, as the door closed behind them, silence.

Father Ambroos turned a large key. 'We'll have an hour's peace in here, my son, before I have to open up to the public.' The old man led Eric into the main nave and up the central aisle until they reached the benches directly in front of the high altar. The faint smell of incense reminded Eric of the last time he'd visited a Catholic church, the parish church of Santa Maria, Mojacar in Almeria, Southern Spain. 'Wait here for a moment. I need to turn on the lights.'

While the priest was gone, Eric allowed the sweet aroma to evoke his memories. Inspired by what his Mexican friend Abrim Mendez had told him, Eric had flown to Andalucía to visit cities with a strong Jewish past as well as a respected Jewish present-day community: the three largest were Seville, Cordoba and Granada. However, his search had been discouraging. Most

Jewish communities viewed him with deep suspicion. He didn't blame them. Not after what their ancestors had gone through.

It was not until his journey took him to the Almeria district that his luck began to change. It had been the same story with the city of Almeria as with the others, guarded Jewish communities who were not willing to talk. But as he travelled on around the coast he started noticing a strange symbol. At first he paid no real attention. However, as it became more prominent – on homes, hotels, cut into the desert rock, sprayed on walls as graffiti and even on some clothing for sale in shops – he started to experience a deep feeling of Déjà vu.

He needed to find out what the symbol was.

Squinting at the crowds, he noticed a man unchaining a bike from a railing on the other side of the road. He had the symbol on his T-shirt. Eric ran across the road without looking at the traffic. The man turned to see Eric arriving, panting.

'*Perdon?*' said Eric, in his best Spanish accent, '*Yo tengo una pregunto.*'

He looked Eric up and down and backed away. 'Sorry mate, I'm English.'

Eric smiled. He was going to have to speak English himself then. No chance of the guy speaking Dutch.

He looked like he was in his early twenties. Eric had assumed he was Spanish because, not only was the man olive skinned, he'd already learned that this was a relatively non-touristy and unspoilt part of the coast, where many families from Madrid and other central and northern cities spent their summers.

'It's apparently called the Indalo Man, mate. He's a man carrying a rainbow or something.' The young man got on his bike.

'Wait. Do you know what it means?'

'It's a sign. Well, that's what I was told. The rainbow is a sign of heaven. So this stick man is like a bridge between man and heaven.'

'Fascinating,' said Eric, 'and you say it's called the…Indalo Man?'

'Yes, or…er the Mojacar Man.'

'Mojacar?'

'A little town not too far from here. This symbol is their emblem.'

* * *

The next day Eric had made his way to the little hill-top town of Mojacar situated on the coast, just within the ancient borders of Moorish Granada. It was there, sat outside the parish church of Santa Maria, studying a fold-up paper map and enjoying a cool beer, that he discovered his original family name.

The church doors opened behind him and he was surrounded by a waft of sweet incense. He finished his beer and followed the scent into the church, crossing himself as he entered. It was small and lit with coloured light that glowed through the windows. There were a few people kneeling at prayer benches and twenty or so candles left flickering in front of the Our Lord and Our Lady statues by visitors. And then he noticed it – on one of the walls near the back – the image of the Indalo Man. Next to it was a sign written in Spanish, English and French. It said, *The Indalo Man, Mojacar's Noah.*

When a tourist visits the region of Almeria for the first time, one thing will soon begin to stand out – the so-called Indalo Man. Some call it the Mojacar Man, others still the Rainbow Man, but perhaps the most telling name for this symbol is the Bridge Man. He means many different things to many different people. To some he is a totem, a magical symbol to bring good luck and ward off evil. To others he represents a link, or bridge, to our Iberian past, for he is probably close to 6,000 years old. And to others still he is a sign of hope – the hope of reconciliation, for just as he stands between heaven and earth bringing together God and Man, so he also stands as a bridge between community and community, unifying all humans whatever creed or culture, race or religion.

He has gained popularity ever since his discovery in 1868, where cave paintings were stumbled across in the north of the province of Almeria.

It is now customary in this region of Spain to paint the Indalo Man on the front of houses and businesses to protect them from evil. However, historians have discovered that this practice of warding off evil by having the Indalo symbol above the door has been going on for many centuries here in Mojacar, so the locals clearly knew of the Indalo Man before the cave discovery in 1868.

It is said that, centuries ago, fishermen would scratch the symbol on their boats before going out to sea as a protection against storms and as a guarantee of obtaining a good catch. For the three great Abrahamic religions there is an extra significance: the Indalo symbol shows a man holding an arch above his head. The arch represents either a rainbow or the vault of the Heavens. Thus the Indalo was perceived to be a go-between for man and God, the rainbow providing a bridge between heaven and earth. Some have suggested that it depicts Noah lifting his hands towards heaven and giving thanks to God for seeing him and his family safely through the flood and sending the rainbow as a promise to Noah (and a reminder to himself) that he would never again flood the earth to destroy all living things as he had just done. This has given some of the more enthusiastic researchers the impetus to believe that this pictogram was made by someone who survived the great flood, perhaps even by Noah himself.

Though not by nature superstitious, Eric decided to find a shop where he could buy himself an Indalo Man. A symbol for good luck. He smiled, shook his head to shake away his wild thoughts, and left the church.

The first shop he came across that displayed Indalo Man figurines was within an area of the town called *el Arrabal*. As he bought himself one he also enquired about the name of the area and discovered that *el Arrabal* was the ancient Jewish quarter. He squinted at his little trinket.

Eric decided he had some time left to explore, so he wandered around the network of narrow streets and alleys looking at the very distinctive low wide doors of the Jewish homes. Then he saw them. Some words etched onto the front of one of the doors on what looked like an uninhabited house. They were faded due to years of wear, but Eric was convinced he knew what one of the words said – *Maranos* – the word to which his friend Penelope had first introduced him.

He knocked on the door but no one answered. Just then a neighbour from over the street opened their door. Eric took his opportunity.

Eric walked over. The old man had a whispy beard and knowing eyes. 'I'm so sorry. Do you know who lives or who lived there?' Eric spoke in English and pointed to the door he'd just knocked on.

The old man's brow furrowed.

'Please, I'm just interested, that's all,' said Eric.

His voice was wheezy, like a long-term smoker's. 'Eh, no one, eh live-a there now, but...' He cleared his throat. '...back a-time,

Ben Kerioth family live-a there.'

'Ben Kerioth. A Jewish family?'

'Yes, eh, we all Jews here. Though...'

'Though?'

'*Eh, eis no importanto.*' The man coughed, frowned and closed his door on Eric.

'But...' Eric couldn't keep the man from disappearing back into his own home.

He looked across at the door with the faded wording.

Then he had an idea.

He carefully pulled out his map and, unfolding it, was relieved to see that one side was blank. Remembering how he'd done this with wax crayons as a child, he removed his dusty shoes and pressed the paper against the door, blank side towards him. He then rubbed the sole of one of his shoes lightly across the top part of the paper.

It was working.

Pressing a little harder a word appeared – *Maranos*. Using his other shoe, he then worked on the lower half of the paper, and one by one the letters started appearing.

First a 'K', then an undetectable smudge. Next there was an 'r' followed by something that might have been an 'i' or an 'l'. It must have been that name, Kerioth.

The next two letters he saw appeared together and were definitely 'ot'. Stepping back, he looked at his paper, and his heart leapt.

K r l ot

Eric's mind flew. He already knew that 'Ben' meant 'son of' or, occasionally, just 'of' in Hebrew, a little like 'Van' in Dutch. *Van Kroot, Ben Kerioth. Surely it could not be, but maybe?*

* * *

'She's beautiful isn't she?'

Eric jumped. 'Sorry, I was daydreaming.'

Father Ambroos was walking back up the aisle towards him. 'It's okay. This place does tend to inspire the imagination. Anyway I was just saying, isn't she beautiful?'

'Who?' said Eric.

The priest looked all around him. 'This place, my son. Even when almost empty of people, she is never empty of spirit.' He turned back to Eric. 'I brought you here to talk, because talking here is like walking on feathers. I've never served in such a place as this. It seems to...'

'I can feel it,' said Eric. 'It's a very comforting place.'

'Yes, that's what I've always found.' The older man turned his head once again and glanced from place to place, nodding gently as he did so.

'Thank you, Father. I do appreciate it.'

'Nonsense, my son, I see it not as a duty but a pleasure to help a fellow in distress. Now, you were telling me about a missing daughter.'

'Perhaps I ought to tell you a little more first, Father, though it'll be like a confession and, God knows, I've not sat in a confessional since my youth.'

The priest looked directly into Eric's eyes. His gentle smile seemed to reach out and embrace him. 'My son, God is not as you have heard many proclaim. His mercy is ever-flowing, his love ever widening, his patience everlasting. Tell me as much as you need. You will find no judgement here.'

Chapter Nineteen

South Wales, 1970

'Leave her alone yer lil bitch.'

'Rose, don't you dare use that kind of language!' snapped Sister Simon. 'And what's going on?'

Rose's desk was behind that of a smug-faced girl called Amy, who sat directly behind Lucy. Hannah was off to the side of Lucy and she'd heard everything. Amy had been calling Lucy cry-baby again.

'But Sister, why don't you tell her? She's always being nasty to Lucy,' said Hannah.

'We'll deal with this after class, girls.' Sister Simon looked at Hannah and winked.

Once the groans had faded, the young Sister looked around at the whole class and smiled broadly. 'This morning, girls, we're going to do something a little different.'

Hannah sat upright, wondering whether this was what she hoped.

'How many of you have ever wondered why some women become nuns?' said Sister Simon.

Hands shot up throughout the classroom.

'So, shall I tell you why I want to be a nun?' she said.

'I thought you already were a nun Sister,' said a girl at the front.

'Well, yes and no. Technically I won't be until I've made what's called my profession, and taken vows for life.'

'You're a novice at the moment, aren't you?' said Hannah.

'Yes Hannah, and before that I was what we call a postulant, but let me tell you about my life before even that. Would you like that, girls?'

Hannah glanced around the room and saw enthusiastic

nodding from almost every girl. Then, as she looked towards the door to the corridor, she noticed a shadow moving slowly across the crack at the bottom.

Sister Simon pulled forward her chair and placed it as close to the girls as possible, and, sitting down, she began. 'I grew up in a little village in South Herefordshire, which is just across the border into England. It was a village called Clehonger.'

Lucy put her hand up. 'Please Sister, my cousins live in Hereford.' She sounded on the verge of tears. 'Mummy told me that I was going to live with them but my aunty didn't want me.'

Hannah turned to look at Amy, and then Rose.

The Sister smiled. 'But we look after you now don't we, Angel?'

'Yes,' said Lucy.

'So I grew up in Clehonger,' said Sister Simon. 'We were the only Catholic family in the village. On Sundays we would attend mass at the local Abbey Church, which is a monastery. I loved it.'

Another hand shot up.

'Yes Rose.'

'Is it right, Sister..., ' Hannah saw the girl smirk, '...that yer can never have sex?'

Loud sniggers echoed throughout the room and Sister Simon blushed. 'Rose, I really don't think you should be asking questions like that. I'm sure the girls don't know what you mean.'

Hannah glanced at the door again. She was certain she'd heard a cough coming from behind it.

The Sister tried to compose herself and Hannah put her hand up.

'Yes, Hannah?'

She'd decided to take the opportunity. 'Sister, what do you think Jesus was really like?'

'Oh my word Hannah, you do ask such big questions. And I

was talking about why I wanted to be a nun.'

Hannah gazed at her. 'But surely Jesus is why you wanted that?'

Sister Simon closed her eyes for a moment. Then she opened them again, smiled and nodded. 'Well, let me put it like this. I believe he was the kindest, and most loving person there has ever been, and ever will be.'

'It don't make sense.' Rose was standing.

'Sit down,' said Sister Simon. 'What doesn't make sense?'

Rose sat. 'Well yer say all this stuff about love and kindness. And *yer* always act like it, to be fair. But what about the others?'

Sister Simon looked at Rose, bit her top lip and glanced at the door. Eventually she spoke. 'Rose, I'm sorry. I'm sorry that not everyone who follows Jesus sees him this way. I'm afraid that to some he's more of a headmaster than a friend. And believe me, I know what it's like to be confused.'

'But why are you so different?' said Rose.

Sister Simon let her head drop as she rubbed both sides of her head. For a while she said nothing. Then she lifted her face.

Hannah looked again towards the door. The shadow had gone.

'Girls, as I told you, I grew up in a Catholic family, and I always adored going to church.'

The girls were silent and all eyes were fixed on the nun.

'But I hated my Catholic secondary school.'

Some of the girls glanced at each other.

'As a young girl I'd attended the local village school with all the other children, but once I was eleven it was decided that I should go to a Catholic high school. At first I was delighted because I thought it would be Belmont Abbey, which I'd grown to know through Sunday mass. But the Abbey was a private school, which meant my parents would have had to pay for it and they couldn't afford it, so they sent me somewhere else. I hated it.' Her eyes glistened.

'Why?' said Hannah. 'Why did you hate it?'

A tear ran down the nun's face, which she quickly brushed away. She looked at Hannah. 'I can't say my dear, I really can't.' Then she smiled. 'But when I finally left that school, I needed to ask questions.' She nodded at Rose. 'The same sort of question you've been asking.'

'Really?' said the bigger girl.

'Look, my dears...' The nun smiled. 'I know I can't force you to believe this, but whatever the Church can be like, God, Christ and the Saints are filled with love for you.'

Hannah thought she noticed tears in Rose's eyes.

But then the shadow was back and Hannah could hear talking. Two shadows and movement, and then footsteps clattering off down the corridor.

* * *

Christmas was approaching rapidly. Nights were getting darker, and the dormitory colder. White clouds floated out from the girls' mouths as they breathed. They were each given an extra blanket to help keep them warm.

Hannah was still concerned about Rose. She'd now had three more dropping fits, and her change of character had lasted half the year. She smiled a lot more, was generally much friendlier to other girls and, though still sulky, was far less likely to pick fights with the nuns. Maybe she'd just turned over a new leaf? Or maybe Lucy had given her something to be content about. Perhaps she just needed a friend?

But where was Lucy? For the last few weeks Lucy had gone missing every few days. Different times in the day. Sister Matthew had clearly got the intention of turning little Lucy into another of her 'nuns' pets'. However, she didn't normally take them away from the other girls for hours on end. Where was she?

Just before bedtime the door creaked open and Sister Matthew stepped out of the shadow with a girl.

'Go to bed now my dear,' the nun whispered as she stood at the door and watched Lucy pace over to her bed. Hannah tried to catch her attention, but Lucy just sat on the bed facing the other way. Then she put on her nightgown and lay down, pulling the blankets over herself so that they almost covered her head.

When she awoke, Hannah noticed that Lucy was missing again, but after rubbing her eyes and looking around the room she saw that the little girl was sitting on Rose's bed. Rose was sitting up and they were whispering about something. Hannah made up her mind to talk to Rose as soon as possible, even if just to warn her that the nuns' pets will almost certainly report her and Lucy.

Mass was unusually long due to it being Advent Sunday. Father Francis waffled on about preparing for Christmas by self-denial, which he explained as *not allowing yourself to have something you really want.* He explained that God looks upon his people with extra merit when they demonstrate their devotion to him by self-denial.

Hannah smiled slightly when she heard him say, 'Children, you don't wish your Father in heaven to think you are spoilt, do you?'

He had to be joking.

To mark the beginning of Advent, breakfast was even less of a meal than usual, though Hannah could distinctly smell something delicious coming from beyond the screen.

Lucy sat opposite. Her head was bowed. She seemed much more distant lately. Rose was on another table that morning, with her back to Hannah. What was going on with them?

Afternoon duty was floor polishing for Hannah. She always hated this particular chore. It involved kneeling on the hard floor, which not only gave her pins and needles but also bruised knees.

About half way through her duty Hannah had finished another part of the corridor and was about to begin a new section. To give her knees a short break she sat and leant against the wall while she opened the tin of polish to smear some on a fresh cloth. Then she heard a door opening at the other end of the corridor, but around a bend, so whoever it was was momentarily hidden from view. Hannah quickly got back on all fours. She waited for whoever it was to come, but no one appeared. Surprised by the silence Hannah decided to slide quietly across the floor and take a peek around the far corner. She reached it but, before looking, heard something like a whisper. Slowly she inched her head to the point where she could see.

The shock almost caused her to scream.

Chapter Twenty

The Testimony of Ezra Van Kroot, Amsterdam, 1535

We Jews learn the stories of our past from childhood, which, along with our traditions, gives us stability. This is often the only stability to which we can cling in a world of perpetual change. Yet here was my father saying that we might have to give up our very identity as Jews.

'But Father, why would we do that? And how could we? You have always taught me to – '

He turned to face me, tears in his eyes. 'I know. I have always warned you to be wary of Christians. My son, this is why...' Then he took out from within his breast a cloth bag about the size of a large drinking cup.

'What is it?' I asked.

'Ezra, this is a scroll. It's been part of our family's journey for longer than you can imagine. Most of our family have never known of its existence. Even your mother is ignorant of it.'

'But what is it?' I could feel a fluttering in my stomach.

'All I can tell you for now, my son, is that this could have us killed if discovered, yet some day it will change everything. When that day will be no one knows. For now, all we can do – all we, the first-born sons to whom it has been entrusted, can do – is keep it safe.'

I looked at him and, as though he could sense my confusion, he continued. 'Ezra, I must tell you about something that happened. It will help explain.'

My father reached over to a small sack and took out two pieces of flat bread. Tossing one over to me he tore a piece out of the other. After he had eaten it, he spoke. 'It was when you were very little. I was fishing along the coast, near the little village they call *Al-hawan*. I was with your uncle Reuben. We had enjoyed a good day's catch and decided to row to the shore to see if we could sell some fish before returning home. As usual the waters were as clear as crystal and, as I hopped into the warmth of the sea, I remember seeing a red crab scurrying off into the depths. I don't know why I have never forgotten that.

'We pulled the boat up onto the sand and, at once, noticed a commotion. There, in the distance, was a crowd of people. Some looked like town officials. Others were traders. But others – I didn't know who they were – were sitting and lying on the sand. My brother and I secured the boat, covered our catch and walked over for a better look.'

'Who were they? What was going on?' I said.

'My son, those people lying on the ground, had seen something truly dreadful. They had witnessed a sight they could not purge from their minds.'

'What had they seen?'

My father's eyes closed and he grimaced like a man about to be flogged. 'Inquisition,' he breathed the words as if they were blasphemous.

It was that word again. And this time he explained why it caused him to whisper. 'Ezra those people had fled a city named Seville. They spoke of great processions of people, in robes and other strange costumes, some with conical hats, others wearing images of flames and dancing devils. They told of wooden effigies, carved to look like men and women, being burned. And boxes of freshly dug up human bones being burned. They spoke of men, women and youths, being burned alive on huge pyres during part of a ceremony known as the *Auto de fe*. Their faces turned white with fear as they relived the spectacle and remembered the putrid stench of roasted human flesh.'

'But Father!' I gasped, 'Why were people being burned?'

He opened his eyes and they blazed with fire. 'Because they were once Jews. Jews who had converted to Christianity, and yet the Church had come to believe they were still practising their old Jewish ways. The Church authorities called them Judaizers.'

'But why would that be wrong, father?'

'Christianity is a frightened religion, Ezra. It fears much. It fears that it will have its message destroyed by people who do not truly believe, and who wander back to their old ways. It fears that this will spread, even into the older Christian communities. My son, up there in Castile and Aragon there are many Christians who were once Jews.'

'But why? Why did they change?'

'Self-preservation Ezra. Do you understand what that means?'

'I think so.'

'These Jews were finding themselves more and more unwelcome in the Christian lands. They needed to protect themselves by becoming Christians. And some, it seems, did truly convert, whereas others only became Catholic on the surface, to hide. And now they are being hunted down by the Inquisition.'

Chapter Twenty-One

South Wales, 1970

Hannah's sleep was troubled. After a night of tossing and turning, and occasional jabs from fed up girls who'd dared to tip-toe over to her bed, she was finally in a deep slumber when the morning bell dragged her tired mind out of her dreams and back to the reality of Crucis Home For Girls.

She managed to sit up, eyes still closed, mouth and chin wet with dribble, and stretched her arms out like Christ on the Cross. Bringing her hands to her face she first of all used her right sleeve to wipe her chin, and then rubbed both eyes simultaneously. At last she opened them and, as they began to focus, the reality of the horror before her sank in.

And then the screaming began.

Chapter Twenty-Two

Amsterdam, 1981

Eric hadn't sat in the presence of such undivided attention for years. Perhaps it was Ella who was the last to bless him in such a way. Father Ambroos listened to Eric's story – or as much of it as he was willing to impart – and promised to do all he could to uncover the British order of nuns who may have taken the child. He took Eric's details and promised to make contact as soon as he had any information.

* * *

Eric now lay in his hotel bed hoping, wishing, praying that the old man would find something – anything that could be useful.

He wondered how much longer he could afford to remain in Amsterdam's centre. He was rapidly running out of funds and figured he might have to find a cheap guest house on the outskirts. For much of the previous two decades he managed to survive pretty much hand to mouth, and for the last few years he'd saved as much as he could for his journey to Spain and back to Holland, but the pot was running out fast!

He cursed his father. Damn him, if only he had left him more. Why did he leave most of it to that greedy bastard of a brother?

Restless and worried, he decided to walk back to the area the priest had taken him to the day before. He thought he might even wander back into St Nicholas's Church. Something about it had touched him deeply. He knew it wasn't just the kindly old cleric who seemed so genuine and compassionate; the church itself seemed filled with the same spirit. For Eric it had been a revelation that a Catholic priest and a Catholic church could be so warm. His own father was a Knight of St Augustine, as was his brother, and neither had a compassionate bone in their body.

Eric's walk took him past the famous Sex Museum on *Damrak* and onto *Prins Hendrikkade*. His head was heavy. He visualised the now empty bottle that stood on his bedside table in the hotel room. Spirits had never agreed with him.

Across the road a bus halted outside the busy Central Railway Station and a group of tourists trickled out. To his right were the canal boats and, as it was close to the hour, two of them were almost full of sightseers and ready to pull off on their tour. Another had already left the dock.

Eric reached the top of the road and saw the distinctive seventeenth-century church to his right. He looked up at the cross on top of its roof and its three towers standing out high above the assortment of hotels, restaurants and cafes that surrounded it.

Unfortunately, the main entrance was locked. The notice board offered the usual times for confession, but Eric didn't wish to hang around until the afternoon before he could enter the church, so he wandered back down *Prins Hendrikkade* into the busier part of town and looked for somewhere to have a coffee.

He stood, peering out over the canal boats. The two full ones had left, but another was filling up – and then something caught his eye. Two young nuns were sitting among the passengers on the boat. The picture jolted him, reminding him of his recent discovery. My God, he had a daughter.

He looked down *Damrak*. The bikes were rushing up and down the busy road and the pedestrian walkways were thick with tourists and shoppers. Eric tried to think of somewhere he could get a caffeine fix, and then he remembered a place he'd seen a few days before. He turned and walked into the area known more for its pot houses than cafes. He walked up *Zeedijk*, past a large Chinese Buddhist temple and out into a square.

The place he was looking for was called Ziggy's. It was more of a pub than a café, but he'd seen people sat outside with coffee the other day – and there it was. It looked busy, but there was a free table. He sat down and waited for service.

Then he saw something. Directly across the square, a group of about twenty young people, male and female, were walking silently – arms linked – towards him. They wore black T-shirts and black jeans or leggings. They walked slowly and said nothing. Eric was intrigued and noticed that many shoppers and tourists had stopped to watch this strange group of people. Their silence seemed to infect the whole area. Even the usual sounds of bike bells and chatter had ceased. As they came closer Eric noticed that certain members of the procession were holding leaflets, and a few passers-by were taking them.

'Strange to be doing that in Amsterdam isn't it?' said a voice from beside him. He turned his head to see a waitress hovering, pencil and pad in hand. 'What would you like sir?'

'Oh, a coffee, please,' said Eric. 'And could you make it a strong one please. But, can I just ask who they are? What are they doing?'

The waitress looked to be in her late teens, perhaps very early twenties. She had thick dark brown hair and dark eyes to match. The blue eye shadow ought to have looked tacky, but it worked. Her accent was unfamiliar.

She scribbled something down. 'They are students, and they are protesting.'

'About what?'

'I'll show you,' she said, and added, 'just a strong coffee then?'

'Yes please.'

Before leaving with his order the waitress reached over to another table, retrieved a leaflet and handed it to Eric.

Chapter Twenty-Three

South Wales, 1970

'Shut up!' The nun's blood curdling screech matched her haunted appearance. 'All of you shut up!'

But they didn't.

The noise in the dormitory was like nothing Hannah had ever heard and, as her eyes began to focus, all she could see were girls in various degrees of distress. Some shaking, some covering their faces, some jumping up and down, eyes bulging and hands over their mouths. Most crying, shouting, screaming. And Rose just standing there, trance-like and gazing in the direction of poor Lucy.

Who swayed gently back and forth as she hung from the wooden beam above her head.

* * *

The girls had been dragged into the chapel, still in their nightgowns. This was the only time in their short lives they'd ever sat in front of the sanctuary dressed in such a way. Any other time it would have been seen as sacrilege and an insult to God.

Hannah sat, eyes fixed on the wooden rood screen in front of her, but she was not seeing a wooden screen. Instead she saw a wooden beam, and hanging from it...

A sound was coming from outside. Some sort of siren. More than one in fact. And the muffled voices of the nuns squawking and screeching. The mixture of human and mechanical sounds brought Hannah out of her daydream. She looked up, and around. They were all there apart from that poor girl. Sister Simon at the front and all about her the shocked faces. All but one. A couple of rows behind her was a black-haired girl who sat scowling with her arms crossed tightly over her chest.

Rose's eyes were fixed on Hannah. She was shaking her head very slowly, her nose curled up and her lips pursed. She did not look frightened or sad or shocked like the other girls. The expression on Rose's face was pure hatred. Her eyes were darker than Hannah had ever seen them. For the last few months Rose's previously angry character had been almost non-existent, but this morning it had been resurrected.

Hannah looked back to the front and saw Sister Simon, now with her head in her hands, shoulders juddering and tears dripping onto the floor.

Chapter Twenty-Four

Amsterdam, 1981

Its title was *Abolish The Crimson Mile* and Eric soon realised that it was an anti-prostitution leaflet. The designer had worked out that the entire walk around the whole district was just over 1500 metres, almost exactly an old-fashioned international mile. But that information was the only benign part of the leaflet. As Eric read on he realised that the rest was dedicated to lifting the shutters on this famous tourist attraction, by stating the most shocking facts involving human trafficking, drug induced slavery and even murder.

Though he'd known of it since childhood, and had even been brought to visit back in his secondary school days, he'd never felt easy about what was on sale behind those red-rimmed windows. If anything, his liberal school field trips were an inoculation against the practice, rather than an immersing into the pride of what so many Dutch saw to be Holland's gift to the world – liberation and feminism.

Feminism my arse.

Ziggy's was only metres from the district and the leaflet prompted Eric to pay a visit. Perhaps it wasn't like it was back then? Maybe the leaflets were wrong and things had changed for the better?

He finished his coffee, crossed the square and entered one of the narrow lanes that led to the infamous area. As he walked into the dimly lit alley, the natural light of the square was replaced with the warm pink glow of neon. In front of him was a gang of laughing teenagers, peering into each window as they walked. To his left a man had stopped and was in some form of communication with a girl. She was mouthing something to him and using her fingers to count or depict numbers. He wore a dark tailored suit and held a briefcase. He might have been a bank manager or solicitor. He seemed about Eric's age, though he was decidedly weightier. The glass door swung open and he walked in.

Christ. She was young enough to be his daughter.

Eric walked out into the *Rossebuurt* and the smell almost knocked him out – a dense mixture of hashish and sickly-sweet perfume. It seemed different from his last visit, but that had been over twenty years before when the window girls wore more and the sex shops didn't have display windows. He was shocked by what was on sale in them – dildos the size of traffic cones and S&M gear that looked like something from the Spanish Inquisition.

It was late morning and heaving. Up and down each side of the canal were windows after windows of sex workers. The red lights were less visible in the daylight, but there was no missing what this place was. About a half of the spaces seemed to be inhabited by much older and larger women than the young girl he'd just witnessed strike a deal. And maybe a quarter of them were empty. He figured that this was the period of the day when window rent was cheapest, and the district's *out of date merchandise* was promoted. The shelf life of some of these women was clearly overdue.

Behind him, the alley deposited a constant stream of window shoppers into the street. Across the canal were a couple of clubs, one called the Banana Bar. No guesses what went on there. He wandered down through the crowds, passing one of the open-air urinals that even a blind man could find by sense of smell alone. The stench was so strong that, at close range, it overpowered both the hashish and the perfume.

Amsterdam was such an oxymoron – a city with a charm and a spell of its own, often referred to as the Venice of the North – and yet with more brothels and drug dens than any other part of Europe. Eric was torn, as he always had been, about those two issues. Neither were legal here, but both were tolerated. Amsterdam's liberal policy was always one of turning an official blind eye. The positive side, so the theory went, was the semi-regulation of two of the oldest and most dangerous professions. Yet Eric wasn't sure. As he gradually made his way towards the other end of the wide canal-centred street, looking at the glass windows and their inhabitants, he didn't see regulated, liberated, safe women and girls, but objects of sadness. Even the ones who bounced up and down tapping windows, with beaming smiles and flashing eyes, seemed like nothing more than prisoners begging for the keys to their cells.

And then he saw her.

Chapter Twenty-Five

South Wales, 1970

She looked like a lost soul, sitting there on her own with her head in her hands.

A week had passed since Lucy's death, and every time Hannah had tried to talk to Rose she turned her back and walked away, but today she seemed ready. It was the afternoon break and Hannah noticed her on the other side of the yard, sitting on the ground, leaning against the wall. Hannah walked over.

'Are you okay Rose?'

At first there was no response. But Hannah knew what would get her attention.

'Rose...Rose I think I know why she did it.'

Slowly the older girl raised her head and looked up. Red tear-stained eyes gazed into Hannah's. 'What yer mean?' She pushed the matted hair out of her face.

Hannah sat down beside her. 'I think I know why...' she gulped, '...Lucy did it.'

Rose's complexion crumpled like a piece of screwed up paper and she buried her face in her hands. Her muffled sobs were hard for Hannah to listen to. She'd never seen Rose cry before.

Hannah waited for her to stop. 'Rose, break is almost over, so I'll tell you tonight, when we have more time okay? We'll talk when the others have gone to sleep.' She put a hand on her friend's shoulder and the big girl fell into her arms, sobbing uncontrollably.

A shadow fell across them. 'Stop that. We'll have none of that nonsense here. Get up, both of you.'

Hannah jolted and looked up. The woman's pasty white face surrounded by a tight-fitting black veil looked like the full moon on a dark night. Only, rather than smiling like the man in the sky, this moon scowled like a witch.

Sister Matthew reached down and opened her clammy hands.

Rose whispered something before they were prised apart, but Hannah must have heard her wrong. She'd never do that. Would she?

On the way back to the dormitory Hannah couldn't shake the image from her mind. Ever since poor Lucy was found swinging by that twisted strip of bed linen, the memory had haunted her. Not the image of her little body dangling, but of Sister Matthew forcing her slimy fat lips onto Lucy's. It was how Hannah imagined a mouse would look if it were being eaten by a huge cat.

She would find a time to tell Rose. And then, at least she would know the story being told by the crows was a lie. Lucy was not out of her mind. Lucy was scared out of her wits. She was being hunted.

* * *

Later on that evening they were together in the dormitory toilets.

Rose looked at Hannah, her eyes hollow and empty. 'So, what yer know then?'

'Rose...' Hannah glanced at the floor, then back up into Rose's eyes. 'I think Lucy was being...being um...'

'Being what?'

'Being...touched.'

A flash of horror appeared on Rose's face. 'Yer what?'

'I saw her. I saw a nun – with her.'

'With Lucy?'

'Yes, I saw a Sister smothering her, and pushing her horrible mouth down on poor Lucy's. She looked terrified.'

'What? When? Why dint yer do anything?'

'How could I Rose? You know what they're like. None of them would have believed me.'

'No, but she might have stopped for a while. Who was it? Which one? Tell me.'

'Sister Matthew.'

'Course it wer. Fucking evil bitch.'

Hannah flinched.

'Rose, I had to tell you, but you're not going to do anything are you?'

She looked directly into Hannah's eyes, her own cold and piercing like a viper's. 'I tell yer this. They're gonna get it one day. I ain't gonna forget this ever. That bitch is gonna get it and so is that fucker Dominic. Both of em.'

Rose swung around and stormed out of the toilets.

* * *

The next morning Hannah awoke with a hollow feeling in her tummy.

'Girls I have something to tell you.' Sister Dominic was standing at the door. She walked into the dormitory and looked around, letting her eyes settle on Hannah.

Hannah felt the back of her neck tingle.

'For a few months we've all been looking forward to a splendid occasion, the profession of a new Sister.'

Hannah and Rose glanced at each other.

'We've had Sister Simon with us for five years now and have watched her grow through her postulancy and novitiate. We had waited longer than usual before professing her because of...' She looked up to the ceiling as if inspecting for spiders' webs. '...a certain lack of...how shall I put it? Sisterly obedience.'

Hannah's heart began thumping inside her chest.

'And it seems her unruly thinking has infected some of you.'

Hannah was now standing by her bed, shaking.

'So you will see her no more.'

That was it. No gentle warning. It was as if the nun was

informing them they'd no longer be seeing a nameless dinner lady. But not Sister Simon.

'No!' shouted Hannah. 'That's not true. It can't be true.'

The nun raised her voice, 'Oh but it is, Maggie! It is indeed true.'

Hannah's head dropped.

'Sister Simon, or should I now say Rowena, has gone back to her family. She's not going to be a Sister. You'll never see her again.'

The nun gave a broad grin, swung around and marched out of the dormitory, slamming the door behind her. Hannah's knees gave way and she crumpled to the floor, sobbing.

Chapter Twenty-Six

Amsterdam, 1981

'My God, what are you doing here?' said Eric. He felt a rush of excitement.

'Can't you remember?' The woman was smiling.

'No, remind me.'

Penelope Kruger was a little younger than Eric. She wore her long dark hair tied back in a single ponytail, exposing her high cheekbones. Her eyes were dark like her hair but her skin was pale, making her eyebrows and lashes stand out. She wore jeans and a blue jumper, over which was an ivy green wax jacket. Eric noticed that she still wore no wedding or engagement ring. He remembered she was of Dutch descent, but her paternal grandparents had moved to Oxford, England, back in the days following the Great War. Her grandfather and father alike were scholars and had lectured at Oxford University. Like them, Penelope was an academic. Many an evening had been spent discussing fascinating topics over a tequila and chilli.

'When you were leaving Mexico for Spain,' said Penelope, 'I told you that I intended to spend some time in your home town of Amsterdam, not least because of my own family background.'

'Yes, I remember about your grandparents and the connection to Holland but – '

'And my research Eric.'

Eric shrugged his shoulders and smiled.

'Oh men,' she said. 'After Mexico I returned to Oxford and began work on my thesis. I told you about that right?'

'Yeah, but ...' He felt his cheeks start to burn.

'It's about the Dutch West India Company.'

'Oh yes, of course. I remember now. I told you I knew about the Dutch East India Company from history lessons back at school, but we didn't study the West India Company.'

'Precisely,' said Penelope, 'because there is a distinct lack of high school and college textbooks on the subject. I hope to do my bit towards correcting the balance.'

'Good plan. But why are you in the Red-Light District?'

'Oh, just interested. After all, doesn't everyone head here on their first visit to Amsterdam?' She winked. 'Anyway, why are you in the Red-Light District? You can't use the tourist excuse.'

For a moment Eric was unsure how to answer. 'I was...just taking a short cut. But, my God, it's so great to see you. In fact, why don't you come on a canal trip with me? Please. It's not far from here, we could catch up...and it's the best way to see the city.' He grabbed her hand.

'I don't remember you being this forceful.' Penelope smiled. 'Okay, I'll come, but I need to be back at my flat in a couple of hours. I'm meeting someone and I need to get ready.'

Eric felt a stab of disappointment and, as if she knew what he was thinking, Penelope quickly added, 'A tutor from the university and expert in Dutch history. We're meeting at the Maritime Museum.'

'Highly appropriate to be going on a boat trip now then.' Eric's smile re-surfaced and he led her towards the docks.

As they arrived, a boat had just finished a tour and Eric noticed the little crowd emptying onto the wooden landing port. There were those two nuns again, but he'd got it wrong. They weren't habits and veils but hijabs and chadors.

Looking at them Penelope said, 'Oh I do love this city.'

The boat chugged through the water, under a bridge and out into a harbour, before turning and making for the entrance into the city's amazing labyrinth of interconnected canals. After a while they emerged from under another bridge and the boat slowed for tourists to photograph one of Amsterdam's most famous sights, only seen from this particular point.

'They're breathtaking,' said Penelope.

'Amazing aren't they,' agreed Eric as they both admired the seven nesting bridges and arches of the *Reguliersgracht*.

Penelope turned to face him. 'So, what are you doing here Eric?'

He thought briefly before answering. 'It's been a while since I've seen Amsterdam, Penelope.' Eric pointed across the canal to the terraced houses lining the street. 'Can you see the wooden beams and hooks jutting out at the top of most of the houses?'

'Yes. What are they for?'

'During the Golden Age a clever pulley system was installed in the attics of these homes to hoist up valuables, like spices, cotton or heavier goods like cocoa. They are still used for moving furniture.' Eric thought she might find that interesting bearing in mind her research on the merchant history of the city.

But she didn't take the bait. 'And so you're here alone?'

'You're inquisitive?' He half closed his eyes.

'I'm interested.'

'In why I'm really here?'

Now Penelope smiled. 'Eric I am a researcher. You know that. I could see you were on a mission when I first noticed you. You were studying those women. Like, really *studying* them. You looked like a concerned friend watching an addict score.' She put her hand behind her head and pulled off her hairband shaking her hair out and letting it fall across her shoulders.

'You could read that from the way I was looking into those windows?'

She nodded, and smiled again. A gust of wind blew some of her dark hair across her face and she flicked it out of the way with a sharp toss of her head. 'Eric come on. Why are you really here?'

He lifted his hands and rubbed his face while letting out a long sigh. His eyes remained closed for a moment, then they opened. 'I came here, back to Holland that is, to see my brother. I don't think I ever told you about him. I wanted to make peace with him, over an incident that happened many years ago. And I wanted to show him something. Something I've discovered about our family.'

'And?' she said, patiently.

'And, now I need to find someone else.'

'Come on Eric, less of the cryptic answers.'

'I spoke with my brother. I tried to apologise for what I did to him. I also tried to tell him what I wanted to about our family. But neither of those things matter much now because...'

'Because?'

'Because he told me I have a daughter.'

'Oh Eric, and you had no idea?' She turned and gazed into his eyes and Eric saw in them something deeply comforting.

Chapter Twenty-Seven

The Testimony of Ezra Van Kroot, Amsterdam, 1535

When my father and I spoke that day, I knew something terrifying loomed. I had no idea when it would come and part of me wished I could have remained ignorant, like my younger brothers, but I knew my father had to tell me. He needed me to be strong. He needed me to be brave. He needed me to take on the duty of the first-born son.

'So, Ezra, if we come under Christian rule we will have to make a choice, and both outcomes could be perilous. If we do what my heart wants us to do and remain Jews by appearance the danger goes without saying, but if we decide to do what so many others have done and convert to Christianity we will be placing ourselves under the authority of the Inquisition and open to their monstrous ordeals.'

I saw the anguish in his face.

'And there's another concern.' My father glanced at the wrapped-up bundle in his hands. 'This scroll. We need to protect it – you and me, my son. It is our responsibility. For now it is mine to guard, but it will soon be yours. And this brings me to the most difficult part of what I have to say to you.' His eyes filled with tears, and then he told me something that shocked me to the very core. 'When that happens my son, you will need to leave us. If we remain Jews and are attacked, the scroll will be discovered and destroyed or lost forever. And if we become Christians and are in any way handed over to the Inquisition, they will discover everything. No secret is safe within the walls of an inquisitor's torture chamber. My son I need to know...are you willing to do this?'

This was something I had not, and could not, imagine –

leaving my home, my family, my mother. In the stab of shock and disbelief I looked at him. His tired eyes overflowed with tears as he held out his arms to me. I collapsed into them and we clung to each other, and wept. I will never forget that day. It is as if it were yesterday.

Chapter Twenty-Eight

South Wales, 1975

The week since dear Mother Angelica's death had dragged, and now the girls were assembled outside in dormitory groups. Hannah stood listening as the Head Governor addressed them. She knew what he was going to say. She just knew. And she was right.

'So, children, I would like you all to welcome your new headmistress, *Reverend Mother Dominic.*'

Five years had passed since Lucy's tragedy, and almost the same since Sister Simon had been dismissed. Over the course of those five long years, Hannah had grown to truly despise the bitch who now stood peering from behind her half-moon spectacles. She stood next to the Head Governor looking up and down the rows of girls, from the tiniest at the front to Hannah, Rose and the others at the back of the yard. In truth Rose was probably too old to be there. Girls usually left when they reached seventeen, but the occasional seizures made her seem simple for much of the time, and Hannah suspected the nuns had just forgotten her.

* * *

For a tomboy Rose was not unattractive. Over the last few years her dark eyes had grown deep and captivating. As a child she had been taller than the rest, but Hannah had always put that down to her age. However, now as a young woman she still towered over the others. Indeed, she was taller than most of the nuns. But Hannah knew Rose's entrancing features would never be noticed because she was despised. She always had been.

Hannah had become aware of her own developing beauty

too. Every morning and evening the washroom mirror reflected back her facial and bodily changes. Her deep red locks glistened and her bright green eyes sparkled. She was also aware of her body's shape, swelling in all the correct places. The other girls often teased her, saying the nuns go to bed drooling over her.

Was this the reason the nuns' scorn seemed to be increasing? Mother Dominic called her 'Maggie' constantly.

Ever since Lucy's death, Rose had withdrawn into herself. Hannah could remember a very different Rose: a fiery girl who didn't mind getting in trouble for a laugh, a girl who was unafraid of the black-robed bitches and would answer them back in her coarse and common way, making them cringe and lash out. She remembered back to the period shortly before Lucy had arrived when Rose had knocked over Sister Matthew like an overweight tin solider with a ball bearing. She smiled at the image but then remembered the weeks when she'd been missing from her bed, and the different Rose who'd returned in her place. Hannah's memories continued as she saw images of Rose and Lucy together. She'd always wondered what it was about those two, but now she suddenly knew why it was they'd become so close. Of course. One had needed a mother to cling to, and the other had needed someone to learn to love and take care of.

That evening, after the bitch had been welcomed as the new Reverend Mother, Hannah and Rose were sitting on Rose's bed, talking. Hannah looked at her friend and asked, 'Do you ever think of her?'

'Who?'

'Lucy.'

The older girl looked into Hannah's eyes, a tear breaking forth and trickling down her cheek. 'Every day.'

Chapter Twenty-Nine

Amsterdam, 1981

'So there it is, Pen. I began this adventure back in Mexico when you first mentioned that word *Maranos*, not knowing where it would lead. Then, after talking to Abrim Mendez and getting the distinct clue that it was not just his story but mine too, I followed the path from there to southern Spain and found, by luck it seemed, the town of my ancestors. I even found our original family name – all because I'd asked about a strange symbol that seemed to ring a bell. I then came back here to Holland, armed with all I'd found, and uncovered an amazing written testimony. But...'

'But what?' said Penelope.

'But now I can only think of one thing. I have a daughter and I've missed over twenty years of her life. If I ever find her how can I claim back those years?' Eric gazed into the sky. Was it a prayer or a wish? He didn't know but he hoped that all the magic in the universe would help him find her.

Penelope reached out her hand. Her eyes were moist. They looked at each other as she said, 'Eric I'm going to help. I'm going to help you find your daughter.'

'Hang on a minute. You can't do that. What about your research?'

'I can spare some time and still continue with my own work. Trust me Eric. I really want to help you. We will find your daughter.'

Eric hugged her tightly. 'Thank you Pen. Thank you so much.'

Chapter Thirty

South Wales,1975

Hannah had reached her fifteenth year and, though worn down by the regime at Crucis Home For Girls, she still carried an inner dream of finding her parents. A tiny spark of hope occasionally reminded her that her time with these bitches was gradually coming to an end and that she'd soon be out of the hell hole.

She reckoned on no longer than a year and a half more, though Rose was at least seventeen now and still a prisoner. But then she was different.

Hannah's mind churned on while her body and will weakened. She'd hoped that the new *Mother* Dominic would, like her predecessor, remain largely invisible, but nothing could have been further from the truth. If anything she was more in her face than ever. She didn't visit the dormitory as much, but she was everywhere else – constantly. A day didn't pass without the Reverend Mother saying something to upset Hannah. Only the previous week she'd teased her about the colour of her hair again, and in the most personal way. She referred to her as, 'Maggie, red all over.'

Hannah had all but lost the will to fight. She was now so accustomed to being called tramp, slut and hussy that the only way of dealing with it was to take it all on board and accept it. And sometimes she almost believed it.

Perhaps she was right? Perhaps that's what she was?

The point at which there had been a notable change in how Hannah viewed herself, triggering a near complete loss of will, was when she finally discovered why The Black Crow called her Maggie. It had happened when Hannah was fourteen. She'd been standing up for a new girl from a non-Catholic family who forgot to genuflect on entry to the chapel. The nun on duty had embarrassed the poor girl by calling her a *pathetic Protestant* and Hannah was caught looking at her with dagger-like eyes.

'How dare you look at me like that girl! Don't you judge me!' the nun bellowed and, before Hannah was able to stop herself, she muttered something just loud enough to cause a gasp from the other girls and a look of horror from the nun: 'Jesus would never treat people like this.'

That was all she said, but it was enough to trigger such an eruption that the whole episode ended with the, then still, *Sister* Dominic pouncing out from a side aisle. 'Maggie, you've crossed a line now! No child is fit to question a Sister. You had better prepare yourself for what's coming.'

But Hannah was not intimidated. 'Maggie, Maggie, Maggie! Don't you know my real name? You stupid cow.'

'I'll teach you.' The nun grabbed Hannah by the hair and pulled her from the refectory.

'Why.' They were now in the corridor. 'Why have you always called me Maggie?'

'Are you that dense? Are you so stupid?'

'Obviously I am.' Hannah crossed her eyes and pushed her tongue into her bottom lip to mimic old Sister Anthony who'd lost her wits. Then she tried to pull herself free.

The nun slapped her across the face. 'Magdalene!'

'Magdalene?' The word stopped Hannah from struggling.

'You heard me.'

'Mary Magdalene? But why?'

'Your hair girl!'

'I don't...what do you..?'

The nun grabbed Hannah's arm and pulled her up the corridor and through some doors that were out of bounds.

'Where are you taking me?'

The nun didn't reply. She just kept on dragging Hannah through doors and passageways until they came into a small dark room. The door slammed behind them. Hannah was petrified. She couldn't see a thing and wondered what was going to happen to her.

Suddenly a switch was flicked and the lights came on. Hannah looked around to see a library. The place was crammed full of books. And Sister Dominic was gone.

'Sister. Sister, are you there?'

A sound and a swish, and the nun appeared from behind a large stack of shelves. She had a huge book in her arms and threw it on a table, causing a cloud of dust to fly up in her face.

Blinking and covering her nose and mouth, the nun spluttered, 'Come here Maggie and look.'

Hannah stepped closer and peered down to see a large book, the title of which was simply *The Magdalene*. Then she gasped as she saw on the cover an icon depicting Mary Magdalene, kneeling down, weeping over a pair of sandaled feet.

And wiping them with her long flowing hair, her long, flowing red hair.

Chapter Thirty-One

Amsterdam, 1981

'Thank you Father,' said Eric. 'And thank you for agreeing to let Penelope come too.'

'You are very welcome. The more the merrier.' The priest smiled. 'After all, any extra help we can enlist in finding your daughter is gratefully received, yes?'

Eric and Penelope entered the presbytery. Father Ambroos sat them at a large table and, after bringing in a tray of coffee, he opened a book and placed it in front of them.

'Now Eric, this is why I called you. I have here the lists of all the British convents that took orphaned children from the early 1950s, and that includes Scotland and Wales as well as England of course.'

'What about Northern Ireland?' said Penelope.

'You're right my dear,' said the priest. 'Eric was wise to bring you along. I'd forgotten that Northern Ireland is part of the United Kingdom and, as I recall, there are rather a lot of convents there.'

'So where should we begin Father?' Eric felt overwhelmed.

'Well, we can narrow it down by eliminating all those that were for boys only.'

'Oh,' said Penelope, 'I assumed that orphaned boys were looked after by monks.'

'Yes some monks and brothers, the Christian Brothers for example, did look after boys in various parts of the world, but by and large it was seen as the work of Sisters to look after orphaned children, whether boys or girls.'

'So once we've done that, eliminated all the children's homes for boys, we'll have cut them down by about half?' said Eric.

'Indeed,' said Father Ambroos.

Penelope reached out and touched Eric's shoulder, squeezing it slightly. He turned to her and saw her smiling. He nodded and smiled back.

'Is there anything else you can remember from your discussion with your brother, Eric?' said the priest.

'No not really. Just that some Belgian nuns had taken her to Britain and placed her with a certain order. Oh, and that he'd made sure that her identity would never be given – he'd paid.'

'So how do we move forward?' said Penelope.

The priest looked at her and then at Eric. 'I think I should write to them all, as a parish priest who is pastorally concerned about a member of his flock with a missing daughter.'

'Which is all true, apart from my being a member of your flock Father,' said Eric.

'Ah but even that is true my son.' The priest smiled warmly. 'You became a member of my flock when you gave me the honour of helping you.'

'What will you write?' said Penelope.

'Oh I know exactly what to write.' The priest winked.

'That's a lot of letters,' said Eric.

'Yes.' The priest nodded, and smiled. 'But I don't mind, and I'm sure they'll understand if the letters are photocopied, with a short hand written greeting at the top.'

'Thank you. Thank you Father. I am so grateful.'

'You're welcome. I'll be in touch when I've heard back from them. Now please have hope, but be patient.'

'My only concern is what to do about my lodging. I've stayed about as long as I can in the hotel. I'm running out of funds.'

'Stay with me,' said Penelope. 'I don't know why I didn't offer before. I have a spare room in the flat. It's not much, but it's mine for the rest of the year while I'm researching. You'd be more than welcome to use it if you can chip in now and again. No strings.'

Eric smiled. 'You're all being so kind. Thank you, thank you both.'

'You're welcome,' said Penelope.

Father Ambroos said nothing, and Eric thought he might have detected a tiny flicker of disapproval in the old man's eyes.

Chapter Thirty-Two

South Wales, 1976

Unusually, Hannah was alone in the dormitory. It was late afternoon and she'd been excused from chores after complaining of a bad tummy. It hadn't been deemed worthy of the infirmary.

She lay back on her bed as the door crept open very quietly. She thought it was a draft, closed her eyes and wished her head would stop churning. Her eyes drew heavier and heavier.

My God!

It was the hand that woke her up. She could feel something on her – on the inside of her clothing – touching her bare flesh. Hannah's eyes opened to see the half-smiling, half-leering face of Sister Matthew stooped over her.

What the..? Hannah couldn't take it in. 'What are you doing?'

'There, there my sweet,' said the nun, gently massaging Hannah's tummy. 'I heard you'd been feeling poorly. I was just trying to soothe you.'

Hannah closed her eyes, petrified as images of Lucy stampeded into her head. Lucy the little dormouse, and Sister Matthew the great big preying cat. She thought Sister Matthew had learned a lesson from what happened to that little girl, but obviously not. Maybe the creep was into older girls now?

Then Hannah felt the clammy hand starting to make bigger circles on her torso, until it was brushing the edge of her pants. My God. The fingers were pressing down and trying to slip inside the hem.

'Don't!' Hannah grabbed the fat arm and pushed it away. 'Please. I don't feel well. Leave me alone.'

'That's not very nice is it my sweet?' The nun's voice had a slight quiver to it, as though she were shivering.

Hannah opened her eyes to see the nun leaning even closer.

'No!'

'I'm just going to kiss you goodnight,' said the trembling voice, and Hannah closed her eyes again as she felt a slimy mouth press down on her own.

When Hannah dared to open her eyes again the nun was gone and there she lay in panic and confusion. She could still feel those clammy fat fingers on her bare skin.

Then she could hear Mother Dominic's voice too – in her head. *You're a slut and a tart.* Had she been giving off the wrong signs? No. No, she hadn't. But what if she had without even knowing? She remembered the occasion of a year before, in the hidden library. Maybe she really was a Magdalene? Maybe people just saw her as an evil demon, a whore?

After a while, the doors swung open and the girls started entering the dormitory. Their duties complete, evening meal and vespers finished, they now had half an hour to chat quietly before bed. Noticing Hannah lying there on the bed, Rose wandered over to her. 'What happened Han?'

Hannah's eyes were screwed up and tears were rolling down both sides of her face, down her cheeks and into her ears. 'Han, Han, what's the matter. Has that bitch Dominic been here?'

'No, no Rose, it was Sister Matthew.' Hannah recounted the whole story.

Chapter Thirty-Three

Amsterdam, 1981

Dear Father Ambroos,

It is with regret that we are unable to help you with your request. There are unfortunately no records of orphans from the period you are enquiring about due to a terrible fire that occurred a decade ago, wiping out everything. Our humblest apologies that we can be no help.

In Christ,

Mother Matthew

'Bloody typical.' Eric stamped his foot.

The preceding weeks had been restless for Eric. Penelope had been back into her personal research, but Eric hadn't been able to continue with his ancestral work. His mind was completely dominated by his daughter. However, a telephone call meant they were now back with the priest. After a coffee had been placed into both of their hands, Father Ambroos began reading the letters he'd received. The first one he chose to read was from Crucis Home For Girls, South Wales.

'Wait.' The priest held up a hand with forefinger outstretched. 'I read that letter first for a reason. Now let me read the others.'

Dear Father,

Thank you for your letter. However, we are not sure why you feel the parishioner's daughter came to us. We took no orphans from overseas during the dates you speak of. If you would like a photostat of our records of these years we'd be happy to oblige.

We wish you well in your search for this poor man's daughter,
Mother Ophelia

And another:

Dear Father,
Greetings from the Sisters. We are sorry to have to inform you that the information you've been given about this particular Van Kroot child coming to us all those years ago is incorrect. We've checked through all our records and no child with such a surname ever came to us.
Continued blessings in your search,
Mother Theresa

The letters went on in a similar vein.

Eric was feeling more and more despondent. 'Father, by the tone of your voice on the phone this morning I thought you had something encouraging.'

'I do Eric.'

'Then tell me.'

'I already have.'

'I don't understand.'

The priest turned back to the very first letter and started to read it out again.

'Sorry but you've already read them. They all say no.'

'Eric let me finish reading this one again. If you pay attention, you'll notice that it doesn't say no.'

Dear Father Ambroos,

It is with regret that we are unable to help you with your request. There are unfortunately no records of orphans from the period you are enquiring about due to a terrible fire that occurred a decade ago, wiping out everything.

Our humblest apologies that we can be no help.

In Christ,

Mother Matthew

'It sounds like it says no to me Father. Oh – hang on yes, yes I see.' Penelope smiled. 'Of course, this letter is the only one that doesn't say no.'

'Exactly,' said the priest. 'Now let me read you my letter to the convents.'

Eric frowned, and shook his head.

Dear Sister/Mother,

Forgive me for this unsolicited letter.

I'm the parish priest of St Nicholas's Catholic Church, Amsterdam. I am writing on behalf of one of my flock, who is a man in great turmoil.

Around two decades ago his daughter, a Miss Van Kroot, was taken to your convent and children's home from Holland by some Belgian nuns, and left there to be cared for by your Sisters. Obviously she will have left by now, but her father is desperate to find her and make amends for his inability to care for her. If there's any way you would be willing to offer help in where we might look for her I would be indebted to you.

Yours,

With the richest blessings of Christ,

Father Ambroos SJ

'See Eric, I wasn't asking whether your daughter had been there. I was telling them she had been there, and all but one offered convincing reasons for me to believe she had not been. The first one I read ignored any attempt to do that, merely declaring that there are no records.'

Eric felt a rush of excitement. 'Then that's where she was.'

'I believe it might be, yes,' said Father Ambroos. 'However, we need to wait for the remaining few replies, just to make sure they follow the same pattern. I think we're onto something here, but we need to be certain.'

'Alright,' said Eric. 'But if you are correct and the first letter shows us where she was, you do realise I'm going to have to go there don't you? I'll have to get it out of them. They will have to tell me where she went after she'd left them.'

Father Ambroos smiled. 'Eric, have you ever tried to get anything out of a nun?'

'No.'

'I didn't think you had.'

Chapter Thirty-Four

South Wales, 1976

It was breakfast and the aroma coming from behind the screen was especially delicious.

'Why dunt we ever get anything like that?' whispered Rose. Hannah's eyes widened. Oh no! It had been too loud. Sister Matthew, who was on breakfast duty, pounced on them like a flabby cat.

'Silence!'

'It wu just me Sister,' said Rose. 'It wunt Hannah.'

But Mother Dominic was now intervening.

'Please, Sisters,' said Rose, as both girls were hoisted out of their chairs.

Mother Dominic grabbed Hannah by the hair. 'You insolent girl.'

But Hannah noticed what was happening to Rose's hands – Rose's *fists*.

'Rose. No. Don't,' said Hannah.

'Don't what?' snarled Sister Matthew.

But Rose couldn't hold it back.

'Shut the fuck up you evil molesting bitch.'

There was stunned silence throughout the refectory.

And then a stomp, and a bang.

And another, louder, stomp.

And the beginning of a chant.

'Rose, Rose, Rose.' The girls were chanting her name. And stamping their feet. And banging the tables. 'Rose! Rose! Rose!'

Mother Dominic had frozen, Hannah's hair entwined around her hand. A tiny trickle of something was dripping down Hannah's forehead from where the crow had ripped out some strands.

Rose looked at Hannah, her eyes widening. 'You've made her bleed. I'm gonna kill you, you fucking bitch.'

Hannah looked at the nuns. They were visibly shocked by such defiance.

Mother Dominic's face was like thunder. 'In the name of the Holy Roman Church and Christ Our Lord I command you to stop!'

She might as well have been talking in Latin, because the chanting just got louder and louder. 'Rose! Rose! Rose!'

Suddenly Rose turned on Mother Dominic like a rabid dog. She bit the hand that held Hannah's hair, releasing her friend onto the floor in a heap.

'Quick, get up Han!' said Rose. 'Grab her other arm!'

Hannah was too shocked to question it and the two girls marched out of the refectory, forcing the Reverend Mother along with them. The nun was thrashing around, grabbing out with her hands, trying to grip anything she could, but they overpowered her. The orphans were still banging and chanting.

'Rose! Rose! Rose!'

Rose and Hannah pushed and pulled the squealing bitch into the kitchen, locking the door after them. The place was hot and steamy, and the smell of watery orphans' porridge mingled with the bacon, eggs and fried bread had lingered, making a sickly scent. The kitchen staff were in the washing room.

'Han.' A breathless Rose had her arm around the nun's neck. 'I'll hold her while you lock that other door.'

Hannah ran over to the washing room, slammed the door and bolted it. Now it was just them and Mother Dominic.

'What do you think you're doing?' shouted the nun.

'Shut up bitch,' said Rose.

'Oh God Rose,' said Hannah, 'what are you doing? Please. What's happening?'

Rose's face was as cold as ice. 'We're gonna teach this cunt a lesson she'll never forget.'

'You'll never get away with this,' said the nun. 'You'll both be sent to Borstal.'

Hannah flinched as a flash of an arm whizzed past her face. The scream from Mother Dominic was blood curdling. Rose's punch landed square in the face, her nose now gushing with blood.

Hannah looked at the bloody face and screamed.

'Han, she deserves it.'

'Rose, we have to stop!'

There was banging on the door and shouting from both directions.

Mother Dominic held her nose and mouth, her eyes wild with rage. 'You two are done for. You little sluts. The dunce and the whore. What a couple of freaks you make.'

Hannah was now demanding that Rose stop. Rose was swearing she'd kill the bitch.

'Pure evil aren't you? You always were, and you always will be – both of you,' sneered the blood-splattered Reverend Mother.

Hannah had let go, but Rose was spitting like an angry cobra. She grabbed the back of the nun's veil and pulled so hard that the woman's head jolted upwards, almost snapping her neck. She let out an awful yell and fell to the floor with her veil in Rose's hand.

Hannah looked down at her, dumbstruck, as she lay unconscious on the kitchen floor, almost bald save for her last few strands of *bright red hair.*

'Oh my God,' whispered Hannah, as she grew unsteady herself.

'Jesus fucking Christ,' said Rose.

Chapter Thirty-Five

The Testimony of Ezra Van Kroot, Amsterdam, 1535

Never before had I seen such people. They came in golden robes and carried huge Christian crosses held up on high, with burning torches leading the way. Their priests marched with carved images, some carrying big brass balls on chains that smoked when they swung. Both we and the Moors found such idols sacrilegious. And then came the marching soldiers, followed by others on horseback, waving the crimson red flag of Castile. The entire procession must have been close to a mile long. These Catholics were indeed a different breed.

And so it was that, just a few months after my father and I had spoken, the Moorish leaders of *Muxacra* made obeisance to King Ferdinand and Queen Isabella. Granada itself was not yet defeated but our little town had fallen. With regard to our horrendous choice, to remain Jews or convert, the Governor of *Muxacra* managed to negotiate an agreement with the Castilians. We had no idea that it would only last as long as the remaining part of unconquered Granada lasted as a kingdom, but it seemed that we were promised continued freedom to be Jews, as the Moors were to be Muslims. The Governor, by his courageous assertiveness, managed to impress the Catholic Monarchs who promised him and his people royal protection.

Over the next four years, we saw many changes and a huge influx of Christian families, coming mostly from the old kingdom of Murcia. We realised that our days as Jewish inhabitants of *Muxacra* were numbered.

Rumours began circulating. Over the first ten-year period of the Inquisition, the problem of Judaizers had not gone away, so voices started to call for a total expulsion of the Jews, as if the temptation to heresy would then be eliminated.

I do not believe that either monarch nursed any personal hatred towards Jews. I am told that both employed a large number of learned Jews within their court, mainly doctors and financiers, and that they were protected under them. But pressure was coming from the outside for them to act.

A certain Torquemada, the Chief Inquisitor and Queen Isabella's long-term confessor, who was himself a Jew by bloodline, persistently advocated the expulsion of the Jews to her and Ferdinand. But the monarchs had other goals and priorities: the completion of what they called the *Reconquesta*, the final taking of Granada. So a new motivation to expel the Jews was needed.

Then something happened far away from our home town in the area of Toledo, the repercussions of which were felt throughout the land. According to the tales that were being shared, a Christian infant had been kidnapped by a group of twelve people, six Jews and six Judaizers, whereupon they crucified the little mite and cut out his heart to create a magic rite as a spell against Christians. Clearly this vile nonsense was nothing more than a spiteful tale to slander Jews, but it was taken seriously by the Christian authorities. Hence, by the beginning of the next year, the monarchs issued an edict demanding the expulsion of all Jews from the land, a land that now included old Granada too. The only possible way to escape the edict's rule was to convert to Christianity and be baptised.

The shock waves were immediate and even a deputation of the wealthiest Jews of our land, led by one Isaac Abravanel, set out to demand audience with the monarchs, where they might persuade them to reconsider. Apparently they offered a large sum to the king, but Torquemada burst into the king and queen's presence throwing down thirty silver coins and asking them whether they would be prepared, like Judas, to

sell Christ out to the Jews for money.
And so came the expulsion.

Chapter Thirty-Six

South Wales, 1976

The door swung open with a thud and a crash.

Hannah was coming out of her unconsciousness. She propped herself up against a kitchen cabinet, and as her eyes began to focus, she saw a policeman standing in the doorway. His mouth hung open and he was shaking his head slowly. Another policeman pushed past him into the kitchen.

She called out for Rose. No reply.

'Oh, Jesus. Oh, God! What in Christ's name's been going on here?' It was a man's voice.

Hannah lifted herself up and turned her head to where the voice had come from. A policeman was hovering over two figures.

Blood. So much blood. 'Rose, what have you done? Rose.'

Lying on the hard wooden floor were two bodies, one on top of the other. Rose was sprawled face down upon the Reverend Mother, whose head was turned to face Hannah, eyes wide open and red wisps of hair stuck to her scalp with blood. Her arms were stretched outward, held in place by the sharp blades of the kitchen knives that had been driven through her palms. But the blood seemed to be mainly Rose's, from whose neck oozed a thick crimson stream.

The policeman spoke. 'Christ Almighty. What on earth did – ' He stopped when he heard the sound: a breath and a deep gurgling. 'Quick, get the ambulance men. I think she's alive.'

Chapter Thirty-Seven

South Wales, 1981

The sign was a few decades old by the look of it, paint flaking and words faded. But there it stood next to the rusty iron gates. *Welcome to Crucis Catholic Home For Girls.*

Eric had arrived at the Convent of the Sisters of Golgotha, East Glamorgan. It was only two days since the phone call from Father Ambroos. Bless that priest. He couldn't have done it without him. The old man was so thrilled to report that the other replies had come in, and that they all told the same story.

It struck Eric that this part of Wales was nothing like he'd imagined. For all his travels he'd never been here before, and if he could help it he'd never be back again. It was run down, dreary and damp. Unlike the lush green mountains and valleys he had expected, this industrial wasteland was dark and depressing.

Eric chose not to warn the convent he was coming, but he hadn't realised that the gates would be shut and secured with a thick chain and padlock. It was mid-morning. He'd spent the previous night at a local hotel and was feeling sick with apprehension. But the first hurdle was getting to the main door. How on earth did people get their attention? What did delivery people do?

Then he saw it, protruding slightly from the mossy stone wall, obscured by ivy. An off-white button – a bell. He pressed it and moved to where he could see through the gates, up the driveway. No sign of any movement. He glanced around the inside of the convent grounds. There was no sight or sound of any children. Perhaps they were not allowed in the front gardens.

He looked at the building, which was sideways on from where he stood. He figured it was probably Victorian, with its sharply pointed windows and upper rooms. The sandstone and red brick were both discoloured by the years. It was a bloody gloomy place.

He heard a sound.

The distant unbolting of a door.

Then a figure appeared, dressed in black with a splash of white.

The Sister turned to re-lock the door, as if expecting someone to follow her. She paced forward slowly, aided by a stick, inching her way down the drive towards the gates. She was bent double, but would have obviously been tall in her younger, straighter days. Eric wondered why such an infirm woman had been given this duty. As she drew closer he began to feel a deep sense of unease and, when she finally reached the other side of the gate and lifted her veiled head to speak, he flinched. Her complexion was transparent – like a ghost. Her face was gaunt and skeletal and she had one eye that sagged down, revealing a deep red inner eyelid, made even more vivid when contrasted with the sickly white eye itself, like that of a boiled fish. Enough to scare away most visitors.

'Can I help you?' Her brittle voice was as off putting as her appearance, like nails on a blackboard.

Resisting the urge to turn away and cover his ears, Eric replied, 'Yes Sister, thank you. I'm looking for some information.'

'You've come a long way?'

'I'm sorry?'

'Your accent,' she said. 'Where are you from?'

'Ah yes, I'm from the Netherlands.'

'And what are you looking for here, may I ask?'

'I'm trying to find out...' Eric stopped. This was a children's home. She knew exactly why he was there. 'Sister may I come in and speak to someone who can help me?'

'Have you made an appointment?'

'Um, no.'

'Then I'm afraid you'll have to make one. She turned to leave.'

'Sister, please. I'm looking for information on my child. My daughter. She would have lived here from the mid-1960s.'

Slowly, the nun turned around again and peered suspiciously at him through the iron gates. 'Very well, tell me the name and I'll see what I can do. But you'll have to wait here.'

Eric felt humiliated and tired. 'Her surname would have been Van Kroot, and she was brought here during the mid-60s.'

Chapter Thirty-Eight

South Wales, 1978

Their gormless faces leered at her through the window before slapping each other on the back and staggering away.

Hannah was sitting in a café in Cardiff city centre, still finding the new sights and sounds hard to get used to. Music blared everywhere: workmen blasted it out on radios; shops played it for customers.

And right there, in the café, a speaker system bellowed constantly. The song now playing seemed to be on wherever she went. It was by a group called Queen and Hannah was even beginning to hear it in her head when it wasn't on: *We are the champions, my friends.*

She thought of Rose, her champion. But why had she done it? What made her kill Mother Dominic? She looked out through the window again. The crowd of freakish youths had moved on, but there were many more sights she'd still not adjusted to. The clothes that people wore – the amazing colours. Bright red hair, but not to be ashamed of, as if it were a curse. Men with dyed red hair, and some of them with eye makeup on. In all her years at Crucis Home, never once had she imagined life outside would look like this.

But while the people out there were colourful, the streets themselves were not. They were as dreary as the convent corridors.

* * *

Three months before, Hannah was finally freed from Crucis Home For Girls and helped to find a basic job and a bedsit. Years of convent chores meant the cleaning work was easy, but the bedsit was strange. Though the house was large and full of similarly occupied flats, she felt totally alone.

However, while getting used to life outside had been difficult, it was also exciting. Some of Hannah's spark had returned and she had a new-found sense of purpose. She was about to embark upon a journey that she'd dreamed of for most of her life.

She also now knew what had happened to her best friend, and had written her a letter. Rose was lucky to have survived. The verdict was murder – the crow's death caused by a fatal stab wound to the heart.

While Mother Dominic lay unconscious, Rose had somehow managed to tie down her arms and legs with long strips of linen torn from kitchen aprons. She then apparently sat on the nun's abdomen, as she hammered a kitchen knife through each of her open palms using a heavy rolling pin. It seems the shock of pain had awoken the nun, causing her to thrash about wildly as she tried in vain to release her outstretched limbs.

Rose had then taken a third, smaller knife, and stabbed her numerous times through the chest. However, and this was probably caused by the shock of what she'd done once the euphoria had begun to wear off, Rose then suffered a seizure and fell with the knife still in her hand, collapsing onto the nun and slicing her own neck on the way. She was safe now, but wouldn't be out for a long time yet.

Hannah read her letter through one more time before sealing the envelope.

Prisoner No – 384
HM Prison Holloway
Camden Road, Holloway, London N7

Dear Rose,
I hope you're okay. It's Han. I'm free at last. The crows told me I'd never be able to contact you again but I found out

where you are. And, Rose, I've also found out something else. I know where I came from. Just before I left Crucis Home I asked Sister Matthew for one small favour. I thought she owed me one. I even gave her 'something' in return. Don't despise me Rose. I'd have done anything to get what I needed and you know what she's like. Ten minutes of tightly closed eyes and clammy hands on my body was worth it.

I asked her to find out where I'd come from and what my family name had been when I was first brought there. And she did. She did, God bless her. I'd come from somewhere in Northern Europe and my name is Van Kroot, which I've discovered is a Dutch name. So, I'm going to go to Holland to find my family and, Rose, I wanted to let you know.

I have no address to give you, so I know I won't hear back from you, but I just wanted you to know this, and also that I'll never forget you. One day I'll come back and find you. But before then I'll write again, hopefully from Holland, when I have some news for you.

Your friend forever,
Han.

Chapter Thirty-Nine

South Wales, 1981

Eric waited outside the gates for at least an hour. He was cold, tired and about to give up.

'I've been talking to the Reverend Mother,' said the nun.

He jumped. Where the hell had she come from? He'd been leaning on the wall and hadn't noticed her approach.

'And?' Eric said, noticing that the nun was avoiding eye contact.

'And it seems your Dutch parish priest had already written and received a reply with regard to your question. Did he not tell you?'

Eric's right eye twitched.

'Look, I'm losing patience. What are you people hiding?'

'I'm afraid there's nothing more to say.' She started to turn away. 'We have no records and she would have left several years ago anyway even if she was here. I think the question you should be asking yourself is not where is Hannah, but why was she brought here in the first place?'

He flinched. 'Say that again.'

'Say what?'

'You said *Hannah*. You said her name.'

'But you've been asking about her,' replied the nun. 'Hannah Van Kroot. Whether she was here or not. You ought to be asking why you – '

'I didn't even know her first name.' He grinned at her. 'But now I do. Now I know her name is Hannah *and* I know she was here. Thank you Sister.'

The nun looked startled.

'Next time it will be an appointment,' he said, as he walked away from the gates.

* * *

Eric had paid the hotel manager extra to borrow the phone. 'Yes Pen, I know her name. Pen, I know my daughter's name!' He laughed. 'The duty Sister slipped up. She's called Hannah.' Eric held the receiver close to his ear and used a finger from his free hand to wedge into his other ear blocking out the background noise of the bar. 'No, I'm not sure what to do now. I still don't think they're going to give me much. I mean, bloody hell, it's a creepy old place. You should see it.'

He spoke for a few more minutes before saying, 'Anyway, I'll call again when I can.' He was aware that the manager's eyes were on him. 'I'm on a line from my hotel so I really need to say goodbye now.' He hung up.

He sat down at a free table and had a sip from the pint he'd just bought. He noticed that the manager was still looking at him from across the bar. Eric downed his drink and left for his room. A few minutes after he'd entered, there was a knock at his door. It was the hotel manager.

'Mr Van Kroot, I apologise but I couldn't help overhearing some of your conversation on the telephone this evening.'

Eric shook his head in irritation. 'I'm sorry?'

'Don't worry. I'm not prying, but I thought you might be interested in something. Can I come in?'

'Um, okay.' He noticed that the manager had an old folded up newspaper with him. He entered the room and closed the door behind him.

'Can I ask,' said the manager, 'have you heard about the murder?'

'Murder?'

'Yes, a few years ago. The previous Reverend Mother was killed, quite brutally by all accounts. Apparently it was a teenage girl who'd gone mad. She crucified the poor nun with a couple of kitchen knives, before stabbing her through the heart.'

Eric swallowed.

'She ended up in a mental wing of a prison. I'm not sure which – maybe Holloway. Seems to ring a bell.'

'Christ.'

'Here, take a look. I kept one of these.' The manager gave Eric the newspaper.

Not Always Murder at the Vicarage! A shocking incident occurred at The Convent of the Sisters of Golgotha, South Wales yesterday when the Reverend Mother Dominic Rees was tortured and brutally murdered by a teenage orphan in her care. Miss Rose Philips (17) has been taken into Police custody. Sole witness, Miss Hannah Van Kroot (15), has refused to speak, which has been put down to the trauma of shock. More on this story on page 8.

Chapter Forty

The Testimony of Ezra Van Kroot, Amsterdam, 1535

We were given a few months to decide whether to leave or convert, and prepare for whatever our future was going to be. It was within that period that my father took me out alone once again. I was now in my fourteenth year. The previous four years had prepared me to expect such a moment as this. Deep down I knew what he was going to say. I knew I would have to leave *Muxacra* on my own.

I dreaded leaving my father, my mother, my sisters and brothers, my home and everything I held dear. I do not know what my father did to explain the decision to my mother. It must have been the hardest for her. Other families were split up in the same way, some older siblings desperate to stay, while others saw only a black-clouded future from which they felt they had to escape.

Chapter Forty-One

Amsterdam, 1978

The train creaked to a halt as Hannah arrived at Amsterdam's Central Station. A few months' cleaning work and living mainly on bread and butter had enabled her to save enough for the ferry and train fares. Her passport was the greatest expense. She changed her remaining few pounds into gilders and, with the aid of a map, made her way down *Damrak* towards Dam Square, where she was told he'd be waiting for her.

Cardiff's introduction to wild new human sights rapidly faded in contrast to Amsterdam's. Hannah picked her way through the crowds, glancing this way and that at the assortment of misfits and oddities she passed. There to the right, outside some sort of café, stood a gang of older teenagers with white painted words written all over their sagging clothes, each one's spiked up hair a different colour to the next. Some had safety pins attached to their trousers and skirts and a couple even had them pierced through their ears. Hannah hurried on, only to be slowed down a few moments later by the sight of a young man lying against a doorway on a piece of cardboard. His black eyes were sunk deep into his grey-white face and his bottom lip hung down allowing a glob of drool to drip onto his shirt. Under him was a piece of soiled cardboard and beside him stood a blackboard, on which a sentence had been written in chalk. She stood gazing, trying to decipher the words. *'Ik heb de gewoonte geschopt. Ik ben ziek als een hond, en niemand kan mijn lijden te zien.'*

A voice from behind startled her. 'It says, *I've kicked the habit. I'm sick as a dog, and no one can see my suffering.'*

She turned, but the voice's owner had walked off into the crowd.

Hannah was now at the end of the long road and she could

see a huge monument within a giant open space. She was there at last, in the heart of Amsterdam. As she stepped into the famous Dam Square she felt sick, but couldn't work out whether it was excitement or fear. She'd found her parents. She was going to meet them.

Hannah spotted the café on the street corner. It was exactly as described on the telephone. And there she waited, replaying the phone conversation in her mind. *Yes, yes I've spoken to Mr Van Kroot and he'll see you. He'll send a car to the following address at eleven o'clock tomorrow morning. Will that suit you?*

She watched and waited. A few moments later she could hear a deep thumping, rumbling sound when, from around a street corner, crept a slow procession of motorbikes. People seemed to move out of the way for them as they passed and, as they did, Hannah noticed that each rider had the same image on their backs. They wore a skull with what looked like wings and the words Hells Angels, in red letters, a phrase that could be justly applied to the Sisters of Golgotha.

After a few more minutes, a taxi pulled up and the driver wound down the window. He spoke in English. 'Are you Hannah? Hannah Van Kroot?'

* * *

The journey took about half an hour and neither the driver nor Hannah spoke. They arrived at a set of gates with an intercom system to one side. The taxi driver didn't need to speak through it because the gates opened as he drove near.

As they reached the enormous house, Hannah felt breathless and giddy. It was a mixture of fear, excitement and doubt. What would they be like? Would they want to get to know her? Oh God, should she have come?

The taxi driver reversed into a space, got out and opened Hannah's door. He motioned to her to approach the stone steps that led up to the main entrance. As she climbed the steps, the door opened and a young woman stood in the doorway.

Who was she? Too young for her mother. A sister perhaps? As Hannah looked into the face of this young woman, she realised she couldn't have been a relation; her eyes were clearly oriental.

'Hello Hannah.' The young woman held out her hand and Hannah reached out her own. They shook hands and Hannah entered the Van Kroot residence. 'Would you like something to eat and drink? You must be famished after your journey!'

Hannah was too nervous to eat. 'A glass of water, please. Thank you.'

'Okay I'll be right back. Why don't you take a seat right there for a moment? My name is Suki. I'm Mr Van Kroot's housekeeper.'

Hannah sat down on the luxurious leather sofa and glanced around. Almost directly across from her was a closed door with a fire extinguisher outside. Further down the polished wood hallway were two more rooms, doors closed, and right at the bottom was a swirling staircase leading to the first floor.

What a place. It was amazing. What the hell did he do? She recalled the phone call she'd made from Cardiff. *Is that Mr Peter Van Kroot? Okay, well can I speak to him? I need to talk to him. Can I at least get a message to him? Look, this is his daughter. I need to see him.*

She had tracked him down by spending the whole day in the city's library searching through the Dutch phone books she had asked to see. The only Van Kroot family in Holland was based in Amsterdam. After a long pause she finally heard a voice again on the other end of the line.

He'll see me? Oh that's amazing. I'll find a way to get there. Thank you.

Once again she waited, but now she was in his home.

She looked to her left, and noticed a painting that belonged to a set of portraits. There were others spaced out along the wall.

All of them were male and they were in date order, the oldest was closest to where she was sat. She looked up into the eyes of an oddly dressed man with glowing green eyes and flaming red hair.

Chapter Forty-Two

The Testimony of Ezra Van Kroot, Amsterdam, 1535

I do not exaggerate that the next four years of my life were hell. I can find no better word to describe the experience. You might ask: how can travelling from one country to another be such hell?

Herewith is my answer.

I am told that two hundred thousand Jews fled in 1492. Thousands travelled by sea to Morocco, Italy and parts of the Ottoman Empire. But most of us sought refuge with our neighbour to the West: Christian Portugal, whose king welcomed us with open arms. Indeed at first I thought King João II must have been blessed with at least some of his Christ's famous compassion, but later I learned it was purely self-interest. He had been preparing himself for what he believed to be an inevitable war with the Moors and he needed the tax collectable from the enormous number of Jewish incomers to pay for it.

A second motive was that he did not wish any of the Jewish talent for arms making, for which we were well known, to be made available to the Moors. If anyone was going to benefit from our expertise it would be him.

As it turned out, residence was granted to just a few hundred wealthy families and a few dozen craftsmen, skilled in the construction of weapons. The rest of us were allowed to stay for a period of eight months, after which the king promised he would provide shipping for us to travel to more distant shores.

I cannot begin to describe the terror when I heard tales of what would await us at sea: unscrupulous Jew hating captains, pirates, shipwrecked boats, food that was not only foul to begin with but maggot filled and rotten, and sea sickness that lasted for weeks on end. I had made a handful of friends by that point and one of them, Hagez, still lives near me, here in Amsterdam. The others are all dead. They perished from various ailments along the way.

The eight-month period came to an end, but the king failed to keep his promise. A mere handful of ships were provided, and those of us left behind were made slaves of the crown. Hundreds of Jewish children and youths were torn cruelly from their parents and sent to an island called *São Tomé*, just west of the continent of Africa. Hagez and I were among them.

There we lived as slaves for two long years, during which we were worked like Pharaoh's Hebrews, as well as being forcibly converted to Christianity. Church history and doctrine was rammed into our worn-out heads by monks. I began to wonder why my father had been so insistent that I fled after all. I longed to return and prayed that my family were still safe in my beloved *Muxacra*.

Then, just as our third year on the island approached, something happened. A miracle. Hagez and I had both proven ourselves studious with our ecclesiastical teachers. Hagez had shown great promise at Latin, and I myself had absorbed church history and theology like a sponge. Soon we were back on a vessel heading for Portugal, the reason not yet apparent.

We returned to discover that King João had died and a new monarch had been crowned, his cousin, Manoel. This new king had decided to free all the Jewish slaves. He even refused a gift offered him in gratitude. I know not whether this gesture was self-less or self-seeking like his predecessor, but we Jews of Portugal seemed at last to be gaining favour with the new king.

I asked my friend whether he thought this was why we had been brought back from São Tomé, but Hagez said he doubted it. After all, it was just the two of us. The rest were still out there on that hell hot island. Later we discovered why we had been chosen. We were recognised as more independent than the poor souls who had been physically ripped from their parents' arms and, more importantly, we had also impressed the clergy with our learning abilities. Thus they had persuaded the authorities to bring us back, that we might be used in the inevitable task of mass conversion.

Any new liberty for Portuguese Jews was not to last. King Manoel's claim to the monarchy had become an object of dispute, and he needed a way to make his position solid. So he sought the hand of Princess Isabel of Castile, the daughter of the monarchs Ferdinand and Isabella. Their answer was affirmative on one condition: that he expel all Jews from Portugal.

The king's dilemma was worsened when the Castilian princess herself announced that she would only accept marriage if all Jews were expelled. Reluctantly King Manoel agreed.

Thus we were ordered to leave Portugal by October 1497.

However, King Manoel's mind had not been fully made up. He knew the value of the Jews and believed he could convert them and keep them in Portugal as Catholics. His method led to a set of images of which I cannot bear to be reminded, but must recount here for the sake of this manuscript. My friend and I wished we had played dumb and remained on that island, for we, along with a few dozen other new Christians, were enlisted to help in the conversion of Jewish children.

Parents were ordered to take their children over the age of three to Lisbon. They were told that, on arrival, their children would be given to Christian families to be raised as devout Catholics.

On the appointed day, children who had not been presented were hunted down and seized by officials of the crown. Parents watched their sons and daughters being forced to the baptismal font. But as news spread, many parents, out of desperation, smothered their little ones in their farewell embrace, snuffing out their lives. Others threw them into the deepest wells to drown, for this was seen as a far better option than to grow up with the disgrace of apostasy hanging over them like a spectre. Such was their emotional agony, many of these parents cast themselves from high windows or in front of heavy carts.

Truly it was an unbearable sight and the cries were soul piercing, but it was not just Jewish children who were targeted. In some places even the elderly were dragged by the hair into churches and baptised forcibly by overzealous clergy who had been led to believe that a general mass conversion of Jews had been ordered.

All the while, the final date for departure approached and deportees were commanded to leave from Lisbon's port, causing severe logistical problems and panic. This was when Hagez and myself decided we would escape once and for all. We both agreed that the trauma of working for this vile country's despicable crown was worse than death itself, so we ourselves made plans to flee. If we were to die in the process, then so be it.

And so it was that, late in 1497, around twenty thousand Jews from all parts of Portugal gathered in Lisbon where they were herded into the courtyard of the palace. Hagez and I, as so-called *new Christians*, were there to help. We saw our people bullied into baptism by the clergy under the watchful eye of officials of the Royal Court. Many succumbed to their threats of eternal damnation.

The remainder were kept under guard until the time for their departure had been and gone, whereupon they were once again told that their failure to leave meant they had made themselves the king's slaves. After this shock, more agreed to baptism, while others were forced. They were treated to a shower of Holy Water, which was sprinkled on them from above. And thus Portugal's Jews were Christianised.

We kept to our plans and sought to escape, though we realised it would now be much harder, as we could not simply submerge ourselves within the fleeing masses. So we travelled north by foot until we found another port and an agreeable captain of a small merchant ship, who welcomed the idea of an extra pair of hands for his crew in exchange for a journey.

It was not comfortable and, while not as bad as the rumours, the food was indeed awful. But we had escaped.

During the long journey around the coastline of Portugal, northern Castile and France, the passengers continued to change and I became aware that it was not just a merchant ship. Before moving into French waters, we ported at a Castilian fishing village whereupon two gentlemen boarded who, as I gained their trust, informed me that they were seeking what they had heard was their New Zion. That was the very first time I had heard anyone speak of Amsterdam.

And so, let us speak of my first glimpse of her.

Indeed, nothing had prepared me. After five nightmarish years in Portugal and six more months at sea I arrived and, as the cart I hid in at the port slowed down, I was able to crawl off.

My first sight was beautiful Dam Square.

Chapter Forty-Three

Amsterdam, 1978

Blood, so much blood.

The taxi drove through a pothole, jolting her momentarily out of her daydream, but then she was gone again.

Blood seeping from Rose's neck wound. Blood smothered all over the orange haired bitch's open hands and contorted face.

Blood pouring from her own mother's womb. A blood river carrying an unborn child – barely a couple of months old. A foetus the size of a hazelnut. Hannah. Hannah before she was Hannah. Before she was Maggie. Hannah being flushed away into nothingness.

She let out a scream, startling the driver who slammed on the breaks. 'What the fuck?'

'God. Oh God. Fucking God.' She slammed her fist into the side of her head, again and again, trying to knock herself out. 'Oh God. Oh Christ. Why did you let me live?'

In her imagination she watched her aborted self slither away into the darkness, and peace.

But there was no peace.

'Look,' said the driver. 'I don't know what this is about, but I've been told to take you back to where I met you.'

Hannah didn't answer.

Eventually the taxi pulled up and the driver turned his head half way towards her. Hannah felt so numb she barely noticed they'd stopped.

'Is there anywhere else I can take you?' he asked. 'Is there anyone here you know?' But Hannah said nothing. Her mind was constantly replaying her encounter with the man she had thought was her father.

She had inched her way slowly into the huge study, and there he was, sitting behind his desk like a bloated king, the man she'd dreamed of meeting her entire life. And nothing could have prepared her for the reception.

From her very first glimpse she could tell that he did not share her desire to meet. His bulky frame, his black, slicked-back hair, his oily skin and his smoke-exhaling mouth. And his expression – oh his hateful expression. The frown, the red eyes, the curled up clammy mouth. *Oh my God he doesn't want to see me.*

The shock was too much.

She stood, quivering and looking down at the floor, until he pushed himself up to stand and, arm raised, finger pointing, opened his gluttonous mouth to speak.

She could have been back at the convent, listening to Sister Matthew or Mother Dominic, such was the sneering show of disgust that spewed out from the man she hoped would be her father.

And then he told her that he was not.

'You should never have come here, you little thief. I know what you want. Money. You thought you could ask your rich father for cash didn't you?'

'But…I…no…'

'Shut your mouth.' He screwed up his face, his voice now a whisper. *'You're not my daughter. You're the spawn of my traitorous brother.'*

Hannah had felt her knees giving way, as she sunk to the ground, dazed and unable to take in what she was listening to.

'Your mother died giving birth to you. She was a whore who fucked her own brother-in-law.'

Every sentence had been like a blow to her head.

'My own brother, your spineless father, is a cheating bastard who I hope is dead.' With that last word saliva had sprayed out from his mouth onto his polished desk. *'There's nothing for you here.'*

* * *

The driver got out of the taxi and walked around the car to open the door for her. Still numb and voiceless she got out of the taxi and slowly walked away. Moments later a hand grabbed her shoulder and turned her around.

'Here,' said the taxi driver, who'd left his car running twenty or so yards up the street.

She looked at his face and then down at his hand, which held a small white piece of folded paper.

'You're alone,' he said, 'and this city can be dangerous if you don't know where to avoid.'

The words were hardly sinking in.

'This is the telephone number of someone who will help you.'

She took the paper and walked off into the crowded square.

Part Two

Dam
Origin and Etymology: Traced back to Middle Dutch
A barrier that impounds water
as seen in the names of many old cities such as Amsterdam.

Chapter Forty-Four

North London, 1981

Eric peered into the window, squinting at the bright neon light. He knew the girl behind the glass was still in her twenties, but she could have been in her forties. Her face was drawn and lined deeply. Her staring dark eyes betrayed insomnia and small rough blotches covered various points on her face and neck. Her fingers picked nervously at the loose skin on the side of her thumb nails.

He had to raise his voice to speak through the little intercom in the thick reinforced glass. 'Rose, thank you for agreeing to speak with me.' The prison authorities had granted him a ten-minute visit.

The dark eyes widened slightly. The voice was cold and monotone. 'Han's bin lookin for you.'

Eric felt his heart leap. 'Is that true? So she's been in touch with you?'

The young woman peered at him, some of her black mop falling across the side of her face. Then she snarled, 'If I could, I'd crucify you too. How could yer have given her up to that hell hole? At least my reason for being there wu better. At least my drug addict mother had no choice.'

'Rose.' He looked down, eyes filling up. 'There's so much to explain, but now's not the time.' He looked directly at her. 'Please, can you help me find her? When did you last hear from her?'

'She only wrote twice. The first wa just before she'd found out where to look for yer. She was still in Britain then and had just about saved up enough to get to Holland.'

'She went to Holland?'

'Course she bloody did – yer know she bloody did!'

Eric shook his head, but didn't question it. 'And?'

'And the last letter she sent came just after she'd bin to see you.' Rose curled her face up and looked like she was going to cry. 'How could you?'

'What? Been to see *me*?'

'After everything she'd been through, how could yer have turned her away. Fuckin paid her off with a taxi ride.'

'No, no I – I don't understand.'

'Yes you do, Mr Peter Van Cunt,' she said through clenched teeth.

'Peter?' Eric froze, and then it all sunk in. 'Oh my God. Oh my poor daughter. She went to see Peter, but why didn't he tell me when I saw him?'

Now it was Rose who looked confused.

Chapter Forty-Five

The Testimony of Ezra Van Kroot, Amsterdam, 1535

Though, on the one hand, I was over awed by the splendour of Amsterdam, I was soon introduced to its other side. After wandering most of the streets, I knew which parts not to visit again. One area in particular has always haunted me, a place that stank of debauchery. As a young boy growing up in *Muxacra* I had not been so innocent as to be completely unaware of the harlot Magdo. I admit that, along with other young boys, I would often creep up to her window to see if I could catch a glimpse of the goings on in her booth. But what I saw in Amsterdam shocked me to the core.

You could buy a woman as easy as buying a loaf of bread. I saw girls as young as my little sisters next to women as old as my grandmother dressed in crimson rags that barely covered their breasts, all screaming to be bought for ten minutes at a time.

I even came across an old official decree on the sale of sexual favours, from 1413 and was amazed to read the following words:

Because whores are necessary in big cities and especially in cities of commerce such as ours – indeed it is far better to have these women than not to have them – and also because the Holy Church tolerates whores on good grounds, for these reasons the Court and Sheriff of Amsterdam shall not entirely forbid the keeping of brothels.

The stench of that place – a mixture of sour ale, gin, excrement and a lingering mind- deadening odour that, to this day, I cannot forget.

Chapter Forty-Six

De Stooterplas Island, 1981

'I swear...I'll take it to the Press. You can tell him that he'd better open these gates now or tomorrow morning his name, his big fucking name, will be spread across the front cover of every newspaper in the land. Go on, tell him. It'll make a top story – *Respected hotel chain owner in orphan scandal.*'

Moments later there was a metallic clunk and he began the long walk to the mansion.

* * *

He burst through the door. 'Why didn't you tell me?'

Peter sat expressionless.

'You knew. When I came here a few months ago, you knew. You damn well knew that she'd been looking for her family. How could you turn her away? And you kept it all from me? I know I wronged you and I'm sorry but, Jesus Christ Peter! Where's your so-called Christian compassion?'

The last remark seemed to snap a fuse in the big man's head. His face darkened and his fists clenched. 'Don't you dare, you little shit! Don't you ever use my faith to accuse me, you heathen. Who was it who fucked my wife behind my back? Who was it who got her pregnant with a child that killed her? And who is it now who's trying to coerce me into believing I'm a fucking Jew? Mother of God, I'm a Knight of St Augustine for Christ's sake.' He smashed his fists down on the table.

Eric stood his ground. 'You're a fraud, Peter. You've always been a fraud. Just like our father, you used your Catholicism and holy clubs for all the connections and your own personal gain. You have no real understanding of the deeper meaning of faith.'

'And you do I suppose?' He looked Eric in the eye.

Eric met his gaze. 'I've never claimed to be a practising Catholic. I've always seen it as a sham. Christianity is packed full of hypocrites, and recently I've seen that again in Britain. So yes, maybe I'm more than a little delighted to find out we're Jews.'

'We're not fucking Jews!' Peter was shouting now.

'You haven't read it then?'

'Yes I have and it's clearly a fake – written by someone who wants to discredit our family.' He opened a draw and threw a package at Eric.

'Discredit? My God that's how far up your own arse you are. So, a Jewish connection discredits us? Have you forgotten your Christ was a Jew? Don't you know your Blessed Virgin Mary was Jewish?'

'Don't be ridiculous.'

Eric shook his head in exasperation. 'Look, all that's irrelevant now. And I don't give a shit what you think of me anymore. I came here because I am pissed off how you fobbed off a poor girl looking for her family, and I'm disgusted that you kept that from me. Now just tell me – where is she?'

'Fuck off and rot in hell!'

'Where's your heart brother? Where's your soul? Come on, prove that at least a grain of that Catholic faith of yours has done some good and have a little mercy. Where is she?'

Peter took a deep breath and closed his eyes.

Eric said nothing more.

After a few minutes Peter slowly opened his eyes. 'Okay, I think she's still here in Amsterdam.'

Eric's heart began to race.

'Amsterdam! Where?'

'I don't know. Honestly. But a few weeks ago I used the same taxi driver who'd brought her out here and she came up in conversation. He's someone I can call upon at pretty much any time. Apparently he sees her around now and again. It was about three years ago she came here and he last saw her about a year ago.'

'Did he say any more? Like where she might live or work? Any clues at all?'

Peter's expression changed and a pinkish flush started to wash over his face.

'What?' said Eric.

Peter turned his head away. 'My driver admitted to me that he'd taken pity on her when he dropped her back in the city after she'd been out here.'

'What else did he say? Come on, you must know something.'

'He gave her something.'

'The driver? What? Come on, tell me.'

'Look, he was trying to help. He gave her the only thing he had.'

There was a long silence.

'Peter, what? What did he give her?'

The big man looked directly into Eric's eyes. 'A card. A card on which was written the name and number of one of the local Madams.' Then he sneered. 'So your whore's brat has gone the way of her mother.'

Chapter Forty-Seven

De Stooterplas Island, 1981

Peter Van Kroot, now alone, allowed his oily head to lean back into the leather armchair, a large glass of golden-brown liquid in one hand and a cigarette in the other. The tiniest fluttering of guilt's conscience was like an irritation in the back of his mind. But the louder voice soon numbed it out. *You owe them nothing. Forget him. Forget Ella. Forget their brat.*

And then, after a few big mouthfuls, the brandy began its numbing effect.

* * *

'Where have you been?' The woman clutches the sides of her metal-framed bed so tightly that her narrow fingers are as white as chalk.

'I was as quick as I could be.' He glares at her and curls up his nose. 'Bearing in mind the situation.'

'I phoned because she's on her way,' she says, now holding her swollen belly. A tear runs down her cheek, 'I can feel h – '

'Don't call it her!*'*

'But I know she's a girl. She's lying so high in my – '

'I don't mean that. Just don't personalise it at all.' He walks over to the bed and leans into her face. 'We know damn well what has to be done.'

He paces over towards the window as the woman's head drops back onto the pillow. His will is stronger than steel.

Another contraction. 'Aaaaaaagh.'

Ignoring her cries, he gazes outside. Such a contrast to the tension inside the room. A gentle breeze blows and summer flowers sway to the left and to the right like a few hundred floral metronomes dancing in time to the slowest tempo. The cloudless sky is a brilliant blue and the grass is a vivid green. In the distance a young couple stroll hand in hand stopping every so often to kiss. He waits until the noise behind him has stopped. Then he spins around, feeling like a bull ready to charge.

'I fucking despise you,' he says through clenched teeth, 'and I despise what's inside you. Were it not a mortal sin I'd rip it out with my own fucking hands.' He crosses himself and turns back to the window, in which he can see his own reflection.

He sees a big man, his body matching his head. Though overweight he sees a man who wears his clothes well. His preferred dress is a collar, tie and blazer on which he proudly displays his lapel pin of The Knights of St Augustine.

He studies his own face. His hair is jet black and oiled back in an attempt to add a touch of sophistication, though he can see that he appears more like a cross between a Wall Street broker and a Mafia Boss. His complexion is not dark as such, but a deeper olive brown than the average Dutchman. He has a large wart to the left side of his mouth, which used to obscure his smile, but it's been years since he's done that.

He turns back to face his wife. Ella is the complete antithesis. Pretty and petite *is how she's always been described, though marriage and pregnancy have taken their toll on her looks. Her hair is chestnut brown and her eyes are the clearest blue. Her gentle face, though lined, is pale and appears so fragile.*

He hears a knock on the hospital door. And it opens.

A young woman steps into the room. She has long red hair and is dressed in nothing but a basque and stilettos, like some burlesque girl from a Bohemian night club. The young woman is familiar but her heavy makeup has obscured some of her features and Peter can't make her out.

Now standing next to the bed, she reaches out a hand and touches Ella's arm. 'Hello Mother,' she says.

* * *

Smash. The brandy fell from Peter's drooping hand. The sensation and sound of breaking glass jolted him awake. And gradually he came back to reality.

Chapter Forty-Eight

Amsterdam, 1981

Eric stumbled through the door and flopped onto the couch. 'Christ,' said Penelope, who came dashing from the living room. 'What on earth's happened?' She sat down beside him. 'Have you been drinking. I can smell – '

'Yes, Pen. Sorry, I needed a few.' He leant forward, put his head in his hands and wept.

She grabbed his hand. 'Eric, it's okay. It'll be alright.'

'He shook his head. 'N...no...it won't Pen.'

'What's happened?' she whispered.

'I c...I...I can't believe it.'

'Take your time. I'll get you a drink. You can tell me when you're ready.'

He raised his head, looked into her eyes and burst out crying again. Penelope leant forward and hugged him tightly. She squeezed his hand and got up to go to the kitchen. A few moments later she was back with a glass and a bottle of Jack Daniels. She poured him a large one.

He took a few gulps and, eventually, his sobbing eased. He wiped the tears from his eyes. 'I can't believe it Pen.'

She stood in front of him. 'Go on. You can tell me.'

Looking up at her and shaking his head, he muttered, 'I can't. I just can't say it.'

Penelope waited in silence.

Then he whispered, 'She's working in the Red-Light District, Pen. She's a prostitute.' His head dropped.

Penelope reached out and lifted his face tenderly. She peered into his eyes. 'Eric, whatever's happened to her, we're going to find her. I know this must be beyond anything you imagined, but I promise you, we're going to find her.' She leant forward and kissed his forehead.

Eric looked at her through his tears. 'I don't even know – ' He gently pushed her hands away and let his head drop back down. 'I don't even know if I can bear looking for her now, Pen.'

'Eric!' She sounded shocked. 'Look, something truly dreadful forced her into that life. You have to try to push those thoughts out of your mind. She needs you. You're her father.'

Eric sat on the sofa shaking his head, tears rolling down his face.

'We need to find her,' said Penelope.

'But where do we start? How do we start?'

'We just start Eric.'

'But you've seen that place. Do we just walk up and down the streets, looking in windows? We don't even know what she looks like Pen.'

'Won't your brother give you any more clues?'

'You must be kidding. He's a fucking bastard. He's probably loving this.'

'So we go there tomorrow and start scanning windows for family resemblances. I can look for glimpses of your features, and you can scan for Ella's. At least that will be a start.'

* * *

The next morning Eric arose with a little more optimism. His night's sleep had been deep and he'd awoken with an idea. As they sat at the breakfast table he shared his thoughts.

'Pen, I don't know why I didn't think of this before. Why don't we knock on a few windows and ask if anyone knows a Hannah from Britain?'

'It's worth a try,' said Penelope. 'Do the girls actually use their real names?'

'I don't know, but what other option do we have?'

'You're right, let's try it.'

'I think we need to be careful, though. I mean we don't want to raise too much attention. There must be pimps around. I don't want to end up facing one. On second thoughts, perhaps you had better not come, Pen.'

'Nonsense, we'll stick to daylight hours. And, anyway, this is the safest Red-Light District in Europe!'

'Okay but let's work out some ground rules.'

They agreed that they must stay together at all times, and keep on the lookout for suspicious characters. They also agreed to be completely honest with anyone they talked to.

'I think it's crucial we're totally up front,' said Eric. 'If anyone can smell bullshit these girls can. Of that I'm sure.'

'Right,' said Penelope. 'I've also noticed some paperbacks in local shops written by Amsterdam's working girls. Shall I get a couple? They might well hold some useful information.'

'Good thinking.'

Chapter Forty-Nine

The Testimony of Ezra Van Kroot, Amsterdam, 1535

I soon found my feet and began to understand the city that was to become my new home. Like the new Granada I had left, the Netherlands was a Spanish Catholic province, but this city had a deep openness with an underlying liberality of thought and freedom of expression. I saw no immediate reason to hide my Jewish identity. Jews lived here without fear of persecution. Likewise, it was a haven for many other cultures, probably encouraged by its developing trade and shipping, and it was becoming a centre for the translation and printing of manuscripts, scrolls and books.

I soon began to recognise the signature of a divine hand in the voyage I had made across land and sea. Perhaps we were approaching the time for its release – the scroll I had guarded with my life.

Chapter Fifty

Amsterdam, 1981

'Seriously?' said Eric. The books Penelope had bought made the crimson mile leaflets he'd seen look tame. Far from being an innocent playground for adults they told of a place run by international pimps and lover boys who enslaved women. Eric was particularly shocked to hear of British girls who'd been duped into promises of a modelling career and high life from the other end of a telephone, only to arrive and end up kidnapped, drugged and forced into prostitution.

'I think we should still go ahead. We just need to be extremely careful,' said Penelope.

They approached the alleyway where Eric had seen a businessman strike a deal a few weeks before. His heart was beating as they stepped out of the light and into the gloomy passage. Before them were about ten glowing pink door frames on each side. They noticed that the first few had no occupants behind the windows, but then they saw the first girl. She was in her late teens by the look of it and sat quietly on a stool, dressed in skimpy bra and pants.

As Eric and Penelope stood in front of the glowing door, the girl looked up and smiled. She had black bobbed hair and big brown eyes. Her skin was pale, and probably looked whiter due to the darkness of her hair. Or was it because of the small bruises on the inside of her left forearm?

She looked back and forth at them from one to the other, until Eric stepped closer. The girl got off her stool and reached out for the door handle.

A bead of sweat dripped down Eric's forehead as he prepared to speak.

She smiled directly into his eyes as the door inched open.

'I'm so sorry,' he said. 'I need to ask you a question.'

The door stopped opening and the girl's smile vanished, a look of quizzed concern replacing it.

'Please,' said Eric, 'do you know a Hannah? Hannah from Britain?'

The horror on her face! She slammed the door shut, bolting it from the other side. 'No, no questions,' she voiced through the glass, eyes darting left and right. 'No questions.'

* * *

They had the same response pretty much constantly as they paced the rest of the district. They also knew that they were being watched by eyes hiding behind the shutters high up above the street level windows. At the end of the day there had been nothing. No clues. No looks of recognition as they mentioned the name *Hannah*. Eric was losing hope.

It was beginning to get dark and they agreed to call it a day. Reluctantly, they made their exit from the district across the street towards *Zeedijk*. They were passing Ziggy's when Eric felt a gentle tap on his shoulder. He stopped and turned to see a girl standing there. She looked about twenty-five and she wore a long overcoat. Her heavy eye makeup and bleached hair gave her occupation away.

Could it be? His heart leapt.

'I can't talk for long.' Her voice was soft and her accent was English. 'I hear you're looking for a Hannah – a Hannah from Britain.'

Unable to speak Eric nodded.

'Meet me at this café tomorrow morning at 10.30.' She pushed a piece of paper into his hand. And then she turned and walked off into the crowd.

He found his voice. 'Wait, I need to ask...'

But she had disappeared into the dark and busy streets.

Eric looked at Penelope, and then at the paper in his hand. He opened it and read the words, *Café De Prins, Prinsengracht.*

'Okay,' said Penelope, letting out a huge breath which sounded like she'd been holding it in. 'Progress at last.'

* * *

An almost sleepless night had left Eric feeling tired and edgy. He also nursed a suspicion and expressed his concerns to Penelope. 'Are we being set up? We know nothing about that girl or about the café she's directing us to.'

'I don't know, Eric. But we have to meet her, and at least it's daytime and a public location.'

'And far from that bloody district.'

They walked past the Anne Frank House and Museum, up *Prinsengracht* and crossed a canal bridge to the other side of the wide, water-filled street. Directly in front of them stood *Café De Prins*. Eric glanced at his watch. It was 10.23am.

They entered the café, found a table near the back wall and ordered two coffees.

'We're being joined by someone else shortly,' said Eric to the waitress. 'You may have to take another order in a moment, okay?'

'No problem,' said the waitress.

The café was a small attractive venue utterly in keeping with its situation, which happened to be one of the most beautiful stretches of road in central Amsterdam, just opposite the *Westerkerk*. Inside it looked every bit a typical Dutch 'brown café' with its dark wood interior, low-wattage lights and ceilings and walls covered with decades of cigarette tar. And even at this hour it was busy – clearly a meeting point for students and, by the look of it, local musicians too.

'Look,' whispered Penelope, nudging Eric. Someone had appeared in the doorway. An anxious looking young woman scanned the interior until she spotted them.

Eric stood as she walked over. 'What will you have?' he asked.

'Coffee. Thanks.' She glanced back at the doorway and then pulled out the chair with its back to the entrance and front windows. 'I'll sit here if you don't mind.'

She could have been anyone's daughter. Her heavy eye makeup had been removed and, apart from the dark red nail varnish, she came across as a regular young woman.

'So,' said Penelope.

The girl reached inside her coat, and brought out a photograph. It was a passport type photo of two girls. One was the girl in front of them and the other was someone neither Eric nor Penelope had seen before. She was stunningly beautiful and had auburn hair. The two of them were squeezed together and smiling, a typical shot of two friends in a photo booth.

'Is this who you're looking for?' said the girl.

'I don't know,' said Eric. 'I only know that her name is Hannah and that she's British. Can I have a closer look?'

She handed the photograph to Eric. 'Well that's Hannah. She's my best friend. Why are you looking for her?'

'It's a long story. But I think she might be my daughter. A daughter I never knew I had until recently.'

'That makes sense. Hannah never spoke of a dad.'

'What's your name, dear?' asked Penelope with a smile.

'I'm Rachel. I've known Hannah for a couple of years. We both ended up here for one reason or another and discovered we were both from the UK.' A waitress appeared with one more coffee. 'Thanks,' said Rachel, looking up at the waitress. She then turned and glanced at the door again.

Eric looked too. Nothing. 'Are you okay?'

'Yes, but I can't be long.' She picked up the cup and took a sip.

'So where's Hannah?' asked Penelope.

'I've not seen her for a few months. She went missing and no one knows where she is.'

'Have people been looking for her?' said Eric.

'Yes, well...no...well kind of. Look, things are not what they seem around here. Some of us are free, but most girls have a – ' She stopped mid-sentence and looked once more at the door. And she gulped. Eric saw him too, a smartly dressed man in a dark coat across the street looking directly at the café from the side of the road.

'I have to go,' she said.

Eric reached out to grab her arm. 'No, please, Rachel, a few more minutes.'

A police siren cried out in the distance. The man had gone but the girl still needed to get away.

'I'm sorry,' she said, but before leaving looked at Eric and added, 'No one will talk to you here. They're all too frightened. Search for Hannah at The Hague. It's where the *special* girls end up.'

Chapter Fifty-One

The Testimony of Ezra Van Kroot, Amsterdam, 1535

I had arrived in Amsterdam aged twenty. By twenty-three, I was working as an apprentice printer. I had also become reasonably well known in one of the smaller Jewish areas of the city, which was where I rented a lodging. The apprenticeship afforded me no spare change after my few gilders rent, so life was basic. But I was beginning to enjoy my new home at last, not least due to the lady with whom I had recently become acquainted.

Chapter Fifty-Two

Amsterdam, 1981

Eric watched her run from the café. He and Penelope dashed to the door and looked down the street. They couldn't see her.

'What did she mean, *special girls*?' said Penelope.

'I don't know.' He looked down at his hand. He still had the photograph. 'But at least we have a picture of her now.'

Back inside the café they looked intensely at the photograph on the table in front of them. The girl next to Rachel looked in her early to mid-twenties. She had flame red hair tied back in a ponytail, a pretty smile and beautiful big blue-green eyes.

'So what do we do now? Police?' said Penelope.

'No. The police aren't going to be any use, Pen. After all, this is just hunches and hearsay about someone we don't even know. And when we tell them she's a prostitute it'll just be another missing hooker to add to their list. No, they're not going to help.'

'But Eric, she might be under the control of a very dangerous person. She might even be a prisoner.'

'Well Pen, she mentioned The Hague. I seem to recall that it has a Red-Light District of its own. Let's say we pay a visit, and show the photo to a few girls there?'

Penelope looked at him. Then she smiled. 'You want to get us killed don't you.'

'Okay don't come. You're right. It's too dangerous. And you've put yourself in too much danger on my behalf already. I'll go on my own.'

'Silly fool,' she said, flicking his floppy fringe with her fingers. 'No, I'm coming too, but we're just going to have to be careful.'

* * *

The taxi slowed down, pulling up in a floodlit shopping area of The Hague.

'You just walk down this road to the end and turn left,' said the driver. 'You'll see it from there.'

Penelope held Eric's hand tightly as they climbed out of the car. They watched the taxi speed away until it could be seen no more. Eric turned to Penelope. 'Well, he didn't want to hang around.'

'No.' Penelope's hand was trembling.

'Are you still okay to do this?'

She squeezed his hand, and then let go. 'Yes, come on.'

They headed off in the direction the driver had pointed. At the end of the street they turned left and could see the pink neon haze in the distance. As they continued following the light, it was the smell that hit them first. The aroma could almost be tasted.

'What the hell's that?' said Penelope, bringing her hands up to her nose and mouth.

'No idea,' said Eric. He screwed up his face. 'How vile.'

The Hague's Red-Light District made Amsterdam's look charming by contrast. The lover boys and pimps didn't even attempt to hide, and the window shoppers were an altogether different breed. If most of Amsterdam's were inquisitive tourists of both sexes, these were hardcore male sex addicts – and much older.

After about half an hour of wandering, and clearly being marked by many sets of intimidating eyes, Eric slowed down and turned to Penelope.

'What do you think?' he said.

'Well I don't like it at all,' she replied, as they looked up and around at the red neon lights.

But then Eric saw the poster.

'My God, look at that,' he said, his heart leaping. It was pinned to a wall next to the porn shop they'd stopped by. It was torn and discoloured, looking like it had been there a while. Eric stepped closer. 'Can you see her face?'

Penelope leaned closer. The girl in the advertisement was definitely Hannah. It was a flyer for an exclusive strip club, within The Hague but slightly outside the actual Red-Light District.

'Should we pay a visit?' asked Eric with some trepidation.

'How can we not?' answered Penelope.

'What's the address? Can you make it out?' He took out a pen and scrap of paper.

With their paper tourist map, they discovered to their relief that it was a few streets away from their current location. In no more than ten minutes they'd found the club and, after being looked up and down and smirked at by the two doormen, were allowed to enter. Inside it was dimly lit and there was a deep red glow throughout. Along one side of the interior ran a bar over which leaned six or seven men. The club was clearly a male domain, apart from the bare-chested waitresses and the dancers who gyrated on a stage. A sweet scent hung in the air – possibly patchouli.

'Shall we get a table and order a drink?' said Eric.

'I think that's an idea,' said Penelope.

They found an unoccupied table and sat down. Within a few minutes, a smiling young waitress bounced over to them. 'Drinks?'

'Just two small beers please.' Eric found it hard not to look at her breasts. They'd already decided not to ask for soft drinks, hoping to blend in as much as possible.

She frowned. 'Really? No cocktails? We're famous for them.'

'Just the beers please,' said Penelope.

The girl winked, wiggled her bottom and left with the order.

Five minutes later they were sipping their cold beers. It was then that they noticed someone else coming over. A man. He wore a dark suit and a red satin shirt, though the lighting may have given it its colour. His hair and neatly cropped beard bore distinguished silver flecks and he had a North African complexion. Eric gazed at him as he reached their table.

He greeted them with a big smile. 'Greetings my friends. You look…forgive me but…new to this kind of thing.'

Neither Eric nor Penelope knew what to say. They just nodded guiltily, like kids caught in an off-limit area at school.

The man sat down. 'So what brings you here?'

Eric could see the uncertainty on Penelope's face. He was on the verge of spilling it all out when the man looked directly up and then around the whole interior of the club and said, 'My name's Omar. This is mine. Do you like it?'

Stuck for words they both smiled.

'Just passing then?' said Omar.

'Um…yes,' said Eric. 'Well, kind of.'

'Look,' said Omar, with a smile and a hand on Eric's shoulder, 'I can tell you're not here for kicks. So, do you want to tell me why you're really here?' The cheerful persona changed as his smiling eyes narrowed and his eyebrows descended into a frown. 'Are you here to check up on us? I can assure you we work within the law here.'

'Hey, no! Not at all.' Eric felt his pulse start to throb. He sensed other eyes now marking him – eyes that belonged to a couple of big guys in suits who had appeared by the bar.

Penelope and Eric looked at each other. Eric nodded, and Penelope nodded back at him. 'What have we got to lose?' she said.

'My friends,' said Omar, 'we're not all bad people here. If there's something you wish to find out or ask me, go ahead. I'll help if I can.'

Eric reached into his inside pocket and retrieved the photograph. Holding it out so Omar could see he pointed to one of the girls. 'Can I ask you if you know this girl. I think she might work here.'

Omar took the photo in his hand and held it close to his face so it was easier to see in the dim light. Then he looked away, his eyes briefly closing and his mouth clenched. He slowly turned his head to Eric. 'Yes I know her. Why are you looking for her?'

'He's her father,' said Penelope.

Omar breathed in, shaking his head very slightly.

'What?' said Eric. 'What is it?'

'My friend, I'm so sorry to have to inform you, but she's not with us anymore.'

'What, you mean she's working somewhere else?'

'No...' He swallowed. 'She's...dead.'

The shock caused Eric to jolt. 'What? What do you...how...are you sure? Oh my God, no.'

'I'm sorry, my friend. But yes, I'm sure. Her name is Hannah yes?'

'Yes,' said Penelope.

Eric gazed into the darkness.

'She worked here for a while, yes. But I never really got the chance to know her well, because of her...habit.'

'Habit?' said Penelope.

'Oh I'm sorry. She was a heroin addict. Beautiful girl. Wasted. Such a waste.' He shook his head.

Eric got up. 'I need the bathroom, where is it?'

'Over there.' Omar pointed.

* * *

Eric leaned over the toilet bowl retching and trying desperately not to let his hands touch anything. He flushed and moved through to the basins, where he stood looking at his blood shot eyes in the cracked mirror. He turned the tap, leaned over and splashed cold water on his face. Dead? She was fucking dead. He had found her too late. Why hadn't he come back sooner?

When he re-joined Penelope, Omar had gone, but he'd told her a little more of Hannah's story. She put a hand on Eric's as he sat beside her, stunned.

'Apparently she turned up one night with a…boyfriend. You know what I mean by *boyfriend* don't you?'

'Yes,' he said, looking into his drink.

'Well Omar, if we believe him, seems to be quite a well-respected club owner here, and he asked Hannah whether she wanted to work for him. Of course, the boyfriend objected, saying she was his special girl, which Omar told me means a natural red-head.'

Eric stared at her. 'Hair colour makes girls special?'

'Yes.' She grimaced. 'Apparently natural redheads are especially sought after by North Africans.'

'Oh my God,' said Eric.

'Anyway, apparently Omar paid the boyfriend off. He said he could see potential. But he claims he didn't quite realise just how much she was addicted to the powder.'

Eric hit his forehead with the flat of his palm.

'I'm sorry Eric, I know this must be terrible for you. Shall I stop?'

'No.' He looked up. 'I need to hear it all.'

'Well, after just a few weeks, Omar could see what the boyfriend had done. He'd sold Hannah knowing she was not going to last. And he was right. She died within a month.'

'How?'

'Overdose. She'd made a little money. Enough to score big. And she took the lot. It may even have been suicide.'

'I need to know what happened to her after that. I need to find her final resting place. Are you sure he's telling the truth, Pen?'

She looked into his eyes. 'I'm sorry but yes. Okay I don't know about the story but, yes, I believe she's dead. While you were still in the bathroom, he brought me this from his flat above the club.'

Penelope gave him a folded newspaper cutting which,

when opened, displayed poor Hannah's pretty face, under the headline: ANOTHER DUTCH DRUG DEATH.

'Oh my God. No, no!'

'I don't know what to say,' said Penelope.

He glanced at her, eyes streaming. 'I can't believe it. My poor daughter.'

Chapter Fifty-Three

The Testimony of Ezra Van Kroot, Amsterdam, 1535

The year was now 1507 and I had completed my long training as a typesetter and printer. I had also decided on the way I was going to release the devastating scroll. My father told me it was powerful enough to transform everything, yet I had still not been able to read a single word of it myself. I needed to find a Jewish translator of Aramaic, but I was not certain who I could trust.

All I knew about the scroll was that it was written by a distant ancestor and contained a message of supreme importance, but one that, if released at the wrong time, could destroy its bearer. I wondered whether that time had finally passed. After all, Amsterdam seemed so open, so unguarded, so free.

Eventually I decided the best way forward would be not to entrust the scroll to a translator, but to learn Aramaic myself. So I began my search for a teacher.

Chapter Fifty-Four

Amsterdam, 1981

Eric sat next to Penelope on the sofa in her flat. His eyes were sore and his stomach felt hollow.

Why, why had he allowed himself to be forced away all those years ago? Jesus, Jesus, why? Why had that bastard hidden the truth about her?

He remembered the letter that Ella had left for him.

Dear Eric,

There's no easy way to tell you this, but it's over. I've realised that we've been swept away on some fantasy. But now that I've had time to think, I know that I need to, *I want to*, stay with Peter. He's not such a bad man and he loves me. Eric, this is such a difficult thing for me to write but I beg you to leave me alone now. In fact, leave Holland. I need to make things right with your brother. I ask for your respect and understanding.

Please don't hate me.

Ella

That bastard. Peter made her write that letter. He could see it all now. Why? Why couldn't he have seen it back then?

He remembered his threat from Peter too. *If I ever see you again, I swear I'll kill you.*

'So what will you do?' Penelope asked.

'I don't know.' Eric looked at the small passport photograph in his hand. 'I just can't take it in.'

'She was so beautiful. I think you need to do something for her.'

'What do you mean?'

'Something in her name, something to honour her.'

'Like what?'

'I think you should continue what you were doing when you first visited your brother, and do it in Hannah's name. You need to find out who your family were, who you are and who your daughter was.'

'But how will that make anything right, Pen?'

'It won't bring her back. It won't make it all right, but it will be setting things straight, both for your ancestors and for your descendants.'

'Descendants. You really think I'll have another child now? You must be kidding.'

She looked at him and then looked down, dropping her shoulders.

But the word *descendants* triggered a train of thought. 'Oh my God.'

'What?' said Penelope raising her head again.

Eric sat bolt upright and wiped his eyes. 'You're right Pen. You're right. I must continue. This is the one thing I really must do.'

'You sound very convinced all of a sudden.' Penelope smiled.

'Yes Pen, because what my bastard of a brother will hate more than anything in the world is if it's all proven to be true.'

* * *

Eric tracked down the little grave and memorial stone where Hannah's ashes had been buried. He stood there alone for a while, not knowing whether to say a prayer and, if so, who to? In the end, he spoke to Hannah. 'I hope you can forgive me. If I'd have known for one minute about you, I'd have walked on red hot coals to find you. I don't know what your short life gave you. I can't imagine what you've been through, but I promise to do all I can to find out who we are – the family Ben Kerioth.'

* * *

Back at the flat, Eric and Penelope had been looking at the book his brother had thrown at him.

'So,' said Penelope, 'we know that this Ezra was carrying a scroll that he had been told contained a secret that could change the world.'

'Yes, something like that.'

'But what kind of secret could change the world?' She held it close to her mouth. 'Come on little book. What are you trying to tell us?' Then, flicking to the back pages, she said, 'It's an odd place to finish don't you think?'

'Let's have another look.' Eric held out a hand and Penelope passed it to him.

Though it was an abrupt end, the back cover was intact and... But wait. Eric felt his heart begin to pulse as he noticed that there was a definite gap at the end of the book – a gap between the last page and the back cover. 'Shit. Why didn't we notice that before?'

'What is it?' said Penelope.

'Look. Here. There's more. There's bloody more to this. No wonder it seemed like an odd place to stop. Look, something's been torn out. But where could it be – the missing part?'

'Think back to when you were given it. Was there anything else? Anything that might have been loose pages?'

'Not that I remember. I was just handed a – ' Eric held his breath.

'Eric. Eric. What?'

'My God Pen.' His heart was now beating like a drum. 'Of

course. The archivist. She handed me a leather covered box. The book was inside it. Maybe the extra pages are still there?'

'Okay. That's good. So where's the box?'

Eric looked at Penelope and shook his head. 'She took it back. She let me take the book, but wanted to keep the box, saying it was the more valuable part of the artefact.'

'So we have to go and get it.'

* * *

The archivist stood at the reception desk, watching, as Eric and Penelope studied the box. There had been no extra pages within it. Eric's enthusiasm had waned rapidly. 'Where the hell could they be?'

He was just about to take it back to the archivist when he noticed she'd left her position behind the desk. Perhaps she'd gone to the toilet? 'Pen,' he whispered. 'Any thoughts?'

She replied in the same hushed voice. 'Well one thing did occur to me. What if the missing pages are under the lining?'

Eric opened the box again and felt around the inside, smoothing down the rippled velvet interior. He stopped. 'Pen. Feel here.'

She put her hand where his was and looked at him, eyes bulging. 'There's something there.'

At that point the archivist returned to her desk.

'We're going to have to distract her,' whispered Penelope through the corner of her mouth. Then she raised her voice. 'Excuse me.'

The archivist looked up.

'We're really grateful for your help. But could you possibly do one more thing for us?'

She met Penelope's eyes. 'What is it you want?'

Penelope walked over to the reception desk and Eric continued feeling around inside the box as the two women talked. The fabric lining on one of the corners felt somehow loose. He carefully picked it and a little flap lifted up. There was a false bottom. Christ.

Eric looked at the women. Suddenly the archivist walked back out of the room. Penelope turned and winked.

Without hesitation Eric lifted up the false bottom and there, underneath, was a little stack of loose pages. He took them out and put them quickly in the inside of his jacket, clipping them with his arm.

For the next few minutes they didn't say a word. Finally the archivist returned. 'No, I'm very sorry but I couldn't find anything else.'

'That's okay,' said Penelope. 'Thanks for looking.'

Chapter Fifty-Five

The Testimony of Ezra Van Kroot, Amsterdam, 1535

My relationship with Greta, who was from a Dutch Catholic family, flourished and we married in 1512. Two years later, we were given the gift of a son, whom we named Baruch.

How I loved that boy and how I thanked God that he would not have to go through what I had. Providence had also led me to a good teacher of the old languages and I was well on my way to understanding the basics of Aramaic.

The time eventually came when I decided I would try to decipher the scroll myself for, as yet, I had still not found anyone I felt able to trust with such a secret. There was the natural linguist Hagez, of course, but the thought of putting him in such a potentially dangerous position stopped me from enlisting his help. After all, he had been through as much as me.

It was a quiet evening at home. Baruch was asleep and Greta was busy with her sister and another friend, who had come to play dominoes, a new game the traders had brought back from the East. This was the first time in many years I had seen the scroll. Once, back in Portugal, I had taken it out to check it was intact, and when I first arrived here after the long sea voyage, I did the same, but I had never before attempted to look at the script.

I removed the inner package carefully from the cloth bag. Then I took the leather container out of the velvet wrapping and, opening the fastening, tipped out the scroll gently onto my bed. It all looked beautifully preserved and I wondered what materials my ancestor had used to make sure it did not corrupt.

But when I attempted to unroll it there was the faintest sound of cracking. I knew that it was decaying. It needed preservation and quickly. Luckily I knew just the people who could do it, but I knew not whether I could trust them. They were a Jewish family who owned a library and museum in the city. I had visited before but had not found them overly easy to speak with. However, there was nowhere else I could go. All the other experts I knew were Catholic and, seeing such a relic, would surely inform the authorities.

Before I put the scroll away, I unrolled a small section and read the very first few lines. The translation was roughly this:

I write this, but know not whether it will ever be read, much less believed. Alas, it is all I can do to preserve the truth. I accompanied my teacher Yeshua for three summers during his mission to the Tribe of Judah and witnessed first hand the extraordinary events that followed him wherever we travelled. I will do anything to protect his memory. I owe him everything.

I know not the future, but can imagine an outcome truly unbearable, where all he stood for is threatened by the very people who claim him as their own.

Since my return, I have seen how his followers have cleverly begun stitching together our own Jewish stories to create something truly dangerous. Yeshua did not suffer as a human Passover lamb. He went to the cross because he was the most courageous man the world has ever known. He challenged the very belief systems that are now being re-built in his name.

He fought both the might of Rome and Jerusalem's highest temple powers, and reaped the consequence of doing so.

He was strong yet humble like no other. When people called him 'good' he corrected them and said that only God is good. He gave hope to those pushed aside, downtrodden and trampled upon. My own sister knew what it was to feel his heart reach into her own and rescue her from the self-hatred that tormented her. But he did so not because he was an angel or a god but because he knew that very depth of divine love so deeply within himself. I will return to her story.

I write this knowing that I risk misunderstanding. I have tried, since my return, to balance the exaggerated tales told by those who should have known better. Have they forgotten that Yeshua stood for truth? I despair.

I desperately wanted to read on but, as I attempted to unroll a little more, a crack appeared in the parchment and it split apart in front of me. I cursed and rolled it carefully back, re-housing it within its protective layers.

But I had seen it. I had seen the words of my ancestor, and they were every bit as astonishing as I had imagined. Even if my feeble translation was just half accurate, I knew they were a message from an actual follower of Yeshua the Nazarene, the man the Christians call Jesus and worship as the Son of God.

The next day I decided to risk taking the scroll to the Jewish family who ran the library and museum. I had to do something, for I could not allow the scroll to become too fragile to be of any value. But when I arrived at their premises, I felt the most oppressive instinct, as if I was somehow betraying my own family. I decided instead to ask my Aramaic teacher some innocent questions on how to repair and preserve old manuscripts. I reasoned that, since he had a sizeable collection of old papyruses and parchments, such a question would merely seem inquisitive, and he welcomed the opportunity to explain.

He told me that the best form of preservation was duplication, which made sense. He also gave me some ideas on basic preservation techniques involving various balms, oils and other substances. I decided to attempt both.

By the end of a year I had managed to work enough oil into the material that it unwound without further damage. Within a few more months, I had made my own copy. I still could not achieve a perfect translation in Dutch so I copied it carefully in Aramaic, a challenge for a novice in the language.

* * *

Baruch grew and was joined by sisters and brothers and, as he grew, so I watched and waited for the perfect time to unleash the secret. But the more I saw my children thrive the more I feared for their safety.

There were also great political and religious changes, as the Rome-backed establishment began tightening its grip on our once free land. I saw my beloved Amsterdam turn gradually from its proud open spirit. It was during this period of change that we, along with many other Jewish families, knew we must do what our forebears who remained in Castile did, and convert to Catholicism. Thus we became Maranos. And once again that word *Inquisition* began haunting my thoughts.

Along with the change of religious identity came the necessary change of name, after all, Jewish names were forever going to be a give-away. We settled on Van Kroot because not only was it an unused name, but the letters that make up *Kroot* were hidden within *Kerioth,* and I reasoned this might be a future clue for descendants.

Because my wife was Dutch I thought that our children and grandchildren would have every possibility of concealing our Jewish background. After all, their appearance was far more Gentile than Jew.

By 1525 I was fluent in both Aramaic and Hebrew, and in one sense this was a blessing, for then I knew almost perfectly what my ancestor had written in the scroll. However, it was also a curse, for precisely the same reason; I now knew that what was written in it was potentially far more destructive than I had ever imagined.

I had in my possession a scroll that, if found, would not only shake the very heart of Christendom, which was the world within which my family and I were living, but would almost certainly see us all burned as heretics. Times were changing and religious powerbases had developed in a way that reminded me of long ago. I was terrified. I even began to wonder whether I should have burned the damned scroll.

And then it became clear what I must do. Never would I have believed that I was to endure another torture, worse than the one of 1492. To protect the secret and my family, I decided that I must leave my beloved Amsterdam, alone.

Thus I write these final words to him who now holds this witness. Tomorrow I shall board a ship, which I pray God sees fit to safeguard and carry me to the place where I know I must lay this scroll to rest, the place of the Rainbow Cross.

Chapter Fifty-Six

Amsterdam, 1981

They turned slowly to face each other. Eric's heart was beating rapidly and Penelope's eyes were wide open, like her mouth.

'No wonder they kept it secret.' Eric looked at the paper in his hand. 'Now I get it. The scroll was written by an actual follower of Jesus. My God this is massive, Pen.'

'And the name, Eric, Kerioth. Now you know for a fact that the Van Kroot family were once the Ben Kerioths.'

Eric's thoughts were taken back to that little house in Mojacar. 'Yes. My God, yes.' He shook his head. 'There's just too much to take in Pen. I can't get my head around it.'

'Read it again,' she said. 'All of it. And slowly.'

Eric read the missing pages out loud for the second time.

Penelope touched Eric's arm. 'Christ. So, he decided that, after everything, he needed to leave Amsterdam?'

'It looks like it,' said Eric. 'But to where? Where did he go?'

'Well, wherever he did, that's where he took the scroll. And that's where it might still be.'

Eric read the very last paragraph out loud.

I write these final words to him who now holds this witness. Tomorrow I shall board a ship, which I pray God sees fit to safeguard and carry me to the place where I know I must lay this scroll to rest, the place of the Rainbow Cross.

'*The place of the Rainbow Cross.* What could that mean?' said Penelope.

'I don't know,' said Eric.

Penelope went to the kitchen to make them both a cup of coffee. As the kettle was coming to the boil she called out, 'Eric. Eric, I've been thinking. Why did you go to see Peter? Why didn't you just continue alone?'

'He's my brother, Pen, and I'd wronged him.'

'Not as much as he'd wronged you.'

'I know that now, but I didn't then. I had no idea about Hannah.'

'So you wanted to ask him to join the quest to find this secret?'

'I suppose so, yes.' He smiled at the absurdity of it. 'Of course there was no way he would, but I'm an idealist. I'd have loved us to make up and join on a family adventure.'

'But you left the book with him anyway?'

'Yes, after he'd told me about my daughter, I just left it and forgot it. Something more important had overtaken me.'

There was silence in the kitchen.

'Pen, Pen are you okay?'

Silence.

'Pen? Pen are you there?' Eric got up and walked into the kitchen. Penelope was standing still, eyes closed, deep concentration on her face.

'Pen.' He touched her arm.

'Yes, sorry,' she said, 'I was…'

'Was what?'

'I was…Eric did you say that Peter threw the book back at you?'

'Yes, Pen. What is it?'

'Clearly the journal points to something that your brother hates or fears. Both, probably, as they're almost the same thing.'

'And?'

'Why would it stir such hate and fear?'

'Well he's a devout Catholic. A Knight of St Augustine for God's sake. And, even without the missing pages, Ezra's words suggested we were Jews.'

'But I think it's more than that, Eric. And I think your brother knew it was, too. I think he knows something. Eric, I think – I honestly think – you need to pay him one more visit.'

Chapter Fifty-Seven

De Stooterplas Island, 1981

Eric was back in his brother's house, but this time Peter was unaware. Eric still remembered the layout of the home that he'd grown up in and had managed to find a way in through a small window on the far side of the house that faced the lake. The hardest part had been climbing the high fence. It was 2am.

He'd made his way into Peter's study and, clicking on the lamp by the side, sat at the desk thinking that the drawers might contain some answers. He noted that there were three to the left, three to the right and a long central one, which was locked.

Suddenly he heard a sound. Someone was coming downstairs. Shit!

He jumped from the chair and looked around for somewhere to hide. The only possible place was a cupboard to the right of him. He made a dash and squeezed himself inside.

The footsteps were now echoing on a wooden floor and getting closer. Oh my God. He was coming into his study.

The door opened and there was a heavy thud of feet. Through a crack in the cupboard's double doors, Eric watched his brother enter the room. Peter walked over to the desk and looked at the lamp. His eyes narrowed and he stroked his chin. A moment later he shook his head and sat down.

Then he picked up his phone handset and dialled a number. Who the hell was he phoning at this time of night?

'Hello...um...yes, Peter. Yes, Van Kroot. Can you bring me someone? I really need it. Yes, I'll arrange where you are to pick her up. Phone you back in five minutes.' He hung up.

Then he dialled again. 'Hello, yes. Exactly.' He let out a low wheezing laugh. 'Sure, at the front of the usual place in about fifteen minutes. Great. Thank you.'

Finally, he dialled once more. 'Yes it's me again. Collect her from the usual place in ten to fifteen minutes.'

Eric waited for about half an hour while his brother sat there knocking back brandy from a decanter. At last a buzz came from a small square unit on the desk. Peter pressed a button and, after a few seconds, the glare of some headlights signalled that a car had arrived.

He rose laboriously from his chair, the soft leather making a farting sound as he got up, and left the room. The next thing Eric heard was the door open and close and the same heavy footsteps now retiring back up the stairs, accompanied by a much more delicate sound – narrow heels on wood.

Feeling queasy at the thought of his brother having sex, Eric now knew he wouldn't be disturbed for a while. He crept back out and sat at the desk again, the chair still warm from Peter's fat arse.

He looked down and, to his amazement, the central drawer was still unlocked and slightly ajar. Bingo. Now, what was in there?

When he slid the drawer open he couldn't believe his eyes. Taking it out he placed it on the table so he could make sure it was what he thought it was. Sure enough what lay in front of him was a photocopied version of the Testimony he'd left his brother to read. So Peter *was* interested in it.

The booklet was made of A4 pages that had been hole punched and tied together. He opened the front cover and what he saw made his head spin. Notes. Copious amounts of handwritten notes. He flicked the page, then the next. Notes. The whole of the document had been covered. And the shock was intensified by the words that had been written.

Peter had defaced the entire thing with a single word written thousands of times: TRAITOR.

Stunned and confused, Eric decided to thumb through every page just to see whether anything else had been written, apart from this word. He was about to give up when he noticed something towards the very end of the document.

There, written under the last paragraph, was the strangest sentence. Peter had written *May the words of this traitor lead my traitorous brother to hell.* And under that, written on a separate piece of paper torn from a lined notepad, *Speak to Father Ambroos.*

Chapter Fifty-Eight

De Stooterplas Island, 1981

Eric sat with his head in his hands letting the full significance sink in. No, not him. Not Father Ambroos. He hadn't just bumped into him at the library. The priest had been sent by his brother.

Then he noticed something else. To check he wasn't seeing things, Eric pulled the lamp closer to the desk, which lit up the whole surface. His heart missed a beat, as his eyes settled on the stone figure that lay there in the centre of the desk. It couldn't have been there the last two times he'd visited. If it had, he would have noticed.

But then he realised that it was carved only on one side – the side that faced the sitter at the desk. It was a stone paperweight belonging to his father, on which stood proudly the image of the Indalo Man.

He still had his own in his pocket. Feeling for it through his trousers, he patted it. 'Still there my friend.'

* * *

The following morning Eric knew exactly what he had to do. He was already at the breakfast table when Penelope came in rubbing her eyes.

'You're up early,' she said, 'especially considering your night time exploits.'

He looked up at her from the table and smiled.

'You found something didn't you?' She held a hand over her mouth stifling a yawn.

'Nothing from my brother directly, Pen, but, yes, I found something. You'd better brace yourself.'

She sat down.

Eric took her hand. 'I think Father Ambroos is working for Peter.'

'What?' she gasped.

'I found something in Peter's desk drawer. He'd made a copy of Ezra's words and...'

'And?'

'And had written the word traitor all over them, as if they were the words of a traitor. He'd written a sentence about me too, as a traitor.'

'Well, yes, from his devout Catholic position I can see why he would do that.' She smiled. 'But then – at the end – he had left a note on a scrap of paper with the name Father Ambroos on it.'

'Okay, now that's very weird. Perhaps he knows another Father Ambroos?'

'No, Pen, this is not a coincidence. He told that priest about me and that's why he found me in the library. He's been looking for me. I'm sure of it.'

Penelope touched his arm. 'So, what are you going to do?'

'I'm going to pay Father Ambroos a visit, and I'll ask him what the hell's going on. But that's not all.'

'No?'

'No. Listen Pen. I think I know where I need to go to find the scroll. I think I know where Ezra went. I know what he meant by the place of the Rainbow Cross.'

'Really?' Her eyes widened.

'Yes.' He reached inside his pocket and took out the little figurine.

'What's that?' she said.

'You've never come across one before?'

'No. Well I don't think so. Maybe I saw something similar in Mexico. What is it? Did you take it from your brother's study?'

He put it on the table. 'No, not at all. I've had it since I went to Spain. It's a good luck charm really.'

'And?'

'And I think it's also Ezra's Rainbow Cross.'

'Oh?' She picked the figure up.

Eric explained the meaning of the little figure and that the hoop above him was seen to be a rainbow.

'He's often called the Rainbow Man in Almeria, but I could see why he might also be seen as the Rainbow Cross. Can't you?'

She looked closely and saw the arms stretched out like a crucifix.

'Yes, I suppose I can. And you think this symbol would have been around back in the late fourteen hundreds?'

'Well the historians of Almeria certainly do, and they say that the fishermen even used it as a totem for safety at sea.'

'That sounds very pagan for such a traditional Catholic town.'

'I know. But don't forget, it was a very open-minded place. It was tolerant and home to three faiths, and probably a heap of folk religion too.'

'And you think Ezra would have returned? After all he'd been through? He'd have been prepared to go back to a place where Jews had been banished?'

Eric rubbed his eyes. 'I don't know, but it's where I feel the story leads. And when did he write his final words in Amsterdam? 1535 it says. Clearly he left the journal somewhere safe and set off. Maybe he went somewhere else first and, when he knew it was safer, returned to his *Muxacra*, where he lived until his death, hiding the scroll in his home.'

She looked at him. 'You're going to go back there aren't you?'

He smiled and nodded. 'I have to, Pen.'

'I know,' she said, 'and I'm coming too.'

'But what about your research?'

'It can wait. Oh come on, you can't really expect me to stop now, can you?'

They smiled and embraced. Eric felt a flutter inside, as they held each other for a little longer than mere friends.

Chapter Fifty-Nine

Amsterdam, 1981

Eric heard footsteps coming closer. The sound of a door being unlocked. A brief pause, before it opened.

'Hello Eric, Penelope. Why don't you come in.'

Father Ambroos stood in the doorway to his home, his face in the shadow, making it impossible to see whether his expression matched his cold formal tone.

They entered the presbytery and were led through to a sitting room with an old red Chesterfield sofa. Years of use had clearly worn the leather so that in places the red was all but gone. They sat opposite Father Ambroos who took a pipe from the side table and held his lighter over the bowl to suck it alight. Eric glanced around the room and noticed a familiar image on the bookshelf: a small wooden plaque displaying the badge and arms of The Knights of St Augustine. The priest took a big draw on his pipe, turning his head to the side before exhaling the fragrant smoke.

'So, how was your trip to Wales?' he said. 'Any news of the girl?' The room was tense, as if they all knew the truth was about to come out, but no one quite dared trigger it.

It was Penelope who popped the bubble. 'Father Ambroos, there's no easy way to say this, but we have reason to believe you've been hiding something from us.'

He shuffled in his chair and sucked on his pipe again. Squinting through the smoke he said, 'Eric, when I first met you, I felt for you. Honestly.'

'Met me?' It was all going to come out now. 'You deliberately followed me and blatantly pretended to have simply stumbled across me at the library.'

The priest sighed. 'Look, I'll explain everything, but please believe me that I had, and still have, your best interests at heart.'

'Tell me then. What's this all about?'

'Eric, I know your brother. I've known him for many years. We belong to the same...'

'Order?'

'Yes, I saw you'd noticed the arms. We love our Church and we want to protect her, but that's only part of the story. Your brother told me about your quest, when he called me just after you'd been to see him, but he didn't tell me anything else.'

'What do you mean?'

'He didn't tell me about the child. I'd always thought he'd just gone through a classic case of sibling rivalry. I never knew the real reason you and he had fallen apart all those years ago.'

'So, when you followed me to the library and asked me why I was so worked up, you never knew I was looking for my daughter?'

'No, and I swear on the Sacred Heart of Jesus that's the truth.'

'But you helped Eric find her?' said Penelope. 'Why? When your only concern was to follow him and see where his quest for the scroll was leading him, why help him with another matter?'

'Christian compassion.' The priest beamed a seraphic smile.

'Bullshit,' said Eric. 'I know why. It's becoming clearer now. The only way I was going to lead you to the scroll was if you helped me find my daughter first. You could see that I was consumed by it.'

'Yes, I admit you're right Eric. But I genuinely wanted to help you. I am a priest, a pastor, a shepherd.'

'Yeah. A shepherd who leads his sheep to the fucking wolves.'

Silence. 'Anyway, what now?' said Penelope. 'Eric's quest is over. His daughter's dead. And his heart's not in the search for the scroll any more. The quest's over.'

'Dead?' Father Ambroos recoiled. 'Oh my Lord. No. Oh Eric, how? What happened?'

'It's none of your business,' said Eric. 'Not that you don't already know of course. Surely your spies followed us to the shithole where she died.'

'Eric, trust me. This is the first time I've heard that about your daughter. Oh Eric my son –'

'Shut up. I don't need or want your sympathy. And, Penelope's right...my quest is over. I'm done with it all.'

There was silence again, and then the priest's concerned face turned into a smile. 'Oh but I'm afraid I *know* that's not true.'

'For Christ's sake, you're still following me?'

'No, not me. But you are being tracked. You understand that I had to hand this over to higher authorities. This could become a serious problem for the Church.'

'So you're telling me that we are going to be followed by some clerical private dick until we lead you to a mystery that has the potential to upset the Catholic Church?'

'Upset?' The priest showed his first sign of anger. 'From what your little *family secret* says this could be enough to destroy us.'

'So you don't know what it is yet, the scroll?'

'No. But anything that's been held with such secrecy, and hidden from the Church for so long, must be heretical and therefore dangerous.'

'Why is everything that doesn't fit in with your fucking Church's teaching seen as dangerous?'

Father Ambroos looked shocked. 'Eric! Oh Eric, my son, you do know that heretics will never see God don't you?'

'Oh bollocks. Don't be so fucking superstitious. The Catholic Church – Jesus Christ. I mean if you guys are his friends, does he really need enemies? Do you know what century we live in?'

The priest was on his feet. He'd sprung out of his chair like a man half his age.

Then he roared. 'Don't you dare insult us. Don't you dare insult my Lord and my God, and my beloved Mother Church.' He was shaking and spitting with rage.

Stunned, Eric and Penelope looked at each other, and then at him.

Finally, the old man calmed a little. 'Well, it may not even exist anymore, but…' He looked directly at Eric and pointed, '… if it does, you'll be the one to find it.'

'And you say this is all in my best interests?' said Eric.

The priest sat back down. 'Yes Eric…' he said, quietly, '…the interests of every Catholic. We must protect the Church for all of you.'

Penelope spoke, 'But Father Ambroos, we're not going to lead anyone. Now we know we're being followed, we'll be extra careful. You can't watch us all the time.'

'Ah but that's where you're quite wrong, my child. Whatever you do and wherever you go, we'll be there, even if you decided to leave it a year before continuing. The Church is a patient creature. We know how to allow the passage of time to flow.'

Father Ambroos re-lit his pipe and took another long draw. Eric looked at Penelope and winked as his face was partially obscured by the smoke.

'You're right,' said Eric. 'So we'll be ready too. And we'll make certain to cover our tracks.'

'You can try.' Father Ambroos smiled a demonic grin. 'Just please believe me. We really do want only the best for the Holy Church and for you.'

* * *

They were back at the flat. 'So what's the plan now?'

Eric rubbed his face with both hands. 'We lay a false trail.'

Chapter Sixty

Amsterdam, 1981

'Are you sure they're watching?' whispered Eric.

'Definitely.' Penelope was looking in her makeup mirror, holding a lipstick to her mouth. 'Okay I need to make sure they can see the titles. Can you pretend to show me a book and face the cover this way?'

Eric and Penelope were in the travel section of *Scheltema*, a large bookshop on the *Rokin* near the city centre. The books on Mexico were few, but enough. After about a half an hour of browsing they moved on to the religion section before making their way to the cash desk where they paid for three books.

Outside, they crossed the road and walked up the street until they were sure they were far enough away. Diving into a Gouda cheese shop they waited until they saw the two men pass.

'I think we've done it,' said Eric.

Their next move was to wait until they were sure the men had walked far enough up the street to make their exit. Moving back down the *Rokin* towards the bookshop again, they walked quickly past *Scheltema* and into the south of the city, taking a narrow street through onto *Kalverstraat* where the travel agency was situated.

Once inside, Penelope said, 'Eric do you think we lost them?'

'Yes, I do, and from the pace they were walking I'm sure they're now looking in all the travel agencies around Dam Square for us.'

Eric stood at the counter with their passports and his wallet ready. 'I'd like to book a flight to Almeria please,' he said.

* * *

It was the brand new Boeing 737, flight number KLM2433. Eric, sitting in the window seat, watched Amsterdam drop away as they rose into the freedom of the sky. He felt elated.

'I just hope they bought it Eric,' said Penelope.

He smiled. 'Well Pen, Mexico is as feasible a place as any. I told Father Ambroos that we'd met there. We could easily be going back to search for more clues.'

Now she was smiling too.

* * *

The hotel was a welcome sight as the taxi pulled up. After checking in they were escorted to their room and given two keys. Eric placed a few pesetas in the young porter's hand as they entered their cosy two-bedroom apartment. It had a huge window facing the coast. Collapsing on the sofa they allowed themselves to relax for a while and gazed at the blue expanse.

'So, what's it like looking out at the sight your ancestors would have known?' said Penelope.

'To be honest, it's hard to imagine.'

'I find it awe inspiring.'

'Oh, so do I. Breathtaking.'

'What's the plan then?'

Eric stood. 'I'll make us a drink. I'm sure there's some coffee here somewhere, and then we'll work out what to do. We're only a couple of miles from the place I told you about, but I don't think we should walk. It's a steep climb and the heat's pretty oppressive in this part of Spain. Last time, I took a shuttle bus, but we could call another taxi.'

'Make the coffee then. If you don't mind, I need to stretch out for a bit.'

Penelope leaned her head back and closed her eyes while Eric checked the cupboards for coffee and dried milk. Then he came across a familiar object. At the back of one of the cupboards was a little figure – a stickman with a hoop over his head.

Moments later Eric was staring out of the window at the blue waters, sipping coffee. He thought of young Ezra on his father's boat.

'Pen.'

'Mmmm?' She was almost asleep.

'That must have been where he and his dad had their first conversation about the scroll.' He was looking up the coast to the north. 'I guess it was just about there, adjacent to the old town.'

'Huh, who?' Penelope was fighting to stay awake.

'Ezra.'

'Oh, yes. Sorry Eric, I'm feeling so tired...I need to...'

Eric lifted her feet onto the sofa – he then gulped down his coffee, picked up one of the two keys and left the room.

Outside it was like an oven. The rooms all had ceiling fans, but out in the Almerian sun it was baking.

Eric's thoughts about his ancestor had inspired him to take a stroll down to the edge of the water. He took off his shoes and walked down to the sea, allowing the cool water to touch his toes as it flowed in and out.

As he looked out to sea, he suddenly had the strangest feeling that he was being watched. He turned around and looked back over to the hotel and then up and down the coast. Nothing.

Something nibbled his foot and, looking down, he noticed a little red crab pinching one of his toes. He knelt down and scooped it up, thinking back to Ezra and his father. He held it in his hand for a few moments before crouching down and letting it go again.

* * *

The shuttle bus took around fifteen minutes and the higher they climbed, the more blue ocean they could see.

'It's so beautiful,' said Penelope.

'It is, isn't it?' said Eric. 'No wonder Ezra never wanted to leave.'

'Well let's hope you're right and that he returned.'

The bus crept up the last and steepest stretch on the north ridge of the village. It finally stopped and Penelope stepped off first. 'Look how different this side of the hill is.' She was peering out over the dry desert.

'I thought that when I was last here,' said Eric, who was now beside her. 'But can you hear that?'

The sudden thumping sound of music caused them both to turn.

They followed the sound until they reached the town square, which was bursting with life. People were everywhere, some of them dressed in the most flamboyant and colourful costumes. A brass band marched, playing jubilant tunes, and a couple of male dancers pranced around waving wooden swords.

'I noticed the posters down there on the promenade,' said Penelope. 'But they were
in Spanish and mine's not as good as yours.'

'Yes I saw them too. I think they're preparing for some sort of fiesta. I'll ask someone.'

They smiled when they discovered that they'd arrived during the period when Mojacar celebrated the Festival of the Christians and the Moors when the whole town re-enacted the handing over to Castile in 1492.

'Come on, let me show you the house,' said Eric.

He held her hand as they pushed their way through the crowds, up the narrow streets, making their way to the old Jewish quarter. They stopped at a certain house, the front door of which was bolted with a lock system that looked centuries old.

'This is the place I told you about, Pen. I imagine it's been shut up for years.' Eric reached out and stroked the wood. 'I really feel something here. I can't describe it but...' He pressed his palm against the door.

Penelope frowned. 'Okay but how can we possibly get in? It's not as if we can break in.' Eric ran his fingers over the letters that were scratched on the door.

'It literally means *pig* you know,' said Penelope.

'Pig?' 'Yes it was not just used as an identifying label but was a term of abuse too – for those they regarded as Judaizers.'

'From whom? Catholics I suppose?' Eric sniffed.

'Not just Catholics, but Jews too. The Maranos were hated by both sides, which makes it all the more intriguing as to why the label has been scratched here, bearing in mind it's a Jewish quarter.'

'That's why it spoke to me, and why I asked the chap who lives over there whose house it was.'

'And you're really sure that these Ben Kerioths are your ancestors?'

'Pen, I *know* they are. And you saw those extra pages with your own eyes. It was there in black and white. Ezra Van Kroot was Ezra Ben Kerioth.'

'Well what we have to do then, is find the mayor of this town and claim the house belongs to your family.'

'But I have nothing to prove that.'

'You have your story Eric.'

'That's true. It's worth a try. Shall we go back to the square and ask where we might find him?'

'Yes I think we should.'

* * *

Half an hour later they were standing in the town council office.

'That house has been uninhabited for as long as I can remember,' said the assistant to the mayor, a short plump woman with greying hair. 'In fact it is periodically brought up as a subject within council meetings because no one knows who or where its legal owners are and some councillors wish to sell it. There's very limited accommodation here as you can see.'

'But no one's been able to get it on the market?'

'Precisely. Every time it comes up as a subject for discussion, someone from outside objects.'

'On what grounds?' said Penelope.

'It varies.' She shrugged. 'Usually to do with the belief that the owners will seek to reclaim it someday, and err – the other stories.'

'Other stories?'

'Yes, tales of superstition and bad luck.' The woman shivered. 'Nonsense I tell myself, but this is a superstitious little town. Have you heard about our ghosts?'

Eric ignored the question. 'I am a member of the Ben Kerioth family. In fact, my brother and I are quite possibly the very last of us.'

The mayor's assistant listened with interest as Eric took her through the whole story, including (he thought it might help) the death of his daughter. One ingredient he left out, though, was the scroll.

The woman wiped a tear from her eye. 'You have this document with you?'

'Yes,' said Eric. 'It's in the hotel down by the coast, but I can bring it to you tomorrow.'

'And you feel that this Amsterdam Jew, Ezra Ben Kerioth, who changed his family name to Van Kroot, left his family to come back here for the remainder of his days?'

'It sounds far-fetched I know, but, yes.'

'Well let me see what I can do. I'll discuss it at our council meeting tomorrow evening when the mayor himself will be present, and if you bring me the document the following morning, I'll let you know what the answer is. Is that fair?'

Eric smiled and nodded. 'Thank you.'

* * *

Two days later Eric faced the mayor's assistant for the second time. He watched as the official fingered her way through the document. 'Well this doesn't mean much to me since it's in Dutch,' she said.

Why else did she think he'd let her read it?

'No,' said Eric.

'But let me tell you our decision.'

'Please,' said Penelope.

'The mayor and council have decided that we need to hand this matter to a higher authority, so we shall have to write to the Commissioner of Almeria.'

Eric's heart sank.

'But...' said the woman, 'if you like, we will allow you an hour or so within the premises to have a look around.'

'Oh that's wonderful,' said Penelope, 'isn't it Eric?'

'Yes. Thank you. We're very grateful.' He beamed at Penelope and squeezed her hand.

'We hold a key at the mayor's parlour, so I'll get one of the council staff to come along and meet you at the house in, say, half an hour?'

'Perfect,' said Eric.

Chapter Sixty-One

Almeria, 1981

Eric's heart pounded as he stood by the door and waited. Penelope was beside him holding his hand.

It took an extra tool and a can of lubricant spray to turn the levers inside the huge lock, such was the corrosion, but at last it opened. The council employee removed the large cast iron key, put it in his pocket and stood by the door looking nervous.

'I've been told to stay here and to give you an hour,' he said. 'I have to make sure no one else enters.'

Inside was dark and, as they made their way into the house, Eric found the smell of dust and mold overpowering.

He coughed. 'Bloody hell, I don't know how long I'll be able to last in here.'

Not only was there no electric light, there was little natural light.

'We should have thought to bring a torch,' said Penelope.

'And a facemask.' Eric held his mouth and nose.

'Let's see if we can open a shutter or two.'

Eric felt around and pushed on something that gave way. It was a door. He applied more pressure and it creaked open. Behind the door was a room lit partially by a shaft of light that shot through a hole in the wall.

'Pen, come here.'

'What have you found?'

'I don't know, but there's light coming in.'

Then they were standing in what looked like a sitting room. A few old wooden chairs that must have once been upholstered were dotted around. Strips of moth-eaten cloth dangled from them. The light turned out to be coming through a knot hole in a wide plank of wood that was leant up against the wall.

'Perhaps this is an old window.' Eric pushed and dislodged the plank. The whole place lit up. The window overlooked a drop. He pushed on the glass and the old window creaked open gradually, giving Eric a little relief.

'How you doing in there?' shouted the man on guard.

'All good!' said Penelope.

'Better now!' said Eric.

Looking around the inside of the now well-lit room, Eric then noticed the expression on Penelope's face. Her eyes and mouth were wide open, as she stared at the wall in front of her. Eric followed her line of sight and then they both stood gazing at the same image on the wall in front of them.

'Oh my God,' said Penelope.

'Sweet Jesus,' said Eric.

They were gazing at an upside down Indalo Man.

'What could it mean?' said Penelope.

'I don't know,' said Eric, 'but surely it's a sign.'

'I'm going to have to ask you to come out soon,' said the voice from outside. 'I need to lock up.'

'We can't have been more than fifteen minutes,' protested Eric. 'The mayor's assistant agreed on an hour.'

'Ten more minutes then,' he said.

'Think, think, think,' said Penelope. 'This may be our only chance.'

'Okay.' His right hand rubbed his head. 'What did I say the Indalo Man was?'

'A sign. A symbol.'

'Yes a sign of, um...heaven – of God's promise to Noah... err...of good luck, protection...um...a bridge between God and heaven, and between people of different creeds.' He was frantic, shaking his head, straining to think. Then there was a moment of clarification. 'He directs us to heaven. Pen, he points up to heaven! He's an arrow pointing us!'

'So he's a pointer, like a signpost?' Penelope sounded more

excited.

'Yes, I guess so.'

There was a pause while both minds came to the same conclusion at once.

Eric looked down at the floor. It was littered with the remnants of an old carpet. They both dropped to their knees and pulled away everything so there was just the stone floor under their hands.

Penelope looked up at Eric. 'Can you feel it?' she said, rubbing over the floor with her hands.

'I can,' he whispered.

'Five minutes.' The voice sounded impatient.

'Eric, can we get any more light down here?'

'I think so.' He reached out his foot and kicked over something that was obstructing the light's path, an old chair probably. And then they saw the second Indalo Man. On the floor at the centre of the slab they'd felt with their fingers. And this Indalo Man was unlike the normal ones in that his legs were not apart like a stickman but together like a crucifix.

They looked at each other. *The Rainbow Cross.*

'Two minutes.'

Eric's heart was racing as he tried to prise open the stone slab with Penelope's keys, scraping around the edge and gradually lifting it up. But it was taking too long.

'Come on! Come on you bastard!' shouted Eric at the ground.

Finally, the slab was high enough for Penelope to wedge an old piece of chair leg under it. With a little more effort, Eric managed to lift it. He heaved and slid it over to one side making a loud scraping sound.

They expected the guard to call out again but there was nothing.

They knew he wouldn't come in anyway, due to his obvious superstition and fear of the place, so they figured they had a few extra minutes.

Then they looked into the hole under where the slab had been and saw it.

'Careful,' said Penelope, as Eric reached down to take it out.

Slowly, he brought out a wooden box. It was about the size of a child's shoe box, and just small enough to place inside Penelope's bag.

Still no voice from outside.

They made their way back to the front door and, as they stepped out into the daylight, saw the two men standing there – dark glasses covering their eyes and Knights of St Augustine badges on their lapels.

Chapter Sixty-Two

Almeria, 1981

'Don't try to run,' whispered Eric, 'they're probably armed.'

Penelope nodded. She was shivering.

One of the men whistled the attention of a third, who was standing by a parked car at the top of the narrow street.

When they reached the car, they noticed who was sitting in the back.

'It's the guy who was guarding the house,' said Eric.

He was allowed to get out and one of the men said something to him in Spanish. Cautiously he made his way back down the street. Eric and Penelope watched him re-lock the door and glance back at them before departing the other way.

Then they were pushed into the car.

'What the hell is this?' Eric demanded, but they didn't acknowledge his question.

It took about twenty-five minutes to descend the hilltop town and pull up at a Catholic church in the next town of *Garucca*. All the while not a word had been spoken. They were taken through into the back room – some sort of vestry – and then a priest entered.

'So they did know we were coming here?' said Eric.

'Obviously our decoy didn't work,' said Penelope.

The priest, a middle-aged Spaniard, smiled to reveal a set of cigarette stained teeth, and said in English, 'We have our ways. As a Catholic, surely you know how small a world it is.'

'I take it the men found the travel agency we used then?'

The priest smiled.

'Well,' said Eric, 'it's all been for nothing. We didn't find anything. I'm afraid it was a wild goose chase for us all.'

'Then you won't mind the men searching your girlfriend's

bag?' he said.

Penelope reached for it and nervously passed it to one of the men. He grinned as he felt the shape of a box.

Drawing out what looked like an ancient jewellery box, he handed it to the priest who placed it on the table in front of him and gazed at it in wonder.

But his excitement soon turned to disappointment when he opened the little eroded latch and lifted the lid. Part of the wood crumbled in his hands, and all there was within was dust and fragments of cloth, and what looked like damp soot.

'Shit,' said Eric.

'Well I didn't expect that,' said Penelope.

'*Mierda Y joder*,' said the priest.

Eric couldn't hold back the little laugh. 'I understood that. Is it normal for priests to swear so crudely?'

The priest ignored him. 'So you tried to send us to Mexico, which we saw through. But it looks like your ancestor's gift is no more anyway.' He laughed out loud.

'I guess he hadn't preserved it well enough. But at least you don't have to worry any more,' said Eric.

'Sad though,' said Penelope, as she touched the box with her fingertips. 'All that history and all those years, and after everything Ezra went through.'

The priest muttered something else to the two men in Spanish, and then spoke in English. 'They'll drop you back at your hotel. I take it you're staying in new Mojacar?'

'Yes we are, at the Hotel Indalo.'

* * *

Later on that evening they were back on the shuttle bus as it climbed the hill. Eric faced the window and tried to assess the best place to get off. It was dark but he could see the approaching lights and shadows of the town. They left the bus at the lowest stop, about 500 metres from the town square.

'Okay, let's think about this. Where would the Jewish quarter be from here?'

They looked up at the skyline and agreed it would be around the other side, as the Jews were never allowed to live facing the blue waters of the Mediterranean. Above the skyline it was pitch black. Not even a solitary star could be seen. It had been a cloudy day.

'It's going to be hard to find in this light, Pen, and maybe dangerous. I think you should wait for me here.'

'Not a chance.'

'I knew you'd say that.' Eric smiled. 'Alright, let's stick very close together.'

The road itself wound its way gradually up to the town, like the spiral on a helter-skelter, but they knew they couldn't use it. They needed to make their way to the other side of the hill town at the same level as they were now. It was a long, slow and strenuous walk, with stone walls to climb, thick dry bushes to avoid, and gardens to creep through. And all in total darkness.

Eventually they came across a low ridge that, once they'd hopped onto it, made the remainder of the journey a little easier. They followed the ridge around to where Eric guessed was roughly opposite the bus stop. They looked up to see if they could see it, but it was still too dark. They couldn't even make out shapes of the houses let alone individual windows.

But then something happened. As they were straining to look, the clouds above parted slightly and a beam of the bright full moon's light lit up the whitewashed houses momentarily – and there it was: the outer window of Eric's old ancestral home.

'Right, make a mental note of that direction,' said Eric. 'It's got to be over there somewhere.'

Minutes later they were standing directly under the window where Penelope had dropped the package earlier on that afternoon, but the bushes they were looking in were making a little too much noise.

'Shhhhhh,' said Penelope. 'Someone will hear.'

A dog barked in a nearby garden, and Eric and Penelope froze as they heard the sound of a distant door open and a man's voice shout something in Spanish. But no one came and the dog remained silent. After a moment, they continued their search as quickly and quietly as possible.

At last they found it: Eric's little leather bag. A few hours earlier, when they were twenty-five metres directly above where they now stood, looking in wonder at a small wooden box they'd found under a slab, it had occurred to Penelope that the guy at the door was suddenly far too quiet. So they'd made a calculated decision and taken a risk. Carefully removing the contents of the box and packing it gently inside Eric's bag, they had swept the floor for as much muck and grime as possible and quarter-filled the box with it. Then Eric had dropped the bag out of the window into the bushes below, while Penelope had put the box in her own shoulder bag.

Chapter Sixty-Three

Almeria, 1981

Eric's stomach churned at the rush and lift of the aeroplane as it rose into the Almerian sky. At last they could breathe. They'd been lucky enough to acquire seating at the back of the jet, and it was not a busy flight, so they could talk.

Eric put his hand on Penelope's leg, patting it lightly. He looked ahead at the back of the seat in front. He was smiling and, as he turned to her, saw that she was smiling too.

'We did it,' she said.

'Yes, we did. I can't believe it.'

The cloth bag and its contents were safely hidden within the hand luggage above their heads. They'd decided not to try to look at it until they were through customs the other end, but Eric had removed an extra few sheets of parchment that had been wrapped around the bag.

Eric carefully took out the parchment and unrolled it. The text, in Dutch, was faded but legible

Dear great-great-grandson.

You have found me.

When I returned to Muxacra, the town was barely recognisable. My family had fled. I know not where. I was never able to find them, and thus if a descendant has found this I assume you are a Dutch descendant. May God bless you. You now know what must be done. When I knew the grave approached I made a pact with my neighbours to watch my home and keep it from being sold by any means possible. I left them all my possessions in return for doing whatever they could to keep people away from this house, even if it

meant scaring them with stories of devils, curses or worse.
My child of the future, you hold in your hands something of
unfathomable value. Guard it well and do what you must.
Your great-great grandfather,
Ezra Ben Kerioth

They gazed at each other.

'What on earth have we found?' It was Penelope who broke the silence.

Eric looked up at the air vents and light above their heads, a few inches above which was their luggage.

'I don't know,' he said, 'but I think I might know where we can find out.'

* * *

Back in Amsterdam, Eric and Penelope were at the reception desk of the small Jewish library, Ets Haim.

'Where exactly are you saying you found this?' said the woman behind the desk. She had laid the package on the desk and was studying it with a magnifying glass.

'In a southern Spanish house that has recently been left to my family,' Eric lied. 'My ancestors were Sephardic Jews. I think this might be a Jewish scroll passed down from them.'

'Have you any idea what it might be?' said Penelope.

The woman looked up at them. 'I daren't even attempt to open the outer material. It's so eroded and fragile. If there is a scroll inside it will probably be in very poor condition.'

'So what would you recommend?' said Eric.

'I can ask our expert, Dr Wolff, to have a look and see what he thinks. Are you willing to leave it with us for a while?'

Eric looked at Penelope and back at the woman. 'Give us a

few moments will you?' Eric took Penelope's hand and led her outside onto the street.

'What do you think?' he said.

'Well, what are the other options?'

'We could try a museum or a university.'

'But if it is a Jewish scroll surely this place is going to treat it with the respect it deserves, and they'll probably be quicker because of their own cultural interest in what they might be handling.'

'You're right,' said Eric. 'Let's agree to leave it here with her, on the condition that we're called back in the minute they discover anything of interest.'

Chapter Sixty-Four

Amsterdam, 1981

It was the middle of the night and Eric was back at his brother's house. He'd broken in again. This time he made for the upstairs. He could hear noises coming from one of the rooms, the master bedroom, the room that had been his own mother and father's bedroom. He put his ear to the door. Grunting, wheezing, coughing, more grunting, and then the sound of a man ejaculating. Then another noise. A faint stepping sound coming towards the door – *coming towards the fucking door*. It swung open. And there she stood – naked – and that fat bastard of a brother in the background leaning back on the bed, grinning and smoking a cigarette.

'Hello Father,' she said.

It was like a shock of electricity being injected directly into his head. 'Noooo, Hannah. Nooooooo.'

Another voice. 'Eric, Eric, what is it?' It was Penelope's soothing voice. She was sat on the bed beside him. The minute she heard him she came running from the next room. He was safe now. His vision had eased.

Breathing hard and sweating he looked at her. 'Oh my God. I just had the most horrific dream.'

* * *

They spent the rest of the night together, having fallen asleep after Eric's description of his nightmare.

It was the telephone that woke them.

'Christ, what time is it?' said Penelope.

Eric looked at his watch. 'It's not early Pen, 9am.'

She jumped out of bed and disappeared into the next room

to answer the phone. 'Yes, oh really? Fantastic, we'll be there as soon as we can. About an hour. Great, see you then.'

'The library?'

'They've found something out about the package. It was a scroll. They want to see us.'

'Did she say anything else?'

'No, just that. Come on, we need to get ready.'

Eric pulled on his clothes from the day before, while Penelope made them a quick cup of coffee, and they were out and onto the first tram they saw.

Approaching the library they noticed that it had CLOSED on the door, but someone was waiting for them. The door opened and a young woman introduced herself as Mrs Levy. She locked the door after them.

They were led through to a back room and invited to sit down at a large round table. Sitting there was an elderly man whom Eric assumed to be Dr Wolff. Then another man entered and reached out his hand to shake Eric's.

'Hello, I'm Dr Wolff,' he said. 'You must be Mr Van Kroot, and you Miss Kruger, yes?'

'Yes. Pleased to meet you,' said Eric.

Penelope smiled and shook his hand.

'Allow me also to introduce Mr Chaim.' The other man stood up and shook their hands.

'Let's all sit down,' said Mrs Levy.

'I take it you've found something of interest?' said Eric.

The three others exchanged glances and Dr Wolff leaned forward. 'Mr Van Kroot...'

'Call me Eric, please.'

'Eric.' He took a deep breath. 'We believe you may have uncovered the most important historical manuscript in the whole of Judaeo-Christian history.'

Eric shook his head. 'What? What are you saying?'

Mr Chaim spoke. 'We were able to open the package without

damaging the contents.'

'Fortunately,' added Dr Wolff, 'whoever had hidden the item had also used a preserving agent – some sort of oily herb – and had wrapped the whole thing in fresh cloth, before adding another oiled sheet of material.'

'And there was a scroll inside?'

The two men glanced at each other. 'Yes,' said Dr Wolff. 'In fact two scrolls. One clearly a later copy of the other, both written in Aramaic and, amazingly, still legible.'

'We assume the newer one was duplicated in an attempt to preserve the older one, by whoever the keeper of the scroll was,' added Mr Chaim.

'Jesus,' whispered Eric.

'Indeed.' Dr Wolff smiled. 'The older scroll we estimate as being up to two thousand years old. It's a miracle it survived. Whoever preserved it did a remarkable job. And, though it's worn and damaged in places, the newer one shows us what the worn parts say.'

'And?' said Eric.

'I'm an expert in ancient Semitic languages,' said Mr Chaim.

There was a long silence, with each person glancing at the others, as if waiting for someone to speak.

'Oh come on,' said Eric, 'what is it? Tell us.'

Dr Wolff looked at Eric but used his surname again to address him. 'Mr Van Kroot, I'm told that you worked out your own original family name by cleverly connecting the Dutch Van to the Hebrew Ben. Correct?'

'Correct.' Eric's heart was beating faster and faster.

'Do you know that Kerioth is a place? A location?'

'Well I'd kind of assumed it was,' said Eric. 'I guess somewhere in Andalucía, Spain. Possibly an old Muslim town or village of Moorish Granada. Am I right?'

'You're on the right track, but wrong continent and period,' said Mr Chaim.

Eric looked confused. 'Wrong continent? Are you saying my ancestors were not from Spain after all?'

'Not at all,' said Dr Wolff. 'They were indeed from the Iberian Peninsula, but Kerioth takes us to where they lived before that.' He was grinning with excitement.

'Oh come on,' said Penelope. 'Tell us.'

Mr Chaim spoke again. 'The word Kerioth takes us to ancient Palestine. When you said Muslim town a few moments ago you were strangely close. There was a town called El Kureitein, a modern Palestinian Muslim village about ten miles south of Hebron. It was destroyed by an Israeli air-raid just before the 1967 war. And archaeologists have recently discovered that it was originally a Jewish settlement known as Kerioth.'

Eric's heart thumped.

'It's even more interesting when I tell you what other Hebrew word was used back then as a prefix to denote where a person came from,' said Mr Chaim, 'other than Ben.'

'Yes?' said Eric.

'You see, the Hebrew word *Ben* literality means *son of*, but the word for simply *of* or *from* is *Ish*.' Dr Wolff clapped his hands.

'I don't understand,' said Eric.

Penelope was beaming and quivering a little. 'I think I do. I think I do.'

'Bloody well tell me then.'

'They're saying that the author of this scroll was a Ben Kerioth, but a man who came from ancient Palestine would have been known as Ish Kerioth. Man of Kerioth – Ish Kerioth.'

'Ish Kerioth, Ish Kerioth,' Eric kept muttering the word, and then it sunk in. 'Oh my God. Ish Keriot, Ishkeriot, *Iscariot*.'

Eric and Penelope glanced at each other and then looked across the table. The other three people in the room were smiling.

'Eric,' said the woman, 'we believe you've found a scroll written by Judas Iscariot.'

'I thought that's what I was hearing,' he said, in shock. 'That's incredible. I mean…My God…do you know…Oh God…do you know much about the scroll yet? Like what it's about?'

'That was our second reason for bringing you here so early Eric,' said Mrs Levin. 'Mr Chaim wants your permission to photograph the whole of the scroll, so he can translate it. Meanwhile Dr Wolff will get to work on its preservation. Eric, this scroll could make you a very rich man if you were to sell it to a Jewish or Christian museum.'

'Christian? Will any Christians want to know about it?'

'I guess that depends on what it says,' said Mr Chaim.

'And how long will the process of translation take?'

'Well,' said Mr Chaim, 'even in the newer copy the text is very faded in places. I would say a good few months. Maybe even a year.'

'Let them do it,' said Penelope. 'After all, you can't possibly have got this far without learning what your ancestor wrote.'

Her words jolted him. 'My God, yes it does mean that I'm a descendant too. Ha, I'm a descendant of Judas Iscariot. No wonder I never made a very good Catholic.'

Chapter Sixty-Five

Amsterdam, 1981

That evening, Eric and Penelope were sitting next to each other, thinking about everything that had happened over the previous few months.

Eric turned to her and said, 'Pen, you know how grateful I am don't you?'

She smiled. 'Yes, and I am too.'

'You, grateful? For what?'

'For bumping into you again.'

Her eyes dilated. He raised his hand slowly, delicately brushing the side of her face with one finger. She leant closer to him until their lips met, and he moved his hand to gently cup the back of her head. He could smell the gorgeous scent of her hair and taste the sensual sweetness of her soft lips. For weeks he'd longed for this moment and now it was happening. He gasped as he felt her hand rest lightly on his groin and hardened instantly.

Suddenly there was a knock at the door.

Eric's instinct was to ignore it. He held her more tightly.

Another knock.

Penelope moved her mouth to the side. 'Who could it be at this time?' she whispered.

'Let's leave it Pen. Maybe they'll go away.' He wanted her so badly.

'Eric, it might be important. Maybe someone from the library?'

'It couldn't be, Pen. Not at this time, surely. Anyway they only have the phone number, not the address. Thinking about it, who does have this address?'

As Penelope got up and walked to the door, Eric said, 'I did give it to a few people we'd spoken to in the district a few weeks back.' Then he had another thought. It could be those Knights of

St Augustine bastards. 'Pen. Wait. Don't open it.'

But she already had, though the security chain was still on.

'Hello,' said a voice with an English accent.

'Who is it?' said Penelope, trying to peer through the slightly ajar door.

'Is there a Mr Van Kroot there?'

'Yes, there is. Who is that?' She turned and called for Eric, who walked to the door.

'Yes?' said Eric. 'Can I help you?'

'I heard you've been looking for a Hannah?' said the voice.

'Yes, but she's dead. Who are you?'

'They call me Maggie. I lived most of my life in a convent in Britain, but have been here for three years. My real name's Hannah. Why were you looking for me?'

Eric released the chain and opened the door. Standing in the doorway was a girl in her twenties with long red hair and, though tired, the most beautiful emerald eyes he'd ever seen.

Part Three

Dam
Origin and Etymology: Hebrew for blood
Used more than three hundred times in the
Hebrew concordance
All words that describe the word RED
have a form of the word DAM (Blood) in them
describing the origin of their redness (being blood).
Also – ruddy or red complexion

Chapter Sixty-Six

De Stooterplas Island, 1981

Peter pressed the buzzer and the door clicked open.

'Thank you Vincent,' he said. The housekeeper brought the girl into the study. 'You can have an early evening. See you tomorrow.'

Vincent rarely got away before 8pm, so Peter knew he wasn't going to argue.

'Very good, sir.'

'And please make sure the doors are locked on the way out.'

'Yes, sir.' And he left.

Peter held out a puffy damp hand and the girl responded. She was wearing a long fur coat, which he was already removing. The curtains were tightly closed but the light was on. He wanted to see everything.

'You want it in here today then, sir?' she asked.

He smiled. And then slapped her around the face.

'Hey, what the fuck was that for?' she said, rubbing her burning cheek.

'Shut up and get your kit off.'

The girl was standing in front of Peter Van Kroot in her underwear and, though the room was warm, her knees were trembling. Looking directly into his eyes, she swallowed and reached behind her own back to unfasten her bra. It popped and fell away, releasing her beautiful ebony breasts. Peter's eyes lowered naturally and he felt a tightness in his own undergarment as his manhood started to swell.

He looked up at her face and then down at her bottom half.

'Come on, those too.'

Leaning over she pushed down her pants and wriggled out of them, the fat man studying every move.

With the girl fully naked apart from her stilettos, Peter grabbed her arm and dragged her over to his desk pushing her over it front-ways.

Holding her tight with one hand he fumbled with his buckle and zipper until his belt opened and his trousers burst apart, letting his belly plop out.

'What's wrong with you today?'

'Shut up.'

He spat in his right hand and moistened himself as his left arm pushed her down further onto the desk.

A kick to the back of her knees made her buckle slightly and lower her arse. Then he was inside her.

Ramming. Panting. Thrusting. Wheezing. Pushing harder and harder.

And swearing at her. 'Bitch!'

The fat man bullied his way in and out as she lay over his desk. But he was hurting her.

'Hey, slow down!' she said.

He ignored her. 'Take it, whore.'

'Stop!' Her voice getting louder. 'You're hurting me.'

'Bollocks,' he said. 'You're used to it, you slut!'

'Stop it! Please.'

He leaned forward, pushing down on her back with his hands. All he could think of was release and he wasn't going to stop until he had it.

She tried to push up with her own hands but his weight and strength overpowered her. He looked down at her and spat. Then he reached one hand to the back of her neck. 'You stay there. I'm not done yet.' Her face was squashed onto the wooden desk and her hands were now flailing around searching for a different part of the surface to push against.

The eruption was about to happen. He could feel it. Like an electric current snaking its way from deep down inside him – coming closer and closer to the surface. The feeling. The intensity. Closer and closer. God he needed this.

And then he saw it – in her hand – but it was too late. With one mighty jolt she managed to swing around. And as she did, so he felt himself pop out of her as he spurted his angry fluid all over the back of her legs and onto the floor.

After the flash of bare arm, the very last thing he saw was the stickman figure and the rock on which it was engraved.

And then everything went dark.

Chapter Sixty-Seven

Amsterdam, 1981

As the chain released, the door opened slowly on a man who looked to be in his mid-forties. His mouth hung open and his wide eyes glistened as they peered into her face. She stepped back and, for a moment, neither of them spoke.

Hannah's head was swimming. Who was he? She saw something like recognition in his eyes. She'd been given the address and the name, but wasn't sure why. Obviously he was connected to that bastard's family but...

The man broke the silence. 'Hannah?' His voice was but a whisper.

She studied him. There was a strange familiarity about this man – this Mr Van Kroot. But it couldn't be, could it? She felt her heart thumping inside her chest.

He stepped forward.

'No!' Hannah lurched back, and thrust out her arm, palm facing him. 'I...' she swallowed and turned her head. 'I don't know who you are. What is this? What do you want?'

She looked at him again. He had moved back inside the doorway. He said nothing but smiled, and something deep inside her responded.

'Are you going to answer me?' she said.

And then the words she knew were coming, reached out from him and struck her in the heart. 'Hannah. I'm your father.'

Tears filled his eyes and flowed over. Hannah remembered that terrible encounter with that foul monster. She'd never been able to erase his words. *You're not my daughter. You're the spawn of my traitorous brother.*

'You're Peter Van Kroot's brother!'

He nodded slowly. 'I've been looking for you.' A large tear

rolled down his cheek. He wiped his eyes on his sleeve and smiled, shaking his head. 'And you're here.' He stepped forward again and this time Hannah didn't back away.

'I can't believe it.' Her words were muffled, as her father wrapped his arms around her, holding her so close – so very close.

'I can't either.' He was sobbing now. 'We thought you were...'

'I had no idea it would be you. When I heard a Mr Van Kroot was looking for me, my first thoughts were of that vile hotel owner.'

'You thought Peter was looking for you?'

'At first, yes. But when I heard the description I knew it couldn't be. So I figured it must be one of his extended family, bringing me a message. I even thought he might have died.'

Her father continued to hold her. 'I just can't believe you're here. I thought I'd lost you forever.'

'But I don't understand,' said Hannah. 'Why now? Why come and look for me after all these years?'

'I'll explain it all. I promise. My friend Pen will make us all a drink and then we can sit down and talk. I'm just so happy.' He was beaming. 'You're alive. And you're here.'

He loosened his arms and, moving his hands to her shoulders, leaned back to look at her. He shook his head. 'My daughter. My beautiful daughter.'

'Your brother told me enough to make me hate you, but I can't hate you. I've dreamed of you all my life.'

'How long ago was it you saw him?'

'I'm not sure, two or three years. The piece of shit.'

'I can't disagree there. Look, whatever that man told you about me, I swear I knew nothing about you until earlier this year.'

'Really?'

'Yes.'

'Eric's telling the truth.' It was another voice. Female.

'This is Penelope,' said Hannah's father, as a woman came into the room carrying a tray with three steaming mugs. Penelope smiled at her. They all sat down.

'Your name's Eric then?' said Hannah.

Her father nodded.

'So, where do we begin?' he said.

Hannah shrugged.

'Where do you live anyway?' said Penelope. 'And are you okay to be here for a while?'

'I don't live anywhere.' Hannah looked down. 'I've just been thrown out of my bedsit.' She knew she had to say what was on her mind. 'Look, I need to ask. You do know what I do don't you? I mean I'm assuming you do, bearing in mind where you were looking for me.'

Her father put his hand on her shoulder. 'Yes, we know.'

'Well I've been trying to get out of the scene,' she said. 'I came across a priest a few months ago, and he helped me to see something about myself.'

'A priest?' Her father flinched and shifted in his chair.

'Yes, I'd never met him before, and haven't since, but he helped shift something inside me.'

'What do you mean Hannah?' said Penelope, looking concerned.

'I've despised myself ever since...' She stopped and closed her eyes, breathing in and shivering slightly. '...Ever since I was given the name Maggie by a nun.'

'What?' said her father. 'So the name you've used here was given you by one of those old nuns at the convent?'

'Yes, the black crows we called them. The one who named me Maggie was Sister Dominic. In fact, *Mother* Dominic during the last year. She...'

'I know,' he said. 'I've heard about her. And I've met Rose.'

She felt her heart leap. 'Rose. Rose. You've met her? How is she?'

'Angry.'

'That's Rose.' Hannah chuckled.

'She was angry with me. At first she thought I was Peter.' He smiled. 'I won't tell you what she called me.'

'I can imagine.' Hannah sniggered.

'I visited Rose after I tracked down the convent.'

'You went to the convent too?'

'Hannah, your father has searched so hard to find you,' said Penelope, nodding.

'Were you allowed inside?' said Hannah.

'No, I was left at the gates for an hour waiting for some old white-eyed skeleton to come back out and tell me more lies.'

'Ah. That's Sister Benedict,' said Hannah. 'Who is the Reverend Mother now?'

'I saw a letter from a Mother Matthew. Would that be correct?'

Hannah shuddered, as she remembered those clammy hands. 'Yes, yes that would be right. She's a bitch like Dominic, perhaps worse.' Hannah lifted her head and looked directly into her father's eyes. 'She is the reason why my friend Lucy killed herself.' A tear ran down her cheek.

'You're safe now Hannah. Those monsters can never harm you again.' Her father's eyes were mesmerising. And filled with kindness and warmth.

'There's clearly so much that you two need to talk through,' said Penelope. 'Hannah, can you stay? I could pop out and get us something to eat, and then you two can have all night to talk and listen. How does that sound?'

'That sounds great.' Hannah smiled at Penelope.

* * *

Then it was just Hannah and her father. They were sitting on the sofa holding hands.

For a moment they were silent, the energy between them

tangible. Hannah squeezed her father's hand. 'So, should I call you Dad or Eric?'

'Which would you prefer?'

'No, which would *you* prefer?'

His eyes misted over. 'Dad.'

'Good. I'd like that.'

'I have so many questions.' She was thinking of one in particular.

'Me too, but you go first.'

'Well why did you say I was dead? When I first knocked, you said you were looking for a Hannah but she's dead.'

He squeezed her hand. 'I honestly thought you were. I even went to your grave. Well, I thought it was your grave.'

'Really? How weird.'

'Yes, we, Pen and I, had tracked you down to a club in The Hague owned by a guy named – '

'Omar!' She had heard all about Omar and his special girls.

'You know him?'

'No. I know *of him* and…Yes, of course. The other Hannah. Poor thing.'

'So there was another Hannah from England? And she ended up in Omar's club?'

'Yes, but not another Hannah. She was the only Hannah. I was Maggie remember. I don't recall whether she'd also changed her name. Didn't know her that well at all really. Even though we were both UK girls we didn't chat. I only knew of her through one of her friends.'

'Not Rachel?'

'You know Rachel?'

'Yes, she was the one who told us to look at The Hague.'

'And that's how you found out that Hannah had…which is why you thought I was dead. Of course. It all makes sense.'

'That poor girl,' said her dad. He got up, walked over to the window, and closed it. 'It's getting cold.'

'Amsterdam's always cold,' said Hannah.

He sat back down and took her hand again. 'So, what were you saying about the priest you came across, and how he'd sorted something out in your mind? And how did you meet him? Surely not…?'

Hannah looked down and felt her cheeks start to burn. 'Yes, I admit I was shocked at first.'

'He came to you, this priest, and…used you?'

'Yeah. As I say, I was surprised. He only came the once but it was enough to make me think.'

'Think? About what?'

'Well, ever since those old crows Dominic and Matthew used to torment me, I've felt like I'm worth absolutely nothing. They pushed us so far, with their ridicule and bullying – to the point that we just ended up believing them.'

Eric held her hand tighter as she spoke.

'Dominic used that name Maggie as an insult.'

'Insult?'

'Yeah, in the end she told me what it meant. She called me Maggie after Mary Magdalene.'

'Why?'

'Well, apparently she had red hair.' Hannah laughed. 'Fuck knows how they figured that out, but all the artwork that depicts her with bright red hair – the red hair of a harlot. Like me.'

'But Hannah, you didn't have to – '

'Stop. Dad. I did. When I saw your brother I knew there was nothing else for me. I knew, or I thought I knew, that they were right about me, that my role in life was to live out the Maggie in me.'

Eric shook his head.

'I've only started to see all this since I met that priest.'

'So, tell me,' said Eric. 'What changed in you?'

'I thought long and hard after he'd left me.'

'The priest?'

'Yes, and I wondered what kind of misery he must live with.'

'Misery? You were feeling sorry for him?'

'Kind of. It was the first time I've ever realised that a priest could struggle in this kind of way.'

'What, sexually?'

'Yeah. I knew that some of the nuns back at Crucis were weird in that way. I had my own taste of them. But...'

'But, you somehow never thought the men who supposedly represent Christ could?'

'Well, yeah.'

'And so...?'

'So I started to visit churches. I'd sit right at the back and listen to the masses. Not, you know, take communion or anything. Who am I to do that? But just take it all in, and focus on the ones at the front. I used to imagine them – see them – picture them struggling with their lives, with their many sins.'

'And this made you feel better?'

'Well, no. Not better. But less alone. Less alone with my pain, and my guilt.'

'Oh Hannah.' He reached out his arms and drew her to himself, holding her tight. 'You have nothing to feel guilty about.'

She pushed him away. 'Oh but I do. I'm Maggie Red-Head. I've become her. Dad, you know what I am. You know I'm a... prostitute.'

'But you were encouraged into this.'

'No, it was my destiny.' She plucked up a piece of her long red hair, and looked at it. 'Red- haired Mary Mag the whore, and red-haired Judas the Traitor.'

She saw him flinch. 'What?'

His mouth was gaping open, like his eyes. He gulped, 'Hannah, can I tell you something?'

'Of course, what is it?'

'I didn't think we'd be talking about this so soon, but that name you just mentioned.'

'Judas?'

'Yes, what does that name mean to you?'

She closed her eyes. 'Well, when I think right back, I used to be fascinated by this painting in the convent chapel. They called it a triptych – kind of three paintings but joined together.'

'Yes, I know what you mean.'

'And there was a character on it that always used to intrigue me, maybe because his hair was the colour of mine, or maybe because he was hanging in the second picture.'

'And, this was Judas?'

'Yes, I asked about it, but was told not to think about him. But occasionally I would think about him, and I would wonder about him, and ask silly questions about him thinking, maybe, that he wasn't so bad.' She stopped, and let her face drop. 'But that got me in so much trouble.'

'What sort of things did you wonder about him, Hannah?'

'Well, the worst thing I ever said about him, and this got me the beating of all beatings from Dominic, was that Jesus forgave him for what he did.'

Eric smiled at his daughter. 'Hannah, this might be the craziest thing you've ever heard, but...'

Chapter Sixty-Eight

Amsterdam, 1981

It was morning. Slowly Eric replaced the telephone receiver and turned to face Penelope.

'He's dead,' he whispered.

'Oh my gosh, who?' said Penelope.

'Peter, my brother. He's dead. He was murdered in his home a few nights back.'

Eric staggered over to the sofa and slumped down.

'What happened? Was that the police? What did they say?' Penelope sat down beside him.

After a moment he turned to face her. 'All they know is that he was hit with a heavy object, so hard that he was killed with a single blow. He was found in his study and...' Eric closed his eyes and let out a long slow breath.

'And what?'

'And he was lying on the floor near his desk, with his trousers and underwear pulled down.' Eric took another breath. 'Semen everywhere. All evidence points to him being killed in the act of sex.'

'Heck,' said Penelope. 'I remember you saying that he'd called a prostitute when you were there before. Do you think he...?'

'I don't know, but I'm worried I might have left my own fingerprints Pen, what if their forensic team finds – ?'

'Stop. Look, it's no secret you have been there. You've got nothing to worry about. You just paid your estranged brother a visit. I imagine this was a prostitute he'd called, who'd either decided to rob him? Or just had some sort of grudge against him?'

As she said that last phrase Penelope and Eric slowly turned to face each other and, together, whispered one word.

'Hannah!'

'You don't think…?' Eric mouthed.

Hannah was in the spare room, asleep.

Penelope gulped, shook her head, and whispered, 'I don't know. I really don't. But we're going to have to tell her.' She looked towards the spare room and Eric followed her gaze.

Suddenly the telephone started ringing again but this time Penelope answered it. 'Yes. No he's not able to right now. I'm his partner. Yes, girlfriend. Look can you tell me anything more?'

There was a short period of silence before Penelope put the receiver back down.

'What did they say?' asked Eric.

'They want you to phone them and arrange to go to the police station for questioning!'

A voice from behind. 'What's that? Police station, questioning?'

Eric turned to see Hannah standing in the doorway, rubbing her eyes.

* * *

The three of them were sat on the sofa.

'And no one knows who did it?' said Hannah.

'Not yet, no,' said Penelope, 'but your dad's got to go to the station, so I guess we'll know more later.'

'Well whoever did do it, he deserved it.'

Eric stood up. 'Hannah, look I want you to be very honest with us. Do you know anything about this?'

'What? No, of course not. What are you trying to say?'

Penelope held Hannah's hand. 'Hannah, they think it might have been someone from the Red-Light District. Of course we don't think it was you, but the police might start putting pieces together and come up with the wrong answer, once they know – '

'Know what?' said Hannah.

'About your connection to him,' said Eric.

The telephone started ringing again. 'Oh shit, what now? Look I'll answer it again,' said Penelope.

She got up and picked up the receiver. 'Yes. Oh. Really?' She looked at Eric who was standing up and biting his thumb nail. 'Okay, thanks. Yes, we'll try. If we can we'll call in by the end of the day. Thank you.'

'What was that about?' said Eric.

'You'll never believe it. That was Mrs Levy at the Ets Haim library. They want to see us again. Urgently. Eric they've found something else.'

'Bloody hell,' said Eric. 'Talk about timing.'

'What library?' said Hannah. 'What's going on?'

Penelope moved back over to Hannah and sat down. 'Your dad told me that he'd explained about the book, the scroll.'

Hannah nodded.

'Well,' said Penelope, 'that was the Jewish library who we left it with. They've got some more information and, from the tone of Mrs Levy's voice, some really important information.' She turned to Eric. 'I think you should go to the station and see what they want, and then we all go to the library.'

'I think you're right,' said Eric.

'Can I come with you?' said Hannah.

'What, to see the police? I really don't think...'

'No, not the police station. The library. After all, he's my ancestor too.' She smiled.

Chapter Sixty-Nine

Amsterdam, 1981

By the time Eric had reached the police station, there had been a major development. Peter Van Kroot's personal assistant had handed over information with regard to the taxi driver, who had consequently given details of the prostitute he'd taken to the Van Kroot residence. Now they were looking for her and the description did not, to Eric's relief, match Hannah's at all. For one thing the girl was of African descent.

* * *

Half an hour later and they were back at the Jewish library, and Mrs Levy reached out to shake Hannah's hand.

'Pleased to meet you.' She turned to Eric. 'Of course it's alright for her to come in. She's part of the story too, as a descendant.' She smiled and led the three of them through to the back room where Dr Wolff and Mr Chaim were waiting.

As the experts stood to greet Eric, Penelope and Hannah, their excitement was palpable.

'Lovely to see you again,' said Dr Wolff. 'And how nice to meet you Hannah.'

'I didn't expect to be back here so soon,' said Eric. 'I take it you've found something pretty significant?'

The two older men turned to each other and smiled.

Mr Chaim said, 'Let's all sit down shall we?'

'So,' said Dr Wolff. 'How does it feel now you know who your great-great-great etcetera grandfather was, Hannah?'

'Weird,' she said. 'No, not weird.' She smiled. 'Amazing. Like, I've always loved Judas, and have always thought there was something else about him that hasn't been told.'

'Well young woman,' said Dr Wolff, 'if you found that amazing, you're in for an extra big treat today.'

'And something that could destroy the very foundations of Christianity,' added Mr Chaim.

Eric, Penelope and Hannah all glanced at each other.

'Tell us then,' said Eric.

Mrs Levy reached over to a side table and picked up some sheets of paper, handing one to each person sat at the table. They were photocopies of part of the manuscript.

'I want you to look at the paper in front of you,' said Dr Wolff. 'I know it won't mean anything to you, as it's in Aramaic, but...'

'But?' said Eric looking up at him.

The Jewish expert smiled. 'But these words seem to suggest that Jesus of Nazareth never died on the Cross.'

Chapter Seventy

Oxford, 1985

Eric sat trembling and hoped he would come over as convincing. He gasped as Penelope had one more look at her watch and switched on the TV set.

The screen flickered and settled as the programme was introduced. Eric grabbed the sides of the armchair tightly. Suddenly the TV displayed a close up of a middle-aged man in a navy double breasted blazer and old school tie. A pair of half-moon spectacles hung around his neck, and a kindly smile added a comforting balance to his rather upper middle-class attire.

'Well ladies and gentlemen, 1985 has been a rather eventful year.' Though public school, his voice was warm and kindly.

Eric glanced at Penelope and wondered how the presenter was going to introduce the subject.

'What was his name again?' asked Penelope.

'Douglass James. He's the new presenter apparently. I liked him.'

'In January,' said Douglass James, 'Mrs Thatcher became the first ever post-war Prime Minister to be publicly refused an honorary degree by Oxford University. In March we saw the end of the miners' strike. April saw the appointment of the first ever black council leader. In August the first heart-lung transplant was carried out. And in September the remains of the Titanic were finally discovered.' As he mentioned each event news flashes appeared on the TV screen.

'Yes, we've seen some remarkable things this year...but none of it will compare in magnitude to what Your World Today is going to unveil this evening.'

The camera shifted focus to another man. He was not quite middle-aged and wore a tweed jacket and cords. On screen

Eric's eyes were warm and friendly, though he was biting the inside of his cheek.

The camera zoomed out and brought Douglass James back into view, who was sat on a chair facing the other man.

'This evening, ladies and gentleman, it's my pleasure to introduce a splendid man with an exceptional story.'

Eric glanced at Penelope and smiled cautiously.

'This is Mr Eric Van Kroot. He's a Dutchman who recently relocated to the UK and now lives in Oxfordshire with his wife.'

Again he paused.

'And he has uncovered what is perhaps the biggest archaeological discovery since...well...ever.'

At that point the screen went dark as the familiar title music began, along with the logo of *Your World Today*. Then, as the titles were playing, a picture appeared of a strange sheet of burned brown parchment with dark markings across it. Some sort of ancient language.

As the titles came to an end a voice said, 'The story of the world's most notorious and infamous traitor is as deeply ingrained in the Western mind-set as perhaps any other villain of history, but is it true?'

The screen flashed to a painting of the Last Supper with Jesus confronting Judas.

'Was Judas really the frightful villain we've all taken for granted? Or is it possible that he might have been closer to Jesus than we have imagined? Closer than the other disciples even?'

A painting of a hanged man filled the screen.

And once again the image of a scroll.

'Shocking new evidence has come to light which, if proven true, will turn everything we've ever believed about this story on its head. And we at ITV's *Your World Today* have been given exclusive access to it.'

The screen then went back to the presenter and Eric.

Douglass James faced the camera and spoke, 'Mr Van Kroot,

first of all let me thank you for agreeing to tell us about your remarkable story and your even more remarkable discovery.'

'You're welcome.'

'Do I really sound like that?' said Eric leaning into the screen.

'You do indeed,' said Penelope.

Douglass James spoke again, 'Unlike most of our documentaries and news stories, we've decided to interview Mr Van Kroot in front of a studio audience.'

A close up of Eric's face.

'Ladies and gentlemen this man might well be one of the last surviving direct descendants of...'

The presenter paused for an extra second.

'...Judas Iscariot.'

Eric remembered the tension in the studio when it was recorded. A pin could have been heard dropping at fifty paces.

Douglass James turned to his guest. 'Eric. I can call you Eric, can't I?'

'Of course,' he said.

'Good and please do call me Douglass. Now, tell us how you discovered this astonishing fact about your identity?'

On screen Eric reached down and clicked open his briefcase, out of which he took a narrow hardback book. 'I found something.'

'And what did you find?'

'I found a scroll, an early book if you like. Written by my ancestor, Judas Iscariot.'

'And this is it?' Douglass nodded towards the book on Eric's lap.

'Yes, it took a few years to have it preserved, translated and authenticated by experts. But yes, this is a newly published version.'

'We'll get to why you think you're his descendant shortly. But first let me ask you about the book. You're saying that this book was actually written by *the* Judas Iscariot?'

'I am, yes.'

'I mean, well, that's a huge statement Eric. Wasn't he supposed to have hanged himself after he betrayed Jesus?'

'That's right, he was, but he did not. In fact, I suspect he was murdered much later on.'

'Murdered?' The interviewer's eyes flared. 'This really is very controversial Eric. You do realise that don't you?'

'I do, yes.'

'Okay, so Judas, you say, was probably deliberately killed. But before he was, he wrote this book, this scroll?'

'Yes, and it was taken into hiding by Benjamin his son. Eventually Benjamin ended up in southern Spain and settled among Jews who were already living there. We have evidence that Jewish communities had lived throughout the Iberian Peninsula from before the time of Christ.'

'Fascinating, and the scroll was then guarded by Benjamin?'

'Yes, and passed down the family lineage, usually through the first-born sons.'

'So how did you find it?'

'Well here's where my story becomes something of a confession. But I need to tell this part of it for you to understand.'

'Go on.'

Eric recounted the story of the shameful bust up with his brother over their mutual love for Ella. Then he spoke of his travels, which led him to Mexico and to the community known as Maranos. He moved onto his journey throughout southern Spain leading him to Mojacar and the Indalo Man, and how he discovered his original family name. Then he spoke of his journey back to Amsterdam where he uncovered his ancestor Ezra's book. He had to stop to wipe away some tears with a handkerchief when he mentioned his visit to Peter, and the audience had to wipe away their own tears when he told of how he discovered he had a daughter.

'What did you feel when you heard your brother tell you that you had a daughter?'

On screen Eric flicked another tear away. 'I couldn't believe it. I was shocked, stunned. It was not what I'd expected, and it took over completely.'

'You wanted to find her?'

'Of course.'

'So you stopped your quest for the scroll and started a new quest to find your daughter?'

'Yes.' Eric then talked about the meeting with Father Ambroos, and bumping into the woman who was now his wife. When he got to the point of describing the discovery of Hannah's death, some of the audience wept aloud.

'Many would have given up at that point.'

'I almost did, but thankfully Pen urged me to continue with what I'd started before I'd found out I had a daughter.'

'And so you went back to the words of this Ezra chap and worked out where to look for the scroll?'

'Yes, but by that time we – Pen and I – realised we'd been double crossed by the priest and were being followed. So we had to lay a false trail to get them off our backs.'

'And that worked?'

'We thought it had, but when we'd finally followed the clues and found the so-called Rainbow Man, we realised we were still being watched. In fact, we were, at that point, kidnapped.'

'Good heavens,' said Douglass. 'Do you know who it was who kidnapped you?'

'It was the Church.'

Gasps came from various sections of the audience.

'As I've said, Eric. This is huge, and you're not making any new Catholic friends by telling all this.'

'I know, but I have to.'

'So you were taken. What happened then?'

'By that time we'd already found the scroll but had managed to re-hide it, so there was nothing on us to discover. We collected it later, before flying back to Holland.'

'Where you took it to be examined, and translated and finally produced into this beautiful book?'

'Precisely.'

Douglass turned to the camera. 'You have to agree that this is a remarkable story.'

There were enthusiastic nods of agreement throughout the audience.

He turned back to Eric. 'But, and I don't wish to throw a spanner in the works, haven't there been dozens of discoveries of scrolls and so on, by early Christians claiming to be written by Peter, or Thomas or even Mary Magdalene? What are they called – The Gnostic Gospels?'

'Yes you're right, and over the last year I've read them all. In fact, there's even a Gospel of Judas.'

'So what makes your discovery so unique?'

'All the others, apart from Thomas's, which dates a little earlier, were written centuries after the events they're describing. One reason we know this is that they contain theology that hadn't developed until half way through the second century.'

'But yours is different?'

'Yes. What I found was written around 50 AD or a little after. That's just twenty years after the apparent death of Jesus.'

'Gosh.'

'And further to that, it was written by Judas himself. None of the others were by the person in whose name they were written.'

'So assuming all this is true Eric, what does it tell us? What do you feel this ancient book has for today's world, because clearly you do feel it has something or you wouldn't have come here tonight, because...' Douglass looked into the camera, '...I have to tell you dear audience at home and here in front of me, he's taking no fee for this.'

The screen showed various looks of surprise and approving smiles within the studio audience.

Eric took a deep breath. 'It will destroy and it will re-build. It will be a mighty challenge to the established churches, demanding that they let go of some age-old beliefs and re-formulate their dogma. Some, I'm afraid, may not recover from this. It will be so shattering for them. However, it will also build a bridge between people, and it will also create a new bridge of understanding to what we mean by God, a God beyond the confines of a single religion.'

More gasps. And applause.

'So tell us about it Eric, and,' Douglass turned to the audience, 'let me tell you that it has been accepted by ninety per cent of the respected historians and scholars who've seen it that it's genuine.'

'Well it's really a final testament of a hunted man.'

'Hunted you say, by whom?'

'We're not sure, but most likely some of Jesus's followers who'd become a little, how can I put it, overzealous.'

'Hardline?'

'Yes, and Judas knew they were coming after him, which is why he wrote the scroll, and sent it off with his son to be hidden and safeguarded.'

'Alright, so what does it say?'

'Well to start, it gives us a very different picture of Jesus to the one that became dominant throughout history.'

'In what way?'

'Well there are glimpses of this Jesus even in the Bible but they're usually whitewashed by doctrine. Judas paints a picture of a Jesus who is, for a start, fully human and limited, imperfect.'

'Obviously the scroll was written after the death of Jesus?'

'I'll come back to that but, yes, if you take the traditional view that he died in his early thirties.'

'Eric, this is going to be seen as heretical you know. People are not going to like it one bit.'

'I know. As I said, we had to shake a few of them off our trail when we were looking for it. And they didn't even know what it was going to say then. This book will both destroy and re-build.'

'It will certainly shake the churches.'

'Yes, but hopefully it will not be seen as a threat so much as a gentle correction, something to get them to reconsider the story.'

'Gentle correction?' The audience laughed nervously. 'So what else can you tell us about it?'

'Well, Judas did see Jesus as divine. It's just that he thought we were all divine too. That's what he believed Jesus was about – enabling all people to discover their innate goodness, God-ness if you like.'

'Hence your desire to forward this book as a text to help found a faith beyond the confines of religion?'

'Exactly. But there's more.'

Douglass seemed genuinely surprised. 'More? You mean there's more than all that?'

'Oh yes.' Eric smiled. 'And if you think what I've just said is a threat to the Church, wait until you hear the rest.'

Chapter Seventy-One

London, 1985

A group of elderly men were sat in a semi-circle looking at a flickering television screen through the smoky haze.

One of them spoke. 'Excellency? What could possibly be worse for us than what he's already said?'

The oldest man in the room turned his head to the one who'd asked the question, and then to another. As he stared at him, his eyes narrowed. 'What the fuck haven't you told us Father Ambroos?'

Chapter Seventy-Two

Oxford, 1985

Eric and Penelope's eyes were still fixed on the screen.

'Okay, here it comes,' said Eric. 'The end of Christianity as we know it.'

Penelope squeezed his hand.

On the screen, Douglass was looking concerned and, for a moment, didn't seem to know which camera to look at.

'He had no idea what I was going to say at this point, Pen,' said Eric.

'I can tell.'

'I'd only told the researchers half the story. I didn't know whether they might consider the rest too explosive. But once I began they knew they had to allow me to finish.'

Looking deeply uncomfortable, Douglass invited Eric to continue.

'Jesus never died on the cross.'

'I'm sorry? I must have misheard you. What did you say?'

'The scholars and experts who've translated and studied this scroll are convinced that Jesus did not die upon the cross.'

'I...thought...that's...what...you said.' Douglass took out a handkerchief and wiped the perspiration from his brow.

'Let me tell you this.' Eric stared directly at the camera. 'There have, over the centuries, apparently been many accounts that claim Jesus escaped the cross and fled west or east to continue his mission elsewhere.'

Douglass was on the edge of his seat, but said nothing.

Eric continued. 'Whenever these accounts have been circulated they've quickly been discredited. Usually by Church-backed historians and theologians.'

Douglass slowly nodded. 'Go on.'

'In fact, the ones that suggest Jesus came in this direction, to southern France or even Glastonbury, England, have been discredited – even by non-ecclesiastical historians. They have a very legendary feel about them.'

'But not the stories that claim he went east?'

'No, not all of them anyway. Some are quite clearly myths, but many are historically compelling, even claiming evidence of Hindu and Buddhist scriptures talking of a St Issa, who has a very close resemblance to Jesus.'

'But, you say they have been discredited.'

'By the Church, yes.'

'But not by more general history?'

'Well, over the last few years, I've read as much as I can on this, and have come to the conclusion that the general historical line is that Jesus might have gone to the East during the so-called "missing years" of his late teens and early twenties – or after his crucifixion if he survived it. But because there had never been any concrete evidence, we had to assume that he did not.'

'Ah.'

'But now we do have that evidence.'

Douglass looked at the producers, who were standing and nodding silently. 'Okay, so you better explain. What does your scroll actually say about this?'

Chapter Seventy-Three

The Judas Scroll

I write these words, not knowing whether they will ever be read, much less believed. But it is all I can do. I accompanied my teacher Yeshua for three years during his mission and witnessed with my own eyes the extraordinary events that followed him wherever we travelled. He changed me and I will do anything to protect his memory. I owe him everything.

I do not presume to know the future, but my foresight sees a prospect truly unbearable, where all he stood for is threatened by the very people who claim him as their own.

Since my return, I have seen how they [his followers] have begun stitching together our own Jewish stories, rituals and traditions to create something truly dangerous. Yeshua did not suffer as a human passover lamb. He was sentenced to the cross because he was the most courageous man the world has ever known. He challenged and was punished by the very belief systems that are now being re-built in his name.

He fought both the might of Rome and Jerusalem's highest temple powers, and reaped the consequences of doing so.

So strong was this man, yet humble like no other. When people called him 'good' he corrected them with kindness, reminding them that only God is good. He gave hope to those pushed aside, downtrodden and trampled. My dear sister knew what it was to feel his heart reach into her own and rescue her from the self-hatred that tormented her life. But he did so not because he was an angel or a god but because he knew divine love so deeply within himself.

I write these words knowing that I risk misunderstanding. I have tried since my return to balance the exaggerated tales told by those who should have known better. Have they forgotten that Yeshua stood for truth? I despair when I see what is taking place.

Yeshua saw no need for human mediators. He taught us how to call God Father and speak to him directly.

Yeshua showed us that religious rules were there to guide not cripple, and to release shame not induce guilt.

Yeshua taught us that nothing can separate us from God. Truly nothing. 'God's grace is limitless,' he would say.

Yeshua gave us the ability to see beyond all classifications that divide, even enemy and friend. He broke through all boundaries that separate, whether age, gender, wealth, race or religion.

Yeshua broke through all barriers and would walk with rich and lowly alike, challenging by example rather than laying down stern rules.

Yeshua showed us how to see light within ourselves and each other. He called this 'to be Christed', a Greek term meaning to know our own anointing.

Essentially his teaching was simple and could be summarised in two phrases: 'Love God, and love your neighbour as yourself.'

And therein lies the gauge. Anything that contradicts that can be regarded as unfaithful to the Spirit of Christ.

So when I see structures beginning to form and unbending statements develop; when I see hierarchies who judge and rituals that separate, and when I hear talk of believer verses unbeliever begin to dominate, I fear that all is being lost.

However, before I set down the truth about Yeshua, I will first tell the story of how I, Judah, Ish Kerioth, came to follow him.

My parents were from Judea, a short distance from Hebron in the Southern Kingdom. I was unmarried and still living within my family home. My father was a merchant and, because I was naturally good with money, he allowed me to help him with the accounts. However, my younger sister had married a Galilean and was living on the shores of the lake they called Gennesaret in a little fishing hamlet. As brother and sister we were close, and I occasionally travelled there to visit her. But, as time went by, my visits were increasingly tainted by my brother-in-law's treatment of her. I saw a beautiful and happy girl turned into a withdrawn and purposeless woman.

It was on one such occasion that I first encountered Yeshua.

I know not whether it was just to spite her brutish husband, or perhaps she wanted to taste the forbidden fruit, but my dear sister chose a truly destructive and dangerous path. She took another man to her bed, and I arrived to find the turmoil. Of course I understood her pain. Indeed, I had wished the man dead many times, but her act rendered him worse than dead. By her sin, she declared him no man, and fit for nothing more than pity. By the time I reached the hamlet she had been taken. I learned this from a neighbour, a neighbour who barely contained her own revulsion.

The next day she was forced to kneel before a tribunal, not an official tribunal, but a rabble of self-appointed and self-righteous men, including her husband and her lover.

Others have sought to tell this tale, placing the setting in the Temple grounds in Jerusalem and making the accusers temple officials, Pharisees and teachers of the law, but I can attest that this happened on the shores of the Lake, and the men who hurled her onto the stony dirt were nothing more than a common mob.

The husband had already cast her out for adultery, and the lover had added to her crime by claiming she'd seduced him with a conjuring spell, such was his cowardice and craving for self-preservation.

It was the same time that Yeshua was wandering the dusty roads of Galilee with his small group of followers, giving hope and proclaiming the year of the Lord's favour. He'd been staying with the family of his right-hand man, Simon, in the nearby lakeside town of Capernaum.

News of his insights with regard to our law had reached my sister's hamlet, so the mob sought him out. On finding him, the rabble dragged my poor sister to him in some vain attempt to have her declared unworthy and fit for stoning under law. In truth they were right. What she had done was indeed punishable unto death, but they were fools to take her to him.

These men had no understanding of who he was or what he truly stood for. They had assumed him to be a man jealous for the letter of the law, but were not prepared for either his compassion or wisdom. I will never forget the scene as I watched from a distance. The men were ready to exercise the punishment with their own hands, each one holding a jagged rock.

Yeshua was sitting on the ground in the shade of a date palm. The men gathered around him and pushed the women through, throwing her down and forcing her to kneel in the centre of their circle. Yeshua did not rise to honour them, but remained on the ground drawing patterns in the dirt with his finger.

They tried to attract his attention. 'Rabbi, we have a question for you,' said a man with a white beard and a steadying stick.

Yeshua ignored him and continued to write in the dust.

A younger man spoke. 'Teacher, this woman is a proven adulteress and witch. She cast a spell on this poor man.' He thumped the man next to him on his chest.

Yeshua glanced up. The man who'd been thumped caught his eye, and then slithered away. Yeshua looked back down at the ground, reaching out his hand to touch the dirt again.

'The law of Moses commands us to stone her,' said the older man. 'What do you say Rabbi?'

By this point I realised they were trying to trap him. They seemed intent on doing what they'd set out to do, but had no clear authority. On seeing him as a holy man and teacher of the law they were asking him to endorse their intentions.

But Yeshua continued to ignore them.

With impatience now, another voice called out, 'Rabbi, surely as a teacher of the law, you have to agree her fate must be stoning unto death.'

Finally, he stood.

It was at this point I caught a real glimpse of the man I was to follow from that day forth. Once on his feet the circle of men expanded as each man paced backwards, as if somehow forced away by his presence.

And then he smiled.

It is his smile I most remember and long to see again. It was the smile of heaven and, while pure and innocent, there was within it no sense of superiority or judgement. Just warmth and compassion.

He spoke. 'You are right. The law of Moses commands her impurity to be dealt with by stones thrown from the hands of the pure.'

I could not believe it. He had endorsed them. My sister was going to perish. I opened my mouth to protest and demand them to stop, but then he said, 'So let the one among you who has remained pure throughout his life be the first to throw a stone!'

And once again he sat down to write in the dust.

The men glanced around at one another, exchanging looks of confusion, then concern and finally guilt. This was followed by the slow thud, thud, thud of rocks falling on the earth near their feet. And one by one, they slipped away, beginning with the old man who'd first spoken, until only Yeshua was left with my sister.

He then stood up again and, lifting my sister to her feet, said, 'My daughter, you are safe now. Come and follow me.'

He took her by the hand and led her away in silence.

Before following them I walked over to the date palm, where he had been sitting. Looking down at the ground I saw some words scratched out in the sand, 'only the fallen are caught!'

Truly Yeshua knew our God in a fresh new way. He had discovered that we come to God through imperfection rather than perfection. Consider who he chose to be his closest. Think about his own humble beginnings. Ponder on the nature of his message, which had a clear bias to the poor, the downtrodden, the unloved, unwelcome and unclean, the alien, the despised and dispossessed, the wounded and the rejected.

However, since my return I've heard his followers arguing over who is right and who is wrong, and over who is a true believer and who is an unbeliever. But Yeshua's way was never to separate over beliefs. His way was to challenge the comfortable and comfort the challenged.

Yeshua's way was never a striving after perfection, a climbing of the ladder to God, but a willingness to be fully human and fall from the ladder into God. He did so himself and thus showed us the way.

Yeshua was the bravest of men. Truly I have not witnessed such courage or faith as I did in him. He was faithful to his own teaching when he gave himself up to the cross.

This is why his message spoke to my sister, who had felt disowned by men and by God, and this is why he still speaks to me, a fallen, broken man.

Ever since that day near the lakeside when my sister became his follower, she has been known by the name of the little hamlet in which she had lived with her ex-husband. Magdala. I was told that Mary died a few years ago. Apart from my son, Benjamin, she was the last surviving member of my family.

Her encounter with Yeshua and the way it transformed her was what turned me also into his follower. I have never forgotten those words in the dust, 'only the fallen are caught'.

How abominable therefore, that I return to find his humble teachings of the beauty of brokenness and the glory of human frailty twisted into doctrines of power and might.

I have heard it proclaimed that Yeshua is Divine. That he is God in the flesh, that he had no human father and that his birth was miraculous. I cannot attest to his birth, for I am of similar age, but I can witness to his being the son of Joseph the carpenter. Like his mother Miriam, his father now sleeps, awaiting the resurrection. All those who followed him from the beginning knew his parents and saw his likeness within them.

And yet I agree he was Divine. But when I speak of his Divinity I witness to that which I saw so clearly within him, but also to that which he revealed within us.

He never claimed uniqueness, yet we knew he was unique. But his uniqueness was a quality that enabled us to see with new eyes and hear with new ears. He unlocked us to see ourselves and others as never before, as sons and daughters of the Most High.

Today the Greek word Christos is being limited to him alone, as if some new divine family name were given him, but he would have said, 'see not me as Christ, but all of us as Christed'.

Further, he taught us to see Spirit as present within peoples, places, even lands we were used to seeing as ungodly. I can give many examples of this, but the most vivid was when we were present at a healing of a child, and a Pagan Roman Officer whose servant was sick spoke with Yeshua. Our teacher was so deeply moved and impressed by this man that he declared him a man of great faith, more than he had seen in many of his own people. This was typical of Yeshua. It was never to shame but always to gently challenge us to see more and more through Spirit filled eyes.

Yeshua knew something terrible was approaching. Signs and portents were all around. Shadowy men following us from a distance, whispering figures on street corners, and each of us disciples being offered silver to speak out against him. The authorities had become nervous of his popularity and of the confidence he seemed to be instilling in his followers. They were growing impatient and wanted something done. And done it was, in the most brutal way.

His eventual ordeal of crucifixion was the most dreadful thing I have ever witnessed. The pain must have been unbearable. And it was utterly unjustified. His crime was simply one of giving hope to broken people. He sought no revolution or uprising. He wished no vengeance on either Jerusalem or Rome. He just wanted people to exchange hate for love.

I've never seen a man such with such love in his eyes, love flowing out to the men holding hammers in their hands. It was remarkable.

For three hours he hung there until the effects of the last dose of poison took away his pain and sent him into a death-like-sleep. The rich widower from Arimathea, Joseph, and I saw our plan taking shape. It was working and no one knew of the scheme we had dreamed up, not even Yeshua himself.

We'd given him a mixture of herbs and medicines before the nails were driven in. The Temple guards were happy to turn a blind eye when

Joseph placed those heavy bags of silver coins in their greedy hands.

Now all that was needed was the second part of the remedy, and that we administered via an outstretched sponge on a Roman spear. Again the deal had been done beforehand. Joseph had great influence and in the highest places. Indeed a few more coins granted him the apparently dead body itself, to be laid out in his own tomb. And this is where the real magic took place.

The antidote was another dose of oil-based herbs, harder to administer this time due to the unconscious state of the subject. We managed to work enough of the aloes into his mouth and, eventually, he awakened.

It was not easy to get him away from the place. He was still so frail and had lost much blood. But we managed to take him to one of Joseph's lodges, a safe enough distance to allow full recovery until we were all ready to make the longest voyage any of us had ever undertaken.

Joseph had made his great wealth by means of the merchant trade, though he had not himself travelled far along the tracks and trails. Most of his spices, silks and medicines were brought back via the Silk Route from the East. And that was the path we were to take. There were various Jewish trading settlements along the route, some as far away as the land we only knew in our imaginations, the land where one they called The Buddha had taught similar lessons to those of our Yeshua.

A year later and we had set up a new life for Yeshua in the land named after the great river Sindhu. We found a Jewish settlement which Yeshua considered a suitable base from which to teach, and also learn the traditions of Indikē, for even he could see how similar they were to his own wisdom teaching, particularly those of the school named after The Buddha.

Our plan was never to stay permanently, but Joseph began suffering from a strange fever shortly after our arrival and died within that first year. The years passed and Yeshua gained in reputation as a wisdom teacher and Sadhu. I myself, never really an aesthetic, ended up marrying and soon I became father to my pride and joy, Benjamin.

In the end it was my decision to travel back to our homeland alone. I suppose it must have been twenty years since the dreadful events that drove us away. Perhaps more. My son had grown into a fine and strong young man and was desperate for adventure, but I was unsure whether it would be safe for Yeshua to return with us, so Benjamin and I travelled back to Judea as scouts to look out for danger and traps.

We found a large convoy of traders, paid them enough to take us, and began the long journey home. As I have already described, what I discovered on my return was sickening. How they'd twisted his words. I tried in vain to correct them, and soon I was seen as their enemy.

I never saw my beloved Yeshua again for, had I sought to return to him, surely they would have followed me, which would have placed his life in peril. Instead I wrote this and entrusted it to my son, giving him the responsibility of taking it in the opposite direction, West.

I know not when, if ever, these words will be found. But if they are, all I ask is for you to open your heart and allow them the chance to resonate within. I am certain that open hearts and minds will hear the echoes of truth within them, for they are the echoes of Yeshua's own soul.

Chapter Seventy-Four

London, 1985

A black-robed figure stood and moved forward to switch off the television.

'So what do we do now, Excellency?' said another robed man, as he blew a thin trail of smoke from his mouth and flicked some ash in the cut glass bowl in front of him.

The large room was decorated with rich mauve damask wallpaper. The leather chairs and sofas, which were arranged in a horse shoe around the central television set, were all deep crimson.

The elderly cleric turned to face his auxiliary bishop. His dark eyes were narrowed and his lips tight. Peeling them back to display a set of clenched yellowed teeth he said, in a voice of ice and steel, 'Call the Inquisition.'

'But Excellency, what good can the *Congregatio* do now? It's all out. That damned Dutchman has destroyed us.'

'As I warned you he would,' said an angry voice from the other side of the room.

'Father Ambroos!' The Cardinal was on his feet. 'Don't you dare take that tone with us! We had him followed all the way to Almeria, but he didn't find anything. You know that.'

'But I did suggest we – '

'Yes, you suggested we murder him. For fuck's sake, we don't work like that anymore.'

Father Ambroos grinned, and bowed. 'Forgive me Excellency. My remark was truly out of place.'

'We'll have to find another way,' said the priest who'd turned off the television. 'If I may, I think the Cardinal is quite right. We in the Order have many connections to the *Congregatio*. I think we can influence them to enlist their theologians to do what they always do with dangerous books.'

'They must act fast,' said the Cardinal. 'This grave news is going to spread like wildfire. Do what you can, and do it now. All of you. You're dismissed.'

Chapter Seventy-Five

Oxford, 1985

'Eric,' said Douglass, 'I think you know how this is going to be received by the churches.'

'I do,' said Eric, 'but I'm not concerned about the churches. I'm concerned about the people. The real people who are the churches. And I believe they will listen.'

'Ladies and Gentlemen, I give you...' he stopped mid-sentence, 'oh, but wait, I almost forgot.'

The audience looked expectant.

'One part of the story that Eric did get wrong, understandably, was about his daughter Hannah. Ladies and Gentlemen in the end he did find her, so may I present to you, Hannah Van Kroot. Or should I say Hannah ben Kerioth.'

Hannah walked onto the studio stage with her long red hair flowing and her green eyes sparkling. And the most radiant smile.

Chapter Seventy-Six

North London, 1990

Hannah was waiting for her. 'Rose! Rose!'

The woman peered across the car park from the gate she'd just exited. She was tall and her thick black hair still hung in a heavy clump across her face.

'Hannah! Han, is that you?'

Eric and Penelope stood back as Hannah ran towards her friend and embraced her.

'I had to be here when you were released. I just had to.'

'It's been years, Han, years. You look so well.'

Rose didn't look so well herself but Hannah was determined that she soon would.

'Rose I want you to come with me. Come and stay with me.' She looked over at her father and Penelope. 'My dad found me. Thanks to you he found me. Rose I've got so much to tell you. We've all moved here to England. Dad married a woman from Oxford – she's over there next to him. We live there now. Come and stay with us.'

* * *

That very evening, Hannah showed something to Rose that she herself still couldn't fully take in.

'Rose,' she said, 'Can you remember when that crow Dominic pulled me out of bed in the middle of the night and had me kneeling in front of her and all of you on the floor for hours?'

'How could I forget it Han?'

'Did I ever tell you what it was about?'

'Um no, no you dint.'

'It was about Judas.'

'You mean Judas the one who betrayed Jesus? The Traitor?'

'Well yes, but he wasn't such a traitor.'

'Wunt he? But I thought – '

'Rose, I'd always thought that the nuns were wrong. Wrong to treat us the way they did. Wrong because they'd completely misunderstood what the whole thing was about.'

'What, the convent?'

'No. Well, yes and no. Christianity Rose. They'd got it all wrong and so has much of the Catholic Church. They only ever succeeded in making us feel bad about ourselves – dirty, unclean, sinful and unloved.'

'Well yeah I can't argue there, but int that what Christianity's about?'

'Yes it does seem that way, but I challenged that old crow and I hit a raw nerve. I suggested to her that God was not what they thought and that Jesus was loving to all, even to Judas.'

'Which is why she flew off the handle at yer?'

'Exactly.'

Hannah turned to the left and opened a draw, carefully removing a broad thin leather folder. She placed it on her lap and opened it up to the centrefold displaying about twenty large glossy sheets of photographic paper. On the left page was what looked like regular type but obviously a different language, and on the right was what looked like some sort of old parchment with very obscure markings on it.

'What's that Han?' asked Rose.

'Rose, this, believe it or not, is an actual book written by Judas.'

'Yer what?'

'Yes, it's been verified and proven by experts. This is his actual writing.' She tapped the right side, and this is a Dutch translation,' she said, tapping the left.

'What does it say?'

Hannah flipped over to the last few pages which were a

handwritten English translation that she'd made herself with the help of her father.

'It says I was right.'

'What do yer mean?'

'I suggested that Jesus still loved Judas to the crow, and that he still had time for him.'

'And the book says he did?'

'It does more than that Rose, it proves he was *the* disciple of Jesus's who understood him the most.'

'Really?'

'Yes really Rose, and do you know something else?'

'What?'

'I'm his descendant.'

Chapter Seventy-Seven

Amsterdam, 2017

The mobile phone kept ringing and eventually clicked to voicemail.

'Don't worry,' she said. 'I can listen to it later. Right now you're what's important my dear.'

'Thank you.' The girl had faced the table ever since she'd sat down. She sounded in her late teens – perhaps eighteen, which was forty years younger than the woman.

'I'm not here to judge you my love, or tell you what to do. I'm just here to listen. What's your name?'

'Sophia,' she said, her eyes still lowered. There were no lights on and the curtains were partially closed.

'And that's your birth name dear?'

'Yes.'

'How lovely. You know what it means of course?'

'No. It's just a name.'

'No name is *just* a name, believe me,' said the woman. 'Your name means *wisdom*.'

The girl laughed sarcastically. 'I was given the wrong one then.'

The woman reached over to the window and pulled the curtains apart a little more. A ray of light lit up the girl's face. She looked so young. Her golden hair hung down in loose curls. From what was visible, her skin tone and features seemed South European, though she had an accent that sounded Estuary English. She couldn't have been doing this for long, thought the woman, for she had such an innocent glow about her.

'The thing is, I don't know what to say,' said the girl. 'I don't even know why I'm here.'

'Here, talking to me? Or here in Amsterdam my dear?'

'Both, I guess.' She shrugged.

'Well let's begin with why you're here in this room, shall we? There must be a reason why you came.'

The girl glanced around, looking from place to place. Then she faced the woman. 'I was told about you, by a friend. I was told you were different, and that you really want to help us…us girls. That you understand us. And that …' she stopped, and her face crumpled as she bit back her tears '…you really care about us.'

The woman reached out her hand and the girl grasped it. They sat for a while in silence until the girl was able to speak again.

'But how? How could you understand someone like me?'

'I'll tell you what,' said the woman. 'Let's make a deal. You tell me your story, and then I'll tell you mine.'

The girl sat for a while, with her head down.

At last she looked up and tried to smile. Her beautiful eyes glistened with tears. 'How far back do you want me to go?'

'As far as you like.'

'Okay, but it might take a while.'

'I have all the time in the world.' The woman leaned back in her chair and waited.

After a moment Sophia began. 'I was born in South London, England. My mum was Italian and, since my dad was just a fling, I was given her name. So my full name is Sophia Romano. Mum was only sixteen when she had me and, because my grandparents are traditional Italians, they pretty much disowned her.'

The woman sat listening and nodding.

'When I was older, my mum managed to get me into a Catholic school, hoping it would bring her parents round. But it didn't. And then…' the girl took a deep breath and her bottom lip started quaking. 'Mum died.'

'Oh my darling.' The woman squeezed the girl's hand.

Fighting back more tears, she continued, 'I didn't realise but she'd been ill since I was born. I was only six when she died. It was from some sort of condition caused by having lots of...se – '

'I know. You don't have to say it.'

The girl reached into her sleeve and pulled out a tissue. She blew her nose. 'She loved me. My mum really loved me. She only did what she did to make sure I had enough.'

'Mothers will do anything to protect their children.'

'Mothers yes, but not grandmothers. I was sent to live with them. They couldn't really say no you see. They had their respectable image to keep intact.' She curled her nose up and sniffed.

'But surely they cared about you?'

'No they didn't.' Her voice became brittle and strained. 'They hated me. They hated me even before they had to look after me, but after mum died they hated me even more for spoiling their peaceful home.'

'I suppose it can't have been easy for an elderly couple to take on a young granddaughter?'

'Elderly? Huh, Mum was younger than I am now when she had me. They weren't even retirement age.'

The woman smiled. 'Go on my dear. So what happened to make you feel they hated you?'

Abruptly, the girl stood up and turned her back. Then, ever so slowly, she unfastened the buttons on her blouse and let it drop, allowing the woman to see her bare back.

On which the scars stood out like plough lines on a field.

The woman gasped. 'Oh my word.' The girl re-dressed herself and sat down once again.

'Your grandparents did...this?'

'My granddad.'

'For what reason?'

'Just for being me, and for the sort of things girls normally get up to. His punishments were terrible. It went on for years and he'd always say it was God's way of cleansing me.'

'My darling, you know that's not true don't you?'

'I swear it is. Honestly, shit I knew you wouldn't believe me.' The girl was on her feet again and making for the door.

'Oh no, no I don't mean that at all,' said the woman. 'What I meant is that it's not true that God cleanses people by punishment.'

'Oh.' She moved back to her chair and lowered herself slowly onto it. 'Sorry, I thought…Well, both of them made me believe it. From six years of age all I knew was that grown-ups hated me and God hated me.'

'Surely not all the grown-ups in your life were cruel?'

'Maybe not. Some of them were. Some seemed less so, but the school reinforced what I was getting at home. I grew to hate it all, and by the time I was twelve I knew I needed to run away.'

'And that's what you did? Ran away?'

'Yes, I waited until I was fourteen and able to use what I'd been given to make a living.'

'Your looks?'

'What else could I do? And I knew, from what my grandparents told me, that my mum had survived that way.'

'Oh my dear, that must have been so terrible for you, and so frightening?'

'No more than what I was living with. It's amazing what becomes bearable when you've been treated worse than a dog.'

'And you ended up here?'

'Yes, I soon discovered that life on England's streets was impossible. Everything's against you. But here, at least we are kinda protected.'

'So, how long have you been in Amsterdam?'

'Only two years, and I had to lie about my age to get registered. I hate it, but it's a job.'

The woman looked directly into her eyes. 'Sophia, why are you here? Why did you come and see me?'

'I don't know,' she said. 'I think it's because of who or what you are. When my friend told me she'd spoken with you, and what you are, it made all sorts of thoughts go through my head.'

The mobile phone started ringing again. She ignored it for the second time.

'You think that what I am is important?' said the woman.

'No, well yes, in a way. I just never expected someone like you to give a shit about…well, someone like me.'

'Sophia do you wish to leave this life?'

'Of course I do, but there's nothing else for me.'

'There's everything for you.'

'No there's not. Look you can sit there and say all that, but you've not been where I am. Okay it's great that you come here and try to help, that you listen and stuff. But you cannot possibly know what it's like to feel so hated, so unloved, so ugly that all you feel worthy of is being a fucking whore.'

There was silence.

A tear broke free from the woman's left eye and ran down her cheek, dripping off her chin. She straightened up and ran her hand over her head to adjust her veil. 'My darling I also lived and worked here. Many years ago. But I've never forgotten it and I've never felt able to stop loving all my friends here.'

'You had some sort of ministry here as a young nun?'

'No my dear.' There was a long pause. 'I was also a prostitute. Back then I wasn't Sister Mary. I was Maggie.'

The girl's mouth gaped open like a goldfish. 'Oh my God, really?'

'Yes, really Sophia. Shall I tell my story now?'

The girl's eyes and mouth were still wide open. She nodded.

'I'm also from Britain,' said the nun, 'though I was born here in Amsterdam. My father knew nothing of me. He found me when I was twenty-three, and was working in the district.'

'I don't believe it,' said Sophia.

'My childhood and early teenage years were spent at a Catholic children's home in South Wales and, believe me, I know how cruel adults can be. I was never given visible scars like yours but we were regularly abused in other ways – locked in tiny rooms without food or drink, and no toilet. Then punished for weeing ourselves. Washed in huge bathtubs with tap cold water and Jeyes fluid. Scrubbed in personal places with hard bristled scrubbing brushes. Picked up by the hair, and touched sexually by some of the Sisters.'

The girl shook her head. 'Oh my God.'

'Yes, so I know what religious abuse is like, and I know what it is to hate yourself and feel fit for nothing more than the most degrading of jobs.'

'But how come you're a nun? After all that, why would you want to go into the Catholic Church after – '

'My darling, I'm not a member of the Catholic Church any more. I'm a member of an inter-faith Order, one which combines the beauty of all the major religious paths.'

'I did wonder why you had all the Eastern looking statues,' said Sophia. 'Is that one Buddha?' she said, pointing to a large carved figure in meditation pose with some sticks of incense burning in front of it.'

'Yes,' said Sister Mary, 'and that one over there is Krishna. You know both their stories have correlations to the Christ story.'

'Really?' said Sophia. 'I never knew that.'

'Besides, the most perfect person I ever met was a Catholic nun. Well, a novice...' She closed her eyes and smiled as if she'd just tasted the most delicious spoonful of sweetness. 'Sister Simon was truly beautiful, in every way.'

'She was at the children's home?'

'Yes, for the first few years. But the older Sisters didn't like her. They sent her home in the end.'

'So why did you end up a nun? It seems that religion treated you like shit. How could you want to be part of it?'

'I don't see myself as part of that, Sophia. I will never forget what Sister Simon once said. She said, *Christ Our Lord, is what makes me want to be a nun. His love flows constantly towards us, and I want to help share that love.'*

'I get that but – '

'And there's another reason. I realised that, while Christianity can be dreadful, the originator was a man of ultimate beauty and the deepest compassion, and he knew God within himself like no other.'

'Sorry Sister, but I was always told that Jesus didn't so much *know* God, as *was* God.'

Sister Mary nodded. 'Yes, but I've come to see things differently. Especially after I read the most remarkable book – written by an ancestor of mine.'

'Ancestor?'

'Yes dear. In fact, if you'd allow me, I'd love to read a little to you.'

The girl nodded. 'Okay.'

'By the way,' said Sister Mary, as she reached down into her bag for a book, 'why don't you call me Hannah. I feel like we're going to be friends and I want you to know me by my real name. I chose the name Mary when I was professed but I feel like being Hannah again today.'

'Hannah.' Sophia smiled. 'Okay.'

Hannah placed a narrow hardback book on the table and opened it to a particular page. And started reading.

'*My parents were from Judea, a short distance from Hebron in the Southern Kingdom. I was unmarried and still living within my family home. My father was a merchant and, because I was naturally good with money, he allowed me to help him with the accounts. However, my younger sister had married a Galilean and was living on the shores of the Lake they called Gennesaret in a little fishing hamlet. As brother and sister we were close, and I occasionally travelled there to visit her. But, as time went by, my visits were increasingly tainted by my brother-in-law's treatment of her. I saw a beautiful and happy girl turned into a withdrawn and purposeless woman.'*

'It was on one such occasion that I first encountered Yeshua.'

Hannah paused. 'Yeshua is Jesus,' she said.

Sophia nodded, wide eyed and looking enthralled. The Sister read on from the testimony she knew so well, stopping at the words: *'Looking down at the ground I saw some words scratched out in the sand, 'only the fallen are caught!'*

Hannah closed the book and looked at Sophia, whose eyes were sparkling like polished diamonds.

'You see, Sophia,' said Hannah, 'Jesus knew God in a fresh new way. He had discovered that we come to God through imperfection rather than perfection. Consider who he chose to be his closest. Think about his own humble beginnings. Ponder on the nature of his message, which had a clear bias to the poor, the downtrodden, the unloved, unwelcome and unclean, the alien, the despised and dispossessed, the wounded and the rejected.'

'Who wrote those words?' said the girl.

Hannah reached out and held her hand. Looking deeply into her eyes she said, 'My dear, those are the words of the closest disciple of Jesus, and yet the one who through history had been seen as cursed beyond redemption.'

'Not Ju – '

'Yes.'

'But he was the traitor. He was the one who handed Jesus over for money. He was – '

Hannah smiled and nodded. 'I know. We were all taught that.

But we were wrong. That's what the men of power wanted us to believe, and it's what has kept Christianity encased within perfectionism and superiority ever since.'

'But – '

'And that's why people like you and people like me have lived filled with self-hatred and fear. Sophia, you do not need to fear any more. God loves you as a precious daughter. He wants you to believe in yourself and know that you need no man's approval. And no woman's approval either. You are beautiful as you are.'

Sophia sat, eyes wet with tears, mouth slightly open, slowly shaking her head in disbelief. 'So Ju...Judas was the brother of Mary Magdalene?'

'Yes.'

'And they were both your...' She took a deep breath. '... relatives?'

Hannah nodded and smiled. 'When I first read these words, which was – ohhh, over thirty years ago, I knew immediately that I had been right about Judas all along. I can remember now the trouble I got in for expressing some of those thoughts to the Sisters – my gosh they ruled my life with a rod of iron.'

'Sounds like my grandparents.'

'Well my dear, religion is like the Roman god Janus. It has two faces and can activate two entirely different responses in people. This is what religious practitioners have been battling with throughout the centuries.'

'But.' Sophia half closed her eyes and frowned. 'Something doesn't make sense.'

'What doesn't my dear?' asked Hannah.

'Well surely something like this – something so earthshattering for the Church – would have destroyed it? You said this all came out years ago. Why have I never heard about it before? Why did my grandparents still believe staunchly in Catholicism? I don't understand.'

'Yes, I can see why you're confused. But you don't realise how clever the Church is, and how good at self-protection. They've had near 2,000 years to perfect the art of self-defence.'

'Self-defence?'

'Yes, well actually I'd call it attack rather than defence. You have heard of the Inquisition haven't you?'

'Of course.'

'Well, my dear, it's still alive and well. And that is the reason why you've never heard about any of this. As soon as it became public they used every trick in the book to totally discredit my father and make a mockery of his claims.'

'Can I ask what happened to your dad? Like, is he still – '

'Alive? Oh yes, and he's still trying to prove the truth of the scroll. He's an old man now, but still travelling the earth picking up hints, looking into reports and trying to uncover the truth.'

'He believes he can prove it?'

'Yes, he believes he will prove the scroll's historicity when he uncovers the tomb of Jesus.'

'Shit. That would be amazing,' said Sophia. 'But why did you become a Sister? I mean, after all you've been through.'

'Quite simply, I found what my dear sweet Sister Simon once talked about. And in a way I'm following the call for her. But I'm also following this call for my ancestors. They went through so much to keep alive the truth. And even now *The Judas Scroll* has been published it's making very little real difference. How could I not do what I'm doing when I've gained so much from him?'

The girl smiled. 'I think you're amazing. And self-less.'

'No, there's nothing amazing about me. And I'm most certainly not self-less. In fact, I am doing this primarily for myself you know. Yes, it's for Sister Simon and yes it's for my long gone family, but it's for me because I still love this place.'

'You love Amsterdam?'

'Yes. It was Amsterdam that brought my father back to me and it was Amsterdam where I fell completely into God's love.

As Jesus wrote in the sand, *Only the fallen are caught.* I recognise that had I not fallen so far, I could never have experienced the sense of being caught so firmly. No, I would never wish that life on anyone. But because of it I am who I am today.'

Hannah closed her eyes, and held both hands out palms up. Sophie reached out with hers and joined them. And Hannah said, 'Even in my darkest moments, here in Amsterdam, when I felt the most despised, the most lost, the most useless and pathetic, my God was with me – loving me. And I have come to see that those who try to follow him by duty alone, by self-denial, by pure religious effort – like dear old Sister Dominic from my old home – are climbing ladders away from the very God they are attempting to reach. If they could only loosen their grip, and slip, they'd fall right into his love.'

Hannah opened her eyes and the girl released her hands and stood up. For a while they looked at each other.

'Come and see me again Sophia.'

'I will.' The girl's tear-filled eyes glistened as she smiled. 'I promise.'

And then she left.

Hannah watched the girl leave, and then picked up her mobile phone. She recognised the number instantly. Pressing the call-back button she held the phone to her ear.

'Dad. Yes, sorry I was unable to answer. How are you? What? Where? You're in the…You've found it. Found what? Who? You've finally found…him? Oh my Lord!'

Chapter Seventy-Eight

Kashmir, 2017

Eric could barely take in what he was looking at. His near two-decade search had led him to this place.

It was the loss of Penelope back in the year 2000 that had prompted it. He could have cursed the cancer and allowed himself to die along with her, or use her death to motivate something positive, in her name. And he chose the latter. It was Pen who'd helped him find Hannah and it was Pen who'd helped him find the scroll. Now he'd honour her by finding the final piece of evidence required to vindicate the whole story.

His journey had led him to follow the ancient Silk Route, the merchant path that ran from the Roman Empire through Palestine and Persia, onwards through Northern India and into Tibet, and then back into India. He had visited thousands of monasteries, temples, churches and communities gaining information. It had all pointed to this one small village in Kashmir, where a tomb was said to contain the bones of one St Issa.

He'd known about it for the last seven years but had not been granted permission to excavate. He had not been surprised by this since it was a sacred shrine. However, he had another plan.

For the previous five years, Eric had been fundraising for a special new archaeological device that could see beneath the earth – a sort of high-powered X-ray machine. Eric had raised the required £30,000 and the company had sent the machine over with a small team of three to operate it.

He'd heard about the new technique when it had been first unveiled in 2005 after a certain Professor Thorne was the first to use the technique to analyse Greek and Roman pottery and the inscriptions upon them. A more recent report from the American Physical Society showed how X-ray sources known as synchrotrons could unravel an impressive amount of detail without disturbing the artefact or what was buried beneath. The technique could illuminate so much detail that even the tiny traces made by tools used thousands of years ago become clear.

Eric knew it would be perfect for his own needs and the local authority had agreed in principle that it would be possible to use it, as long as it did not disrupt the tomb in any way – and that the results would not be made public but be simply for Eric's own edification.

Now he couldn't believe his eyes. All the effort, the travelling, the searching, the painstaking detective work and the fundraising had been worth it. He was looking into the screen at the image of the skeleton...clearly a stooped skeleton of an elderly man... an elderly man with visible marks in his wrist bones and feet.

He had to call someone. He had to speak to Hannah. Where was his phone?

Epilogue

The lizard re-emerges and this time the fugitive sees it. The tiny flicking fork evokes images of the serpent himself. A movement from behind, and a shadow. The lime-green portent is gone. His accusers have arrived.

'You've found me.' He peers up at the figures hovering over him.

'We have.'

He stands, knowing what must happen. 'You'll never find them,' he says, 'Benjamin has left no trace. My words are safe.'

They step towards a ridge where a single olive tree stands, one branch hanging over the edge.

'Maybe not,' said one of the men, 'but once the other stories have been completed, your name will never be trusted and will stand always for *traitor*, and your son will just be seen as a traitor's child.'

The rope is thrown over the branch, and the noose placed over his head. A push, and he drops, the motion and jolt causing his turban to come loose.

And fall away, revealing his hair – *his thick, red hair*.

Historical Notes

Judas
The Judas of History

Very little is known of Judas Iscariot as a historical figure. The name Judas (Greek Ioudas) is a Greek form of the Hebrew Judah, which means 'God is praised'. According to the New Testament there were two among the twelve disciples of this name.

Within my story I used the (scholarly) theory that the surname Iscariot refers to 'Man of Kerioth'.

There are, however, other theories with regard to the origin of his name. One is that it is a corruption of the Latin 'sicarius' meaning 'murderer' or 'assassin'. There was a First Century group of radicals known as the Sicarii, some of whom would have been seen as dangerous terrorists. However, some historians claim that this radical Jewish group arose in the 50s CE, which would be too late for Judas.

Another theory suggests an etymological connection to the Aramaic word for 'liar' and still another to the word for 'red', and yet another to the term 'to deliver'.

I like the idea that it depicts his home town Kerioth. It feels the most convincing to me.

This would also make him stand out as something of a 'foreigner' to all the other main disciples, who were all Galileans.

* * *

The Gospel of Judas

The Gospel of Judas is an almost certainly fictional collection of conversations between Jesus and Judas Iscariot. Most scholars date it to the late Second Century because the largely Gnostic theology it contains comes from that period. Thus it was not written by the protagonist Judas.

Further, there is only one copy in known existence, a Coptic copy that has been carbon dated to 280 CE, plus or minus a few decades.

Unlike the four Canonical Gospels (Mark, Luke, Matthew and John) *The Gospel of Judas* does not portray Judas as the great traitor and betrayer of Jesus, but as the one who completely obeyed his Master's request to hand him over to the authorities. It sees Judas as the only member of the twelve disciples who understood Jesus's mission and suggests that Jesus did not teach his secrets to the others, but just to Judas.

One of the most telling contrasts between the theology of the *The Gospel of Judas* and the theology of the Canonical Gospels concerns the crucifixion. Whereas the Canonical Gospels see the crucifixion of Jesus as a blood atonement for the sins of humanity, *The Gospel of Judas* sees the idea of 'substitionary atonement' as irrelevant to the true God, who is utterly grace dispensing and does not demand sacrifice.

While I have used some of the character traits attributed to Judas within *The Gospel of Judas* as inspiration for my book, I have not based my 'Judas Scroll' on it. The Judas within my story is not a Gnostic but a devout Jew who sees Yeshua (Jesus) more in terms of a Prophet than the Son of God.

* * *

The Judas Scroll

This is entirely fictitious. I decided to write a short booklet to use as my own source material for what I have called *The Judas Scroll* (discovered by Eric within the house at Muxacra). I considered using *The Gospel of Judas* (see above) but decided against it because of its clear late authorship and theology. I also wanted my Judas to come across as far more real and human than the voice that speaks through the Gnostic *Gospel of Judas*.

I would say that the Judas of my book is far closer to the

Judas of the wonderful Tim Rice and Andrew Lloyd Webber musical *Jesus Christ Superstar* than any of the popular depictions based on *The Gospel of Judas*. The most well-known of these is the astonishing book by Nikos Kazantzakis, *The Last Temptation of Christ*.

I thought it would be interesting for readers to have a copy of the entire booklet, hence it being printed in total as Chapter Seventy-Three. However, I do not wish any readers to mistake it for an actual historical book – it is fiction.

* * *

The hometown of Judas – El Kureitein / Kerioth
Kerioth in the south of Judea is indeed identified with the ruins of El-Kureitein, which is roughly ten miles south of Hebron. During my research I have discovered many scholars who believe this was Judas's historical hometown.

* * *

Mary Magdalene
It is almost impossible to distinguish between fact and fiction when it comes to Mary Magdalene. She has enjoyed a huge surge of interest over recent decades, not least due to popular fiction (Dan Brown's *The Da Vinci Code* etc.) and New Age conspiracy theories based on rather dubious Victorian pseudo-history.

As with Judas, when it comes to actual history, we know very little about Mary Magdalene, and even the things we feel we do know about her are often not even Biblical. For example, she is never once referred to as a prostitute within the New Testament.

However, because of her long history as 'redeemed harlot' I chose to use her symbolically within my story. Also the red hair, which has been used to depict Judas within art too, is often seen as an anti-Semitic symbolic mark of Jewishness. I wanted to take this often negative use of the colour red, and use it as a beautiful colour as well as to mark a connection between my main characters.

* * *

Muxacra / Mojacar

Modern day Mojacar was called Muxacra under the Moors and, when I visited, I found it an enchanting place and the perfect setting for Ezra's home. Much of its Moorish past is still evident, with the narrow labyrinthine streets and archways.

Populated since 2000 BCE, it has witnessed the arrival of many and various tribes and peoples, from Phoenicians and Carthaginian traders to Greek conquerors, when it was called Murgis-Akra. This name was later Latinized to Moxacar, and became Muxacra under the Moors.

The North African Moors settled in Spain in the early eighth century and the province of Almeria was ruled by the Caliphate of Damascus. Later it came under the authority of the Umayyads of Cordoba and Mojacar quickly grew in size and importance.

With the growing tension between Muslim Granada and Christian Castile, Mojacar found itself on the frontier with the Castilian forces to the east.

During the fourteenth century, Watchtowers and fortresses were set up but Christian incursions occurred and fierce battles were fought. In 1435 much of the population of Mojacar was put to the sword by the Christian army.

My use of the year 1488 to set Muxacra's submission to Castile is historical, as is the initial agreement of freedom to practise any of the three Abrahamic religions.

* * *

The Indalo Man

The Indalo Man is an ancient symbol found in Almeria over a hundred years ago. Any new visitors to this area of modern Spain will immediately notice this image on road signs, T-shirts, bookstores, souvenir shops and elsewhere.

It was first discovered somewhere in the Las Velez mountain range of northern Almeria in a cave known as La Cueva de los Letreros by Antonio Gongónia y Martinez in 1868.

The symbol dates back to Neolithic times and depicts a man holding a rainbow over his head.

Historians tell us that the Indalo Man became a local good luck charm and was used to ward away bad luck.

In the 1960s the local government began to offer free land to anyone that would agree to construct a dwelling as long as they obeyed certain conditions. This offer and the growing popularity of the region (especially around Mojacar itself) attracted international artists and counter-culturists who were looking for somewhere special. Mojacar was just the place and to many of the new residents the Indalo Man was recognised as a perfect mythical icon to represent their new home.

Since then, the Indalo Man has become even more popular and has been incorporated into the ever-increasing number of businesses and hotels etc.

The Best Indalo Hotel which Eric and Penelope stayed in within my story is an actual hotel. Indeed, I've stayed there myself and even performed a wedding ceremony for my step daughter in the beautiful grounds.

Over the last few decades, the Indalo Man has been painted on the front of houses and businesses as a good luck charm. It has very much become the symbol of this region of Almeria and of Mojacar in particular.

* * *

The Jews in Iberia

It is believed by some that the first Jews arrived in Seville in the sixth century BCE and were from David's family. However, the more definite history of Spanish Jews dates back at least 2,000 years, when the Romans destroyed the Second Temple in Jerusalem and brought many Jews back to Europe with them.

Since then, the Jews have experienced times of great oppression and hardship in Spain, as well as periods of relative tolerance, freedom and growth.

Known as Sephardic Jews (Sephardi means 'Spanish' or 'Hispanic', and derives from the word Sepharad), this community suffered persecution from the Visigoths during the sixth century AD, followed by a period of harmony under Moorish rule, during which Jews, Moors and Christians co-existed, respecting each other's religions and holy days – the so-called Conviviencia, which I mention in my story.

Sephardi Jews once made up one of the largest and most prosperous communities under Moslem and Christian rule in Spain, numbering well over 200,000, before the majority were forced to convert to Catholicism, be expelled or be killed when Catholic Spain was unified following the marriage of Isabella of Castile to Ferdinand of Aragon, the Catholic Monarchs.

* * *

The Islands of São Tomé

As I detailed within Ezra's story, many thousands of the Jews who were expelled from Spain in 1492 attempted to make homes within the neighbouring country of Portugal. However, in 1496, to punish the Jews who could not or would not pay the required head tax, King Manuel forcibly removed 2,000 Jewish children from their parents, had them hastily baptised and then deported to the islands of São Tomé off the west coast of Africa.

Because the children belonged to those families who could

not or would not pay the required tax, they were declared slaves of the king. They were aged between two and ten years.

The king's intention was Portuguese colonisation of the islands, but he did not want to risk the lives of his own men. A year later only six hundred of the children were found alive.

* * *

The Spanish Inquisition

In an attempt to 'purify' Catholic Spain, the Inquisition was introduced in 1481, the same year that I set Ezra's birth. By 1492, up to 200,000 Jews had fled Spain. One hundred years later, the remaining Muslims were also expelled.

Decades of persecution had shown Jews that they could be baptised and outwardly Catholic, and yet still hold to and practise their Judaism in secret. These 'conversos' (converts to Christianity) or New Christians, as they were also called, were often referred to as marranos (swine). Thousands were discovered and burned at the stake. Many other thousands were 'forced' to convert.

Many of the Jews (some of them conversos who still practised Judaism) who left Iberia in 1492 headed to Western Europe. Others travelled as far as Latin America, where the converses could revert to the open practice of Judaism. Amsterdam became a major city for Sephardi Jews to settle within, and was known by some as The New Zion.

Though a feared institution, the popular image of the Spanish Inquisition has been questioned by revisionist historians. Consequently, much of what people think they know about the Inquisition is simply not true.

Many urban legends surround the Spanish Inquisition and they come from Reformation-era Europe.

There were indeed terrible abuses committed in the name of the Church, and at the hands of the Church, but the urban legends have drastically exaggerated them. Many historians now say that, although the evils committed during the life of the Inquisition were very real and must not in any way be defended, many historical misunderstandings and falsehoods have been based on anti-Catholic propaganda – known as the so-called 'Black Legend'.

I suppose the most obvious images that come to mind when hearing the term Spanish Inquisition are those of torture. The Monty Python parody used this image for its hilarious comedy sketch.

However, the revisionist historians, who've studied the well documented cases in detail, now claim that most of the torture and executions attributed to the Church during the various inquisitions didn't occur at all.

Torture was indeed used during some Inquisitional trials. However, unlike much of secular Europe at the time (which used torture frequently), the Inquisition had strict rules regarding its use that made it far less severe than contemporary use outside the Church.

However, having read through many of the cases that these historians refer to I still find the whole concept and practice of the Inquisition truly horrific. The fact that people were tortured at all, and some burned as heretics – which is fact – proves to me how far an organisation can stray from the values of its founder, Jesus of Nazareth.

The Inquisition was finally abolished in 1834.

* * *

Amsterdam (Dam)

The Anabaptists in 1535

As I put in the first section of Ezra's journal, 1535 was the year that forty Anabaptists processed naked through the streets of Amsterdam and ended up paying the price for this act of anarchy with their own blood.

It was a non-violent protest to the religious establishment that they regarded as being in league with the wealthy, the privileged and the powerful. This, to them, was a clear contradiction of the Bible and of Jesus, whose bias was to the poor and the marginalised.

Anabaptists held to a vision of equality and the sharing of property. At this point in Dutch history, unemployment was high and there was much unrest. The rich and powerful thus saw this group as potential trouble makers because the poorer classes were becoming attracted to and stirred up by their teachings.

It was a time when heretics were generally left alone as long as they didn't cause trouble, but these forty Anabaptists did cause trouble walking naked through the streets to the town hall.

The following day the authorities had them massacred. All forty were killed by having their hearts cut out in the centre of Dam Square, after which their bodies were quartered and their heads were stuck on poles and displayed at each of the city gates as a warning.

* * *

Jesus's Survival of the Crucifixion and Journey East

There has indeed been a long tradition of Jesus either travelling east during the so-called 'missing years,' which refers to the period after his last New Testament mention as a child (when he visited the Jerusalem Temple as a youth and impressed the rabbis and teachers with his knowledge) and his first mention as an adult of around thirty years, or after surviving the cross. There is too much about this to discuss here but a quick internet search will throw up an enormous amount of information, resource material and further reading should this subject interest you.

**ROUNDFIRE
BOOKS**

FICTION

Put simply, we publish great stories. Whether it's literary or popular, a gentle tale or a pulsating thriller, the connecting theme in all Roundfire fiction titles is that once you pick them up you won't want to put them down.
If you have enjoyed this book, why not tell other readers by posting a review on your preferred book site.
Recent bestsellers from Roundfire are:

The Bookseller's Sonnets
Andi Rosenthal
The Bookseller's Sonnets intertwines three love stories with a tale of religious identity and mystery spanning five hundred years and three countries.
Paperback: 978-1-84694-342-3 ebook: 978-184694-626-4

Birds of the Nile
An Egyptian Adventure
N.E. David
Ex-diplomat Michael Blake wanted a quiet birding trip up the Nile – he wasn't expecting a revolution.
Paperback: 978-1-78279-158-4 ebook: 978-1-78279-157-7

Blood Profit$
The Lithium Conspiracy
J. Victor Tomaszek, James N. Patrick, Sr.
The blood of the many for the profits of the few… *Blood Profit$*
will take you into the cigar-smoke-filled room where American
policy and laws are really made.
Paperback: 978-1-78279-483-7 ebook: 978-1-78279-277-2

The Burden
A Family Saga
N.E. David
Frank will do anything to keep his mother and father apart. But
he's carrying baggage – and it might just weigh him down …
Paperback: 978-1-78279-936-8 ebook: 978-1-78279-937-5

The Cause
Roderick Vincent
The second American Revolution will be a fire lit from an
internal spark.
Paperback: 978-1-78279-763-0 ebook: 978-1-78279-762-3

Don't Drink and Fly
The Story of Bernice O'Hanlon: Part One
Cathie Devitt
Bernice is a witch living in Glasgow. She loses her way in her
life and wanders off the beaten track looking for the garden of
enlightenment.
Paperback: 978-1-78279-016-7 ebook: 978-1-78279-015-0

Gag

Melissa Unger

One rainy afternoon in a Brooklyn diner, Peter Howland punctures an egg with his fork. Repulsed, Peter pushes the plate away and never eats again.

Paperback: 978-1-78279-564-3 ebook: 978-1-78279-563-6

The Master Yeshua

The Undiscovered Gospel of Joseph

Joyce Luck

Jesus is not who you think he is. The year is 75 CE. Joseph ben Jude is frail and ailing, but he has a prophecy to fulfil ...

Paperback: 978-1-78279-974-0 ebook: 978-1-78279-975-7

Tuareg

Alberto Vazquez-Figueroa

With over 5 million copies sold worldwide, *Tuareg* is a classic adventure story from best-selling author Alberto Vazquez-Figueroa, about honour, revenge and a clash of cultures.

Paperback: 978-1-84694-192-4

On the Far Side, There's a Boy

Paula Coston

Martine Haslett, a thirty-something 1980s woman, plays hard on the fringes of the London drag club scene until one night which prompts her to sign up to a charity. She writes to a young Sri Lankan boy, with consequences far and long.

Paperback: 978-1-78279-574-2 ebook: 978-1-78279-573-5